THE REMAKE

AS TIME GOES BY

Forge Books by Stephen Humphrey Bogart

Play It Again
The Remake: As Time Goes By

THE REMAKE

AS TIME GOES BY

STEPHEN HUMPHREY
BOGART

A TOM DOHERTY ASSOCIATES BOOK
NEW YORK

THE REMAKE: AS TIME GOES BY

A Forge Book
Published by Tom Doherty Associates, Inc.
175 Fifth Avenue
New York, NY 10010

Forge® is a registered trademark of Tom Doherty Associates, Inc.

Library of Congress Cataloging-in-Publication Data

Bogart, Stephen Humphrey.
        The remake: as time goes by / Stephen Humphrey
    Bogart. — 1st ed.
            p.   cm.
        "A Tom Doherty Associates book."
        ISBN 0-312-85666-0 (alk. paper)
        I. Title.
    PS3552.O4334A9   1997
    813'.54—dc20   96-33982
                                             CIP

First Edition: April 1997

Printed in the United States of America

0 9 8 7 6 5 4 3 2 1

THE REMAKE

AS TIME GOES BY

CHAPTER 1

It was spring and there was a manic energy turned loose in the city, an energy that made everybody bounce a little when they walked. Even though it was still too cold for all the bad smells to thaw out, people were starting to unbutton the top buttons of their coats and look with a special spring gleam in their eyes for new ways to hurt each other.

But it was spring, and R.J. didn't mind. He liked the fact that all New Yorkers are predators. It was why he lived here. He'd grown up with the sun-tanned, veggie-loving mood-ring kissers on the West Coast, and he would just as soon take the knife in the front, New York–style.

It was spring in New York and R.J. was alive, healthy, and he had enough dough tucked away that he could tell just about anybody to go to hell if he felt like it. Which he frequently did these days.

The last six months had been hard. Especially for a guy trying to make a living by being tough. Ever since his mother, film legend Belle Fontaine, had been killed, he had been up to his neck in two of his least favorite types: lawyers and reporters. The lawyers would probably be with him for a while, at least until he got Belle's estate squared away. The reporters—that was another matter.

It had taken the media buzzards most of that six months to get the message: R. J. Brooks wasn't talking. Didn't want his picture on any magazine covers—although he'd been on eleven without his permission when he gave up counting. He didn't want to appear on any TV shows, with their hysterically sincere hosts and brainlessly enthusiastic studio audiences. Wouldn't give an exclusive to any of the network soft-news magazines. Wouldn't cooperate in any Movie of the Week— although a couple had been made. Wouldn't say anything to anybody with a press pass.

Except Casey Wingate, of course.

Casey. He sighed just thinking about her.

Most of his life he'd been able to handle women with no problem. He could take 'em and leave 'em, and he'd done that with his fair share. More than his fair share. Enjoy them for what they could give, and when cling-itis developed, walk away with a smile, no hard feelings.

Casey was different. And that was an understatement. Six months into their relationship, and there were days when he still didn't know if they had a relationship.

He tried like hell to get back to his old attitude. Accept whatever Casey offered, which was plenty, and let it go at that. Tried like hell, and failed miserably. She was under his skin and he was stuck with it. Worse, he wanted to stay stuck.

And Casey was a TV producer. They had met when Belle died. Casey had been working on a story about Belle and she had ended up helping R.J. catch Belle's killer.

It had been hard to say no to Casey's project on Belle. In fact, it had been so hard R.J. hadn't even tried. He'd gone meekly in front of the camera and said his piece. Because that's what Casey wanted. He was a tough guy in a tough job, but when Casey wanted something . . . Somehow he just wasn't tough enough to say no to her.

So there was his face, all over network TV. And the show got terrific ratings, which was great for Casey's career. But for his, it was a kiss of death. Because every time he showed up to do surveillance lately, some bozo would light up with a goofy grin, point a finger, and shout, "Hey! You're that guy on TV!" And there went the job.

To be fair, he had to admit that Casey had been helpful finding a solution. Had helped him get ready for the job today, in fact, and so far everything was going smoothly.

Until now.

R.J. snapped out of his thoughts when he realized he was being followed. More accurately, he was being stalked. He stopped in front of a store window and looked inside for a moment. It was a butcher shop. R.J. pretended to be very interested in a duck and a pair of rabbits hanging in the window, headless and skinned. Of course he was really just looking in the glass. It was an old trick, but it still worked, especially on the kind of punk who seemed to be following R.J. right now.

In R.J.'s business, if somebody was following you it was never good news, and it could get very bad. Outraged lovers have long memories, and R.J. was good at his job. He'd been a private investigator specializing in marital problems long enough that he'd made quite a few enemies. But this didn't look like one of them.

Reflected in the butcher shop window was a young guy with baggy clothes, baseball cap backwards—a real cliché. Probably hadn't been watching MTV and didn't know that New York punks weren't wearing that stuff anymore. Very sad, no sense of being on the cutting edge of society's deterioration. But this punk was definitely following him.

R.J. hid a grin. The kid was in for a surprise.

R.J. moved slowly down the street. What the hell, make it easy for the punk. Get it over with. And sure enough he was no more than half a block further when the little shit made his move.

"Give it up, bitch," came the voice. R.J. could tell the kid was fighting to keep his voice from cracking. He felt a tug on his shoulder bag, but held on hard. "Come on, old lady," the kid said, "just give it up."

R.J. struggled for a minute, getting real pleasure thinking of the surprise this creep was going to get. Then the pulls on his shoulder bag got to be too much and R.J. spun on the balls of his feet and planted his fingertips in the punk's gut, right under the rib cage. The creep grunted, "Uhhk," and collapsed onto the sidewalk.

The people on the street had been moving casually around them. R.J. pulled out The Big E, his .357 Magnum, from its resting place in the waistband of his dress, and the people gave them a slightly wider berth, but traffic moved on undisturbed. Nobody screamed, nobody yelled for a cop, nobody tried to wrestle him to the ground—nothing. Just a quick glance and a slightly faster pace.

I love this town, R.J. thought. He knelt and put the nose of the huge gun into the punk's earhole. "Us old ladies are getting tired of punks like you," he said in the quavery little voice he'd been practicing. "We're learning to fight back."

R.J. pulled the hammer back on his pistol. It sounded loud even to him. To the kid it must have sounded like God's footsteps. "Pass the word, punk," R.J. quavered. "Old ladies are off-limits. Next time I pull the trigger."

The kid's eyes were basketball-sized when R.J. stood up. Just for luck, he planted a hard kick in the punk's crotch and watched him shrivel up, writhing on the sidewalk like a worm on a hot plate. "Remember: Hands off old ladies, or else," R.J. said, and walked away grinning.

It was good to know the disguise worked well enough to fool a punk like that. It would be plenty good enough for his job this afternoon, too. And even better, it had been fun to put it on.

Casey had sat him in a chair and worked on his face for over an hour, using all the little makeup tricks she'd picked up in a career in TV. When she was done and showed him his reflection, R.J. was stunned.

"Holy shit," he'd said.

"Why so surprised?" Casey had asked him.

"I look like a little old lady, for Christ's sake."

She took the mirror away. "There's a little old lady in all of us, just waiting to get out. Stand up."

She'd dressed him in a housedress, padded out with stuff she'd borrowed from a friend in a costume-rental house who owed her a few favors.

And just like that, he looked like an old lady.

He stepped to the big mirror to take a look. He stopped after two steps when he heard Casey groan. "What?"

She shook her head. "Not like that. Jesus, R.J., you walk like Lawrence Taylor."

"Why shouldn't I?"

"Because you're an old lady, schmuck. Here—"

She'd put her hands on him, bending him over.

"You're *old*. This whole area hurts. So you walk like *this*. Yeah. Now the legs—knees are shot, keep 'em locked. Better. Walk across the room. Again."

And he'd practiced. After about forty minutes, she nodded. "All right. That's pretty close."

"Jesus," he complained. "I didn't know you were Method."

"I don't want you to get caught."

R.J. grinned. "Thinking of me in a holding cell dressed like this?"

"No. It might hurt my career if they knew I hung out with a cross-dresser," she said.

"Thanks, Wingate. I'll remember this."

"Just remember how to walk. *Hmmp*," she said.

"*Hmmp* what?"

She shook her head. "In a really weird kind of way—it's very . . . attractive," Casey said, her tongue resting on her lip.

And before he really knew what was happening the costume was all over the floor, and he was an hour later than he thought he would be to his stakeout.

It was worth it. Something had gotten into Casey, into both of them, and they had been all over the floor, completely wild. Maybe it really was the costume, and maybe the costume was just an excuse. For whatever else was going on—the moon, or maybe Aquarius was in Jupiter or something. Maybe it was just the weather. Sure, that was probably it; the change in weather. It was spring, goddammit.

R.J. grinned. Spring in New York. He loved it.

CHAPTER 2

Reverend Lake was terribly afraid his wife might be "seeing" someone.

He sat in the chair across from R.J.'s desk, shaking hands with himself and knotting his fingers as he tried to think of how to say it.

"She's somewhat younger than I," said the preacher. He self-consciously jerked a hand up to his salt-and-pepper hair, more salt than pepper. "And I'm afraid that I, well—" He shrugged. "It is sometimes hard to be as attentive as one might think ideal. I am shepherd of a large flock, all with their own problems, which are my problems. And Cassandra . . ."

"Cassandra would be your wife?" R.J. prompted.

The reverend looked away. "I'm sure it's all very innocent. I just worry about her so very much. She is not too much of the world," the good reverend said. "Many of us Baptists have the same failing, of being somewhat otherworldly," he said with a modest smile. "My wife is one such. I should like to know that she is all right. That's all."

"That's not quite the way I work it," R.J. told him. "What I can do is keep an eye on her, and get some photographs of who she's seeing and what she's doing."

"Photographs? I don't— Is that really necessary?"

"Yeah, it is," R.J. said. "Otherwise, you won't believe me. You won't know what I've been doing for your money, and you won't like that, because it's going to be a lot of money."

"What do you mean by a lot?" he asked, and R.J. knew from the way he said it that the guy would pay.

Sure enough, the check had cleared, and R.J. had been tailing Mrs. Lake for a week. The reverend had been afraid Mrs. Lake might be seeing somebody, and after two days R.J. knew the reverend was wrong. Mrs. Lake wasn't seeing anybody. She was, however, screwing everything that moved, including the albino dwarf she was with this afternoon.

It had taken R.J. two days of surveillance in his old-lady outfit before he could believe what he was seeing. The woman was definitely not normal. Either she was a full-fledged clinical nymphomaniac or—

Or what? Hell, it wasn't any of his business, or what. He would take the pictures this afternoon and that would be the end of it. But if this daily afternoon orgy stuff had started recently, the woman was no nympho. That kind of thing didn't start suddenly, like from a bump on the head or something. It was a lifelong pattern. No, if Mrs. Lake had suddenly developed a taste for sex—more sex every day than most people have in a month—it probably meant she had found the good reverend cheating and was getting her revenge. That's just the way people were.

But Reverend Lake was the client, so it didn't matter who or what *he* was screwing. Just so long as the check cleared, the reverend could be getting it on with the whole cast of *Tommy*. He wasn't in this business to moralize or make people better. He was in this business to take a guy's money for snapping pictures of the guy's wife with no clothes on, doing the wild thing with a stranger.

Life was funny.

Maybe because it was so full of people.

R.J. stopped outside the small hotel in the East Twenties where Mrs. Lake had taken her "dates" every afternoon this week. A nighttime photo session was easier. He could just sneak in, flash the pictures, and be off. Everybody was half-asleep, a little stunned, confused by the bright flash.

But in the afternoon, just getting past the desk could be tricky. And then when he took the pictures people were more likely to object, try to grab the camera, hit him with a chair. Maybe they were more full of adrenaline in daylight. Who knew? Still, a lot of people seemed to check into cheap hotels with strangers in the afternoon, so there really wasn't any choice.

To avoid the desk, R.J. took the service stairs in the alley beside the hotel. He had wedged a wad of tinfoil into the lock yesterday so the door would open. He waddled up to the third floor, holding his skirts out to one side. No wonder old ladies walked so slowly. How did they move at all dressed like this?

He got to the third floor landing and almost tripped as he dropped his skirts. He caught himself and staggered quietly down the hall, pulling his camera from his shoulder bag and checking it over one last time. He paused at 304 and listened. Yeah, that was passion going on inside. He'd heard it often enough. Even felt it once or twice. He moved on to the end of the hall, where through the window, he could reach the fire escape.

Glancing back to make sure nobody was watching—Look, mom, that old lady is jumping out the window!—R.J. slid the window up and stepped down onto the fire escape.

Room 304 was about halfway back the way he'd come. The fire escape was an old one, and rickety. The hotel was probably paying off the inspector. Cheaper than replacing the thing.

As R.J. made it about halfway to 304 the fire escape gave a terrible dry creak and swung out from the wall several feet.

It hung there, swaying like a spastic dinosaur for what seemed like hours, but was probably more like thirty seconds. R.J. held his breath, waited for it to hold still again, then moved on, swearing. Once he got to the next steel section, the thing behaved itself.

R.J. counted windows along the wall, hoping not to be seen but not really caring, until he came to 304. Then he flattened himself against the wall to the side of the window and reached into his shoulder bag. He pulled out a kid's toy, a small plastic periscope made of bright yellow plastic. The thing made him look and feel stupid, but it worked.

He poked the head of the periscope around to peek into the window. The window looked unlatched—why not? It was on the third floor. And they'd want to let some air in between rounds.

Over on the bed there was a dim shape and R.J. squinted through the cheap lens to make out the details. Sure enough, the beast with two backs. Except one of the backs was small, white, and stuck up like a camel's. The dwarf.

R.J. tucked away the periscope and got the camera ready. Holding it in his right hand with one finger on the trigger, he slid the window up with his left hand, swung around into the room, and started shooting.

"Hiya, folks," he called out cheerily, snapping pictures. "Everybody ready? Okay, sequel to *The Wizard of Oz*, take one."

Long experience had taught R.J. not to try to guess how people would react when they were caught, literally, with their pants down. Even so, he hadn't expected trouble. Not from a preacher's wife and a dwarf.

But at the sound of his voice the dwarf had jumped straight into the air as if he'd been burned with a branding iron—and came down on the run, headed straight for R.J.

Mrs. Lake, too, had come off the bed, grabbed the lamp from the bedside table, and yanking it from its socket, began swinging wildly, apparently trying to take off R.J.'s head, since she was swinging too high to hit the dwarf.

Instead of a smooth, quick retreat out the hotel room's door, R.J. was instantly snagged into a fight with a naked dwarf and a Baptist. The dwarf started winging wild haymakers, right at crotch level, and R.J. was hard put to fend him off and duck the lamp at the same time.

But more through luck than skill, R.J. managed to swing his heavy shoulder bag and connect with the side of the dwarf's head, and the little man went down.

At about the same time, though, the lamp caught R.J. on the cheek. He could feel the skin split, and then he got a hand up and yanked the lamp away from the outraged Mrs. Lake.

"How *dare* you," she said in her genteel voice, in spite of the fact that she was standing there stark naked after trying to decapitate what looked like an old lady.

"I was wondering the same thing," R.J. said. He nodded to where the dwarf was struggling to a sitting position. "Your friend could use a hand, sister," he said, and as she turned to look, R.J. bolted for the door.

Hurrying down the stairs, he tore a strip from his dress and held it to his cheek. It wasn't too bad, might not even need stitches.

He pushed out onto the street and the cold air slowed the bleeding. After a block or two he didn't feel too bad at all.

"Jesus, lady, are you all right?"

R.J. turned to see a black man in a nice suit, holding a small girl by the hand.

"I'm fine," said R.J. "Just a scratch."

The man looked startled as he heard R.J.'s male voice.

"You're not from here, are you?" R.J. asked him.

The man shook his head numbly. "What the hell—" he said.

R.J. grinned. It made his cheek hurt, but he grinned anyway. "It's a New York thing," said R.J. "You wouldn't understand."

CHAPTER 3

Angelo Bertelli was waiting for him in his office when he got there. Wanda, his secretary, sighed and said, "I tried to stop him, but he lit one of your cigars."

"Thanks for trying," R.J. said. "He probably has a warrant for the cigar. Nothing you could do." R.J. looked toward his office and sure enough, the blue fumes of one of his Cubans were trickling out the door of his inner office.

R.J. hadn't smoked in a lot of years, but he kept a supply of good stogies in his desk. When he was thinking, chewing on a cigar helped him think. Besides, no matter how much he hated the smell of burning tobacco, a good cigar–*un*lit— smelled great.

Bertelli was the only person who smoked his cigars, and it pissed R.J. off, but Bertelli just smiled with his shiny white teeth and earthy Guinea charm. When it came down to it, he could do what he wanted. He was a cop, and he had become a damned good friend. A guy in R.J.'s business needed friends on the force.

Besides, R.J. hated bullshit, and Angelo was a kindred spirit. Bertelli spent most of his career energy fighting it in the NYPD. "I go to work every day," he had told R.J. one night over the best Italian dinner R.J. had ever eaten, "and I got to surf in the shit. Shouldn't be that way. They should let a cop be a cop."

R.J. agreed. Most of his run-ins with cops had swamped him in the same waves of bullshit Bertelli spoke of surfing on. They also found they both liked the Knicks, the Giants, and bad musical theater. Still, the cigar smoke was annoying.

R.J. swung the door wide and stepped in. "Jesus Christ, Angelo," he said, waving a hand at the smoke. "Is this some kind of Sicilian peasant de-lousing technique?"

Bertelli was seated behind R.J.'s desk, his feet up, the stogie smoldering in his mouth. He glanced at R.J. and looked him over carefully before letting out a long wolf whistle. His tough but handsome features were carefully set in a poker face. "Well, well," he said. "Spring is in the air. Is there something you need to talk about, R.J.?"

R.J. looked down at his dress. Bertelli was, in fact, sitting on his clothes, which he had stacked neatly on his chair. "This whole joint is going to stink like a pool-hall spitoon for three weeks," he said indignantly, "and all you can talk about is my wardrobe?"

Bertelli blew out more smoke. "I'd have to say it needs talkin', R.J. Have you been doin' this long?"

R.J. yanked his clothes out from under Bertelli and started to change into them. "About a month now," he admitted. "Ever since that damned TV thing Casey did. I can't show my goddamn face anywhere in town without some dimwit shouting, 'Yo! You that TV motherfucka!' Help me with this thing in the back, would you?"

Bertelli undid the snaps.

"Thanks, Angelo. You practiced that, huh?"

"Never on somebody with your physical charms, thank God," Bertelli said, leaning back into the chair. He picked up the cigar again and blew out a large purple cloud with a satisfied look.

"You're ruining a perfectly good chewing stogie," R.J. told him, pulling up his pants.

"These things are supposed to be *smoked*, R.J. Not chewed. Chewing is an abomination in the eyes of decent society. I'm just like restorin' the delicate natural balance here." He blew out more smoke, looking even happier. "Besides, I didn't figure you'd mind, considering what I come down here for."

R.J. sat in his client chair. "Jesus, don't tell me. They finally caught Lieutenant Kates molesting a choirboy, and he shot himself rather than go to jail."

Bertelli grinned. "It ain't quite that good, but it's all right." He slid a hand into and out of his slick Italian silk suit and threw a small white envelope on the desk. "Knicks tickets."

"Have another cigar, Angelo," R.J. said scooping up the tickets. "When are they for? The Bulls?"

"For tonight, R.J. Phoenix, and it's breakin' my fuckin' heart not to go see Charles Barkley. But I got a date who only likes indoor sports, if you know what I mean."

"Aw, Jesus Christ, Angelo," R.J. moaned, tossing the tickets back on the desk. "I can't go tonight, it's Casey's birthday. Put that goddamned cigar out, would you?"

"Hey, you shoulda said. Now I gotta get her something quick," Bertelli complained, ignoring R.J.'s request to snuff the stogie. "What you got planned?"

"I have reservations at Tavern on the Green. Then I figured a carriage ride through the park."

"Sure, the whole tourist thing. Everybody should do that oncet." He took the cigar out of his mouth and reflectively dumped an inch of ash into R.J.'s pencil jar. "You two doin' all right, ace?"

R.J. snorted. "What do you get when you cross an elephant with a rhinoceros?"

"Helifino?"

"Exactly. Hell if I know, Angelo. Sometimes I can hear the angels singing, and sometimes I think that's just a trick of the acoustics, there's no music at all. I don't know. I just don't know. I think we're okay. She helped me with this disguise."

"She dresses you up like an old lady—and you think that's a good sign? R.J., you're in serious trouble if she ever turns against you."

"For all I know, she has turned against me. I just can't tell with her." He shrugged. "So, I take it for what it is, which is pretty damned good most of the time."

"That's all what matters," Bertelli said. He stood up and threw the stogie at the waste basket. "Gotta go. This was supposed to be my lunch hour, and now I gotta find a present for Casey. I'll see ya, R.J. Sorry 'bout the Knicks."

"Me, too, Angelo. See you later."

R.J. opened the windows wide. A cold wind blew in and took the cigar smoke out. He still had two hours before he was to pick up Casey at her office. He used the time to go over the books with Wanda and dictate a few quick letters.

He enjoyed the time with Wanda—they both did—and it never felt like they had to play any of the typical office games that plagued most boss-secretary relationships.

Besides, Wanda was so fast and efficient, with her shorthand, typing, filing, everything, that they could kid around, take it easy, and still get all the work done in record time.

Wanda was a real treasure, there was no doubt about it, and he felt lucky to have her. He let her know that by giving her unscheduled bonuses as often as he could. The money went to her kid in Buffalo. R.J. had never met the kid, who lived with Wanda's mother. Wanda took long weekends twice a month to go visit and beyond that never said a word about the kid, the kid's father, or how the whole situation had happened. She never said, and R.J. was smart enough not to ask.

He looked at her across his desk. She perched on the chair, relaxed but alert. He really was lucky.

"Okay," he told her. "We're ready to bill Reverend Lake." He pushed a roll of film toward her. "Get that developed first thing tomorrow. Try not to peek; it's ugly."

"If I wanted to stay away from ugly I'd move to Vermont," she told him. "I sure wouldn't work for a seedy Manhattan gumshoe."

"If it bothers you, try the florist on the corner. Maybe he's hiring."

"No good," she said. "I'm heterosexual, and I'm not Korean. You want the bill to go out first, or you calling him in for show and tell?"

"Show and tell," R.J. said, hating it. It was what they called the procedure when they had a case wrapped and the client came in to review the evidence. The evidence was generally very graphic pictures proving that a loved one didn't return the tender sentiments. It could get very dicey. R.J. had a feeling that a Baptist minister looking at pictures of his young wife screwing a dwarf might turn just about as bad as it could get. "But like I said, it's ugly. Have the Kleenex ready. The big box."

"Sure, boss. You want the handcuffs, too? Or can you handle an aging preacher without them?"

"Quit needling me. One of these days I'll get *you* in the cuffs."

She stood up, gathering her steno book and the ledgers. "One of these days I'll let you." She spun away briskly, her short, dark red hair snapping, and was already into the outer office before R.J. could hit her with a comeback. He snorted. Not that he had one.

CHAPTER 4

Casey had an office in a midtown production company run by a Pillsbury doughboy look-alike named Pike. R.J. called him "the Slug" because he was pale, blubbery, and slimy. But this slug had teeth, and he liked chomping them onto R.J. Any time he caught R.J. in the office he'd call for the security guard, a former heavyweight contender, who had stayed in shape. The guard liked R.J. and didn't like Pike, but a job was a job and he'd given R.J. one or two rough trips down in the elevator.

So instead of taking the elevator up to Casey's office, R.J. called up from the lobby. There was no place to sit in the lobby, so R.J. looked through the window at the people on the sidewalk outside. A man with a briefcase pushed a woman with her arms full of packages. The woman sat down in a slush heap. The man grabbed her cab and closed the door.

A young guy in shorts and a tank top started preaching and singing on the corner. An old lady walked slowly past, bundled up in so many coats and sweaters and scarves that she could barely move.

A large woman on roller blades whizzed by. She grabbed at the old woman's purse, snapped the strap, and was gone. The old woman stood watching for a moment, then opened her mouth and started screeching. It was a high, thin, dry wail with no words that R.J. could make out. People walking by moved a small step further away from her as they passed. In case she was crazy, R.J. thought. And in case it was catching. Which it sometimes was in this city.

The elevator doors slid open behind R.J. and he turned. His eyes met Casey's and she smiled. R.J. could feel it all the way down to his toes. Not that it was such a huge smile, but it was aimed at him, and that made it seem like it was bigger than Times Square.

"Hello, Grandma," she greeted him, planting a small kiss on his cheek. "How's the dirty picture trade?"

"I could ask you the same thing," R.J. said, looking her over. She was dressed in a cool blue spring power suit with a ruffle showing at the throat and she looked like a million dollars. "You look great," R.J. told her. He wanted to say she took his breath away, she made him hear music, just looking at her made him want to do handsprings, something like that. But she didn't go for what she thought of as flowery compliments. Telling her she looked great was pushing the limit.

Still, she linked her arm with his and they stepped out onto the rush-hour-packed sidewalk to find a cab.

It took awhile. There were plenty of cabs, but there was even more competition. By the time they got a cab crosstown and pulled up in front of Tavern on the Green it was close to 7:00, which was the time R.J. had made the reservation for. There was the usual crowd in front of the restaurant, maybe a little bigger than normal.

"We're on time. You may not have to wait for your table," R.J. said.

"That's too bad. I wanted the full experience."

And maybe the crowd looked a little different, now that he thought of it. As they got out of the cab onto the sidewalk, R.J.

noticed a lot of cameras. "The newshounds are out," he said to Casey.

Casey shrugged. "They all have someone on the payroll at these places, to let them know who's eating there every night."

"Well," R.J. said. "Tonight there must be some—"

He was going to say "celebrity" but that was chopped off by the shout of "There he is!," and before he knew what was happening he was in the center of a mob. Pushing, elbowing, foot-stomping reporters clonked one another with microphones as they clawed their way toward him, bellowing his name and whinnying questions.

"What the hell—" R.J. managed to sputter.

Casey, clinging to his arm, seemed coolly amused by it all. "Quite a birthday surprise, R.J.," she said, putting her head to his ear. "Did it take you long to work this up?"

"Mr. Brooks—!" yelled a woman with short blond hair and a long microphone.

She was shoved brutally out of the way by a guy with smarmy, blow-dried good looks. "R.J.!" the man yelled. "How about it? How do you feel?"

"Jesus Christ," R.J. grunted as the crowd pushed them back. "What the hell is all this?"

"It must be the sequel," Casey got out between shoves. "I didn't think they'd land on you like this."

It made no sense to R.J. But for the next two minutes he was too busy to think about it, as he tried to get them into the restaurant alive. The reporters didn't seem to care if they got their story, whatever it was, from a live person or roadkill.

About ten feet short of the door it began to look like they weren't going to make it. R.J. put Casey behind him, with her back to a wall, and faced the mob.

"All right, goddammit," he snarled. "What is this all about?"

The hysterical babble rose a notch as they all tried to get the first question.

"One at a time! You—with the mustache." R.J. pointed to

a young black man with a mustache and gold-rimmed glasses.

"Mr. Brooks," the man said with a smug glance at the others, "what were your feelings when you heard about the sequel?"

"I'll let you know as soon as I hear. What sequel?"

There was actually a moment of near silence.

"You haven't heard?" asked the short-haired blond.

"For Christ's sake, heard *what?*"

Almost in unison, R.J. could hear the TV people muttering "Move in tight" to their cameramen.

Blow-dry tried to shove a microphone up R.J.'s nose as he said, "Andromeda Pictures is making a sequel to *As Time Goes By.*"

R.J. couldn't think of a single word worth saying.

He tried to think of a cuss word strong enough, and couldn't. He tried to believe that somebody was kidding him, and he couldn't do that, either.

A sequel to *As Time Goes By?* It wasn't possible. It wasn't even thinkable. It was maybe the single greatest movie Hollywood had ever made—a sequel to perfection? No way; how could anybody, even in Hollywood, think they could get away with that?

But R.J.'s feelings didn't have a lot to do with his appreciation of good cinema. *As Time Goes By* had been the picture his parents had been working on when they first met. The script had been first-rate, the direction terrific, and the chemistry between the members of the cast—especially his parents—had been the stuff that acting dreams are made of.

The movie had turned his father from a star into *the* star. It had brought his mother, too, into the front rank of Hollywood's starlets. And as he now knew from his mother's diaries, he had been conceived on the set during the filming of the movie.

And some soulless, money-hungry, brain-dead baboon was making a *sequel?*

Some greedy half-wit was trying to cash in on his father's lifeblood? Trample on something that was almost sacred, just for a couple of cheesy fast dollars?

No. By God—

"How about it, Mr. Brooks? You have a comment?"

"I'll say I do," R.J. snarled.

The microphones hovered close, the lenses zoomed in, the jackals held their breath.

"I hope the goddamned animals responsible for this die a nasty death as soon as possible. Now get the hell out of my way."

R.J. pushed through the reporters, holding Casey's hand. They bleated for more, but he was too angry to talk. He was so mad he didn't have any idea how he got to the table, but a few minutes later he was sitting there with a menu in his hands.

Casey was saying something, but he didn't hear it. He looked up at her. She sat across from him, cool and amused.

"You knew about this?" he asked her.

She shrugged. "Sure. It's been gossip around the industry for a while."

"Why didn't you tell me?"

She just looked; not unfriendly, not mad at him, but not really registering how much this bothered him. She did not understand, would never understand, the turmoil this was making him feel. He wasn't sure he understood it himself. All he knew was that he hadn't been this mad in a long time.

"Honestly, R.J., what does this have to do with you?"

He couldn't answer that, not without going deeper into himself than he wanted to. So he didn't answer. He tried to shrug it off, tried to enjoy a birthday dinner with Casey.

But it was harder work than he could do on such short notice. No matter how hard he tried, no matter how good Casey looked in the carriage ride through the park, the wind in her hair and a rosy glow in her cheeks—no matter what, he couldn't shake off the feeling.

R.J. was mad and didn't really know why or what to do about it. But the dinner was spoiled, there was no question about that.

Somebody was spitting on his parents' graves, and he didn't like it.

CHAPTER 5

The morning *Post* had him on the front page. The *Times*, of course, had to play it low key and stuck him in the Arts section. R.J. didn't dare turn on the TV. He knew he'd be all over the dial.

He hadn't slept much. The final part of his birthday present to Casey had left him tired, but as she drifted off to sleep almost purring, R.J. remained wide awake. He looked at the gorgeous face pillowed on his shoulder and thought, What the hell have I got to complain about?

Casey's face in sleep had taken on a softness that it never had when she was awake. All the defenses were gone; it was just pure Casey now, and that was amazingly good. As R.J. traced the lines of her face with a light fingertip, he had a quick vision of what their children would look like.

He thought about that and sat up. Casey grumphed once and rolled over.

Children, hell. Casey didn't want children. She didn't really even want a long-term relationship of any kind as far as he could tell. And what the hell was he going to do with children? He couldn't handle the son he already had. Hadn't even seen the kid in a couple of years, and his mother was sending frantic letters that the boy was out of control. Well, that was her fault, and her problem. She'd made that choice when she had shut him out of raising the kid. He sent the checks and a present at Christmas and his son's birthday. If that wasn't enough, well, sorry. He'd done all he could.

R.J. was wide awake now. He realized his mind had spun him off onto other things that worried him because he couldn't figure out why this business of the sequel should bother him at all.

He got up and paced in the next room. It wasn't his problem. It had nothing to do with him. He stood by the window and stared out for a while, then just sat on the couch and tried to figure out why, since it really didn't mean a thing to him, it bothered him so much.

Okay, big deal, a sequel. So what? It wasn't his movie. It wasn't even his dad's movie, legally speaking. Dad had been paid for it, and the money had helped put R.J. through school, and probably paid for his first bicycle. Wasn't that enough? Why should he feel connected to the goddamned thing? The suits on the coast owned it, it was theirs, he hadn't even thought of the movie in years.

R.J. had left Hollywood behind him years ago, and if it was trying to catch up to him—well, he didn't have to let it. Just shrug it off, keep plugging where he was, forget about it, right?

Only he couldn't forget about it.

Morning came and found R.J. slumped on the couch, finally asleep, when Casey came out to go to work. Her hand on his shoulder woke him. He blinked up at her, feeling stupid and thickheaded.

"Do I snore?" she asked him.

He tried to answer but had to clear his throat a couple of times first. "What?"

"Do I snore? Bad breath? Anything like that?"

R.J. didn't get it. His head hurt and his eyes were puffy and he couldn't get his brain to tell him anything beyond an urgent request for coffee and this was a hell of a way to start what looked like it was going to be One of Those Days. He had no idea what Casey was talking about.

"No. You sleep quietly and your breath is great," he said.

"Is the bed too lumpy?"

"For Christ's sake, Casey."

She tugged his ear playfully. "I woke up alone in the middle of the night. I had no idea where you were."

"You were worried?"

She nodded and gave him her small cat smile. "Yeah. It took me over five seconds to get back to sleep." She let go of his ear and gave him a little slap on the cheek. "Your loss, hoss. You could have helped me stay awake. See you later." And she was out the door before he could think of an answer.

R.J. took a shower, hoping the hot water would wash away some of the sand in his head. It did, but it left the anger. He didn't feel like eating anything, so he got dressed and headed for the office, stopping to pick up some doughnuts and cinnamon rolls in case he changed his mind.

"My, my," Wanda greeted him, cocking an eyebrow at the doughnuts. "What's the occasion? Or is this just what celebrities eat for breakfast?"

He flung his coat at the coat rack. "Celebrities eat their young for breakfast," he said. "For lunch they eat whoever is closest, and for dinner they eat themselves." He dropped the doughnuts on Wanda's desk.

"We are very profound this morning," she said. "Especially for somebody who is the lead teaser for most of the news programs and front page of the *Post*."

"I saw it," he snarled.

"And did you see this?" she asked quietly. She pushed the Business section toward him. There was a photograph of an attractive but hard-looking woman under the headline AN-DROMEDA CEO IN TOWN. Under the picture it said, JANINE WRIGHT TO SPEAK TO STOCKHOLDERS.

R.J. looked up at Wanda. "What's this?"

She smiled. It was almost mean. "Boss, we both know you were going to stomp into your office and sulk for an hour and a half. Then you'd stick your head out and snarl at me to find out who was making the goddamn sequel. Then you'd fret for a while, trying to figure out how to get to them." She tapped a neat red nail on the picture in the paper. "Here she is, gift-wrapped. Staying at the Pierre."

R.J. stared at the picture. Then he stared at Wanda, who just stared back, looking cool, amused, and in control. R.J. finally had to laugh. "Doll, you're amazing, you know that?"

"Of course I know it," she said.

R.J. picked up the newspaper, grabbed a cinnamon roll and headed into his office.

He sat at his desk, munching the doughnut and reading the article. Janine Wright, president of Andromeda Studios, had arrived in New York yesterday. Although she was allegedly just in town to talk to a group of concerned stock owners, the rumor was that she was using the trip to plant some publicity seeds for the studios' hot new project, the sequel to *As Time Goes By*.

There were also a couple of hints about Andromeda's disasterous previous year, all their prospects having withered at the box office. Janine Wright herself had gotten behind this sequel and pinned a lot of Andromeda's hopes on the project. She was sunk, and maybe the studio, too, if it didn't fly.

There were one or two references R.J. didn't get about Janine Wright's "legendary way with people." From the tone of the piece, R.J. gathered that Wright was an ogre. Well, he wasn't expecting to meet any saints. Not from Hollywood—especially not the head of a studio. They didn't get the job by being sensitive to people's feelings; they got the job by killing everyone else who wanted it. That hadn't changed since his father's time.

None of that bothered R.J. He had cut his teeth with these people, and he would—

Would what? Wait a minute, what did he think he was going to do? Show them the error of their ways? Politely suggest that they give up the idea of the sequel and do something else, instead? And if they refused, threaten them with his camera bag?

R.J. couldn't see any scenario that might work. He pulled a cigar from his desk and began to chew it thoughtfully. Only one thing motivated these people: money. To get them to do something you either had to give them money, or threaten to take money away from them.

R.J. was pretty flush right now, for him. That meant he could buy a steak for dinner if he wanted it. It didn't put him in Janine Wright's league. So if he couldn't offer them any significant cash—

An idea flitted in. He thought about it. It might work. The odds weren't good, but maybe he could bluff it out without having to play the hand.

He knew he looked like his old man. And thanks to the jackals of the press, everybody knew who he was. Maybe, just maybe, he could threaten them with so much bad publicity and so many bogus lawsuits, they would cut their losses and give up the idea of the sequel. If they were in such bad shape, they might back away from any legal tangle that could keep them from scoring quickly at the box office.

It could work. It probably wouldn't but it could. If he could get together all the fans, film buffs, nostalgia freaks, and cranks, he could sure stir up a shit storm—maybe enough of a shit storm to get Janine Wright to back down.

Anyway, she might swallow the bluff. R.J. leaned back in his chair and threw the mangled cigar at the waste basket. Let's just see what she's made of, he thought with satisfaction.

R.J. picked up the phone and dialed the Hotel Pierre. A very smooth voice, sounding like it had just been oiled, answered. "Hotel Pierre, how may I help you?"

"Albemarle Florist," R.J. said. He always used the name *Albemarle* because it was impossible to understand; no one could look it up because they could never quite piece it together. "We have a very large basket for a, uh—" He rattled a sheet of paper on his desk, just for effect. "—Jasmine White?"

There was a pause so short R.J. wasn't sure he heard it at all. "We have a J*anine Wright* registered."

"Uh . . ." said R.J., taking a stab at it, "is that in the Presidential Suite?"

"That's correct, sir."

"Yeah, do I gotta carry it all the way up to the, what, the top floor?"

"The top floor, yes. No, sir, if you will deliver to the Sixty-first Street entrance we will take it from there."

"Beautiful," said R.J. and hung up.

He was feeling smug, first that his little scam had worked and second that he had guessed right about the suite. Of course, the Presidential. Where Nixon had stayed. That's the way these moguls thought. President of a studio, president of the U.S., what's the difference? Except the President of the U.S. didn't make a quarter of what Janine Wright would make. And if any U.S. president did to the national budget what the studios routinely did to theirs, he'd be out of office and into Leavenworth.

It didn't matter. He had a plan. It wasn't much of a plan, but it beat the hell out of sitting around the office, eating cinnamon rolls.

R.J. stood, stretched, and strolled for the door, snagging his coat as he went by Wanda's desk. "Reverend Lake will be here at two," she warned him.

He shrugged into his coat. "If I'm not back by then, you can show him the pictures."

"If you're not back by then," she threatened, "I'm taking a sick day."

R.J. grinned at her, waved, and headed out the door.

CHAPTER 6

The Hotel Pierre was a swanky old place on 61st and Fifth. It had the kind of old-school big-dollar feel to it that always made R.J. want to blow his nose on one of the thick Oriental carpets, carve his initials in one of the Colonial writing desks in the lobby, throw dirty socks up to hang from the chandeliers.

But right now his problem was more immediate. If you stepped in through the door on Fifth Avenue you'd find yourself in a lobby swarming with attendants in white gloves, wearing gray uniforms with gold trim; a dark-suited concierge, bell captain, valets, clerks—hell, the place was a discreet, charming, posh, tastefully understated Gestapo headquarters. And one did *not* simply waltz in and head for a guest's room. One would find oneself waltzed out the door again by a white-gloved bouncer in record time.

But getting into places like this was R.J.'s job, and he had come prepared.

Holding a clipboard he'd brought along, loaded with a

computer printout, a small stack of index cards, and a pen stuck through the clip, R.J. approached the staff entrance on 61st Street. The printout was nothing more than some blank business form he had on the computer at his office, but nobody had to know that.

He was not even two steps in the door of the staff entrance when a gray uniform blocked his way.

"We're not hiring this week," the uniform told R.J.

"Oh, really," said R.J. He decided to run with the lead he'd been given and quickly took out the pen and held it poised over his clipboard. "And have you filed the forty-two-dash-twelve-slash-four-eleven B with our office explaining why not? Considering what our files say this ought to be good."

R.J. looked up at the uniform and watched his smooth superiority fall from his face and hit his shoes. "Uh, what?" he said.

R.J. glared at him under one raised eyebrow. "So you *haven't* filed a forty-two-dash-twelve-slash-four-eleven B?" He slammed the pen back under the clip. "I'll have to see your Minority Hiring Report."

"Um," the man sputtered out, "I, it—the personnel office is back there." The uniform moved quickly away, no doubt looking for something to polish.

"Have a nice day," said R.J. grimly, and headed back the way the uniform had pointed.

I ought to move, R.J. thought. Tahiti, maybe. Or Sri Lanka. Anyplace where a clipboard is a free pass to be a bully is no place to live.

Going through a large gray door, R.J. found himself in a hallway. At the far end he could see the glowing red letters of an Exit sign. It hung over a gray metal door. R.J. went through the door and found a flight of stairs next to a service elevator. He pushed the Up button, and a moment later the doors slid open.

R.J. rode up to the top floor without interruption. He got

out of the elevator, and looked around for a clue to the whereabouts of the Presidential Suite. The Pierre wasn't the kind of
place to put a brass plaque on the wall and let a hard-working
guy know which room was the right one. Naw, they were way
too tastefully discreet. R.J. would have to work at it.

About halfway down the hall there were two large oak
doors. They looked fairly presidential to R.J. The rest of the
rooms on the floor had single doors.

A large serving cart was parked to the side of the double
door. The ruins of a presidential-looking breakfast were lying
all over the cart. R.J. stepped forward to survey the contents.
A bill was tucked under a plate of half-nibbled lox. There was
an absurd total at the bottom, and next to it, a scrawled signature: *J. Wagt*, it looked like. But hell, a signature is a signature.
R.J. was willing to bet the ranch that *Wagt* was really Wright.

Somedays, R.J. thought, being a detective was a lot easier
than others. He knocked on the double door.

Just as he was getting ready to knock for a second time, the
door swung open. Inside stood a girl, no more than twenty-
one. She was medium height, slender, with black hair that was
obviously dyed from a lighter shade, and dressed in deliberately slashed, baggy clothes. The girl stared at R.J. with an
empty expression. Then suddenly, a look of recognition swam
into her pale blue eyes.

"Oh," she said.

"Is Janine Wright here?" R.J. asked.

The girl nodded. "Come on in," she said, with an air of
who-the-hell-cares that made R.J. certain Janine Wright
wouldn't like it.

He went in, anyway.

Janine Wright was sitting on a settee that probably cost
more than any car R.J. had ever owned. She was an elegant-
looking woman with short blond hair and the hardest eyes R.J.
had ever seen. She was dressed in a two-inch-thick terry-cloth
robe and had a telephone glued to her ear, and as he walked

into the room she glanced up at him like he was a piece of second-hand furniture.

"Fuck that," she said into the phone, "and fuck you." She looked away, to a sleazy-looking, mean-faced little guy in a three-piece suit sitting on the opposite end of the settee. She snapped her fingers at him and he delivered a cigarette, then lit it for her.

Janine Wright looked back at R.J. And spoke into the phone. "No. You're dead, you hear me? You don't work, ever again. You want me to spell it? I own your balls now. Well, eat shit and die, asshole," and she hung up. "Fix it, Murray," she said to the weasel.

Her eyes now locked onto R.J. "Well," she said, and her voice was doing the same thing her eyes had done, talking to him as if he couldn't really understand words. "You look just like him."

R.J. had expected to start off by telling her who he was. Now he hesitated. The way she had said that had boxed him in, dismissed him at the same time it identified him. He felt like a pet caught pissing on the rug.

"Well?" she prompted.

"A lot of people think I look just like him," he said. "A little makeup, the right clothes, I *would* look just like him." He was about to add, "And that could cause you some bad publicity," but the weasel didn't let him.

"Do you know how much trouble you're in, coming in here like this?" the little guy barked. R.J. corrected his first impression. Not a weasel; one of those scruffy, obnoxious little terriers. The kind that only bites you when your back is turned.

She cut him off. "Shut up, Murray." And then to R.J., "How much do you want?"

There she was again, pushing him off balance, jumping around so he would stay confused. He had grown up watching that technique used by people like her, and he didn't like it, but it still worked. "How much *what?*" he said, pushing back a little.

She blinked. "Who's your agent?"

R.J. grinned. A stock comeback like that meant he'd won one. He had *her* confused.

"I don't have an agent. I don't believe in agents," he said. "I like to do everything myself." And he cracked his knuckles.

"That's enough, asshole," said Murray, and he stood up. R.J. took a step toward him and he sat down again.

Janine Wright frowned. The girl giggled. Janine looked at her briefly, coldly, then looked back at R.J. She shook her head, just twice, and turned to the girl who had let him in. "You let him in. Get this shithead out of here."

"I'm not your fucking slave," the girl said.

"Don't use that language with me," Janine Wright said.

"Oh, for God's sake, what language am I supposed to use? All I've ever heard from you is fuck this, shit on that, piss on you—"

Janine Wright was up and across the floor in two steps. She slapped the girl once and the sound of it was loud enough to make R.J. jump. "I'm still your mother, you little bitch," Janine Wright said.

The girl took a step back, rubbing her cheek. "That's my problem," she said.

Janine Wright hissed out a breath and raised her hand again. The girl didn't flinch, just stared at her mother. Janine put her hand down.

"Sometimes you're so much like your father I could puke," she said.

The girl just looked at her. "Considering some of the things you've done," she told her mother, "I doubt you could puke at all anymore, no matter what." Then she looked once at R.J., and there was something funny going on in her eyes, a kind of idea or recognition that R.J. was being included in, but didn't get. Then the girl turned and walked out of the room.

Janine Wright watched her daughter go. "Murray," she said.

The terrier got up and scuttled away. "I'll talk to her," he said.

"Do you have kids?" Janine Wright asked R.J., without looking at him. "If you don't, stay lucky. Never have kids. They're fucking awful. The whole thing is a—"

Suddenly she turned and looked at him, as if seeing him for the first time. "Who the fuck are you, anyway?"

R.J. stepped forward and handed her his business card. "My name is R. J. Brooks," he said.

Janine Wright did a double take, looked at the card, and stared at him again. "Oh," she said. "You're that guy. That's why you look like him."

"That's right."

"I thought you were an actor."

R.J. grinned at her. "Nope."

"I thought you were auditioning."

"No, I'm complaining."

She looked at him for a full thirty seconds. Once again, R.J. felt like he was a wrinkled drapery, or a chair with a stain on the slipcover. Finally she nodded and said, "Sit down."

She turned and moved back to the settee. R.J. perched on a chair that would probably make a down payment on a place in the Hamptons. He opened his mouth to start his pitch, but she cut him off.

"How much do you make?" she asked him.

R.J. blinked. "None of your goddamned business."

"You grew up in Hollywood, right? Why'd you leave?"

"There's no air and I hate the people," he said, wondering where this was going.

"Ever think about going back?"

"Think about it? No, I have nightmares sometimes. Look, Ms. Wright, I'm not applying for a job—"

"Then why the fuck should I care if you look just like him?"

"I can't imagine why the fuck. You brought it up, not me."

A door slammed and Murray came scuttling back rubbing

his face. He slid into his place beside Janine Wright so fast, R.J. had to blink to be sure he wasn't seeing things.

"I'll pay you two thousand a week to come work for me," Janine Wright said.

"I advise against that," said Murray.

"Twenty-two-fifty," said Janine Wright.

R.J. felt the breath leave him and for a few seconds he couldn't get it back. Finally he managed to shake his head. "Can we start over? I don't think we've been in the same conversation since I got here."

"So what do you want?"

"I want to talk about this picture you're making, the sequel to *As Time Goes By*."

"You don't have a leg to stand on!" Murray barked. "We own all worldwide rights to this sequel and if you think—"

"Shut up, Murray," Janine Wright said.

"I'm not going to sit here and—"

"Yes you are," she said, and looked at him briefly. He shut up. He seemed a little paler than he had been.

Janine looked at R.J. and smiled; not like she was happy or amused, but like he was a brain-dead kid she had to talk to. "Twenty-five hundred dollars."

"Jesus Christ, lady, for what?"

"For looking like your father."

R.J. could feel something happening on his face, almost as if he was watching it, not like it was his face at all. It was somewhere between a snarl and a sneer. Everything about this woman and her pet lawyer made his skin crawl, made the hairs stand up on the back of his neck, made him want to grab her by the lapels of her $500 bathrobe and shake her till her teeth rattled.

"Listen," he told her, fighting for control, "I'm not going to plug your sequel for you. If I put on a fedora and call in the cameras, it will be because I want to stop the picture, not because you're paying me to make people want to see a half-wit, brain-dead, watered-down, scummed-up, weak, sick, silly, stupid copy of something that's more important to a hell of a lot of people than—"

"Including you?" she asked. She hadn't even blinked at the name calling. "It's important to you?"

"Including me," R.J. said. "And since I do look like him, I think I can get you a lot of negative publicity if you go ahead with this thing."

She just looked. "Negative publicity?"

"Yeah, you know. Look-alike son calls project a lame sack of shit, scion of great actor heaps scorn on greedy, brainless, soulless studio—that kind of thing. Get the fan magazines involved. Organize protests. Maybe a nuisance suit. Hell, lady, I haven't even thought about it and I know ten ways to pee in your soup."

Janine Wright smiled. "Okay. Great. Do it."

"Gotcha," said Murray.

R.J. blinked. He had thought he was getting somewhere, really felt like he was on a roll. "What?"

She leaned back. "I said, go ahead. Do it. Call your press conferences. Organize boycotts. Sue the shit out of me. You're gonna do for free what I would have paid you for, shit-for-brains."

R.J. was surprised to see his hands were trembling. He'd never wanted to hit somebody so badly. "You would have paid me to sue the shit out of you?"

"Absolutely. Including court costs. Now you can pay for it yourself. This is fucking great."

"Why?"

She stood up. "I don't have time to teach kindergarten to half-wits. You ever hear the expression, no such thing as bad publicity?" She moved toward the door.

"I've heard it."

"Well, the way things are today, it goes even further. Bad publicity is the best kind. People hear you hate this movie, they'll go see it just to find out why. They'll buy a ticket just so they can agree with you." She opened the door. "Assholes. And they say TV is stupid. I wonder why. Get out."

R.J.'s head was spinning. He felt like the private eye in an old movie, realizing somebody had slipped him a mickey. It was in the drink, he thought, except I didn't have a drink.

"Come on, get out," Janine Wright repeated. "Before I have to call security. Forget the white gloves, those cocksuckers are mean. Move your ass, ace."

Murray jumped up and leaned around her, yapping at R.J. "Sue us, you dumb loser. You have to file in California, and that's my private pissing grounds. I guarantee it'll take you twenty years to see court, and you won't have a penny left. And when you *do* get in court, it'll be *my* court and *my* judge and you, you pathetic loser, *you*—"

"That's enough, Murray," Janine Wright said.

"Loser," Murray yapped, and then he flinched away as if expecting a kick.

R.J. found his way to the door. "You're a tough lady," he said.

She gave him that look again, that used-furniture look. "You're only half right, half-wit," she said. She gave him a push and slammed the door.

R.J. stood in the hall and looked at the beautiful oak door. She was right. She was no lady.

R.J. made it back to his office in plenty of time for the session with Reverend Lake and it was as bad as he had figured. The reverend wept when he saw the pictures and fell to his knees on the office floor, yelling out pleas for forgiveness and blubbering like a baby. Then he looked at the pictures some more, a little too long, R.J. thought, and a little too interested, before he caught himself and went back to praying and snuffling on the floor.

R.J. sat through the whole performance without blinking. The check had already cleared. Even when the reverend got a little more specific than he should have about some of the things he wanted forgiveness for—something about one of the teenage boys in the youth group—R.J. just sat and watched. He'd seen it before. Besides, he was still churning over the whole thing with Janine Wright. He was so burned up about it that he couldn't really enjoy the reverend's performance as much as he should have.

And when that was over, he didn't even enjoy banking the fat bonus check Reverend Lake left with him in exchange for the envelope with the pictures. The good man left, clutching the envelope like he would have paid even more for something that good. R.J. should have enjoyed the way the man's sweaty knuckles turned white as he gripped that envelope, but he didn't.

In fact, although he didn't know it then, it would be a good long time before R.J. really enjoyed anything again.

CHAPTER 7

R.J. was in a long hallway lined with doors. There had to be a couple thousand doors, and his father was behind one of them. But inside the one he opened there was just a pile of bones, and then the door slammed shut behind him and he knew the bones were his father's and as he tried to back off, the bones got up and danced and the door started to slam open and shut to set the beat for the dancing bones—

—and he woke up covered with sweat and somebody was pounding on the door of his apartment.

R.J. shook his head to clear it. It didn't work. The pounding on the door didn't stop, either. He got up and splashed some water on his face. Anybody who pounded on the goddamn door like that at—what was it, 3:45? Hell, let 'em wait.

He let them wait until he got a bathrobe on. Then he opened the door. There stood Detective Don Boggs.

Boggs was a square guy with a low forehead and a lower IQ. He had a widow's peak that almost touched his eyebrows and was wearing one of the ugliest suits R.J. had ever seen.

Even more amazing, it was different from the one he'd been wearing last time they'd met, which until then had been the ugliest R.J. had ever seen.

R.J. had met Boggs on several occasions and they would never be doubles partners at the country-club tennis tournament. In fact, R.J. would cheerfully spit on Boggs's grave and he knew the detective felt the same about him.

So it wasn't a pleasant surprise to see him, especially with that righteous scowl on his face.

"What the hell took you so long?"

"Gee, I'm sorry I didn't hear you," said R.J. "I was reading Tennyson and just lost myself."

Boggs frowned. "Is that funny?"

"No, Don, Tennyson is very serious stuff. I think it's poetry. You want to come in and I'll read it to you?"

Boggs pushed past him and into the apartment. "You'll have plenty of time to read poetry where you're going. It'll make you real popular."

Annoyed, R.J. closed the door. "Where am I going, Don? And what couch cover did you make that suit out of?"

Boggs turned and glared at him, then shook his head and looked righteous again. "I've waited a long time for this, Brooks. Get dressed. You're coming with me."

"Didn't I hear a rumor about a law somewhere that said you need a warrant or due cause or something?"

"This time I can get the warrant, Brooks. I can have it here in half an hour. But it might go easier on you if you cooperate. Maybe we can get your sentence reduced."

"That would be swell, Don, I appreciate it. By the way, what did I do this time?"

Boggs smiled like it was his favorite crime. "Murder One, Brooks. And this time we got you dead to rights."

R.J. sat on the arm of his sofa. On top of that dream, this was just a little bit too much. He knew it was serious, but if he wasn't careful he was going to bust out laughing. "Who'd I kill? I forget."

"Murray Belcher, smart-ass. Like you didn't know. Now get dressed or I'll take you in your goddamn robe."

Murray Belcher. Murray Belcher. Who the hell was Murray Belcher? Whoever he was, he was dead now, and the cops had to have a pretty good reason to think R.J. killed him. Otherwise they would have waited until morning and sent Angelo to get him.

R.J. got dressed, with Boggs hovering nearby to make sure he didn't slip a howitzer into his shoe. They left the apartment a few minutes later and R.J. still didn't have a clue who Murray Belcher was.

He still didn't know when they got down to Lieutenant Kates's office.

If there was one guy on the NYPD that R.J. got along with less than Boggs, it was Lieutenant Kates. They'd never actually swung at each other, but R.J. figured that was just a matter of time.

"Sit down, Fontaine," Kates greeted him. The lieutenant liked to needle him by calling him Fontaine, after R.J.'s famous mother. He thought it showed wit, and R.J. figured he was half right.

"Thanks, Freddy," R.J. said. "Say, the office looks real classy. Who's your decorator?"

Kates came around the battered desk and perched on the front of it so he was only a few inches away from R.J. "You're going to answer some questions, Fontaine, and your smart mouth is not going to get you anywhere this time. Except maybe Attica." He crossed his arms and sneered at R.J. "Your high-priced show-biz lawyers aren't getting you off the hook, either, Fontaine."

R.J. was getting annoyed enough to wish that he had really killed this Murray Belcher, whoever he was. "Sure, Freddy, that's a beautiful speech. I know how hard you must have practiced it. You didn't even stutter once. But I got some bad news for you."

"I'll bet you do," Kates sneered. "But not as bad as what I got for you."

"Number one," said R.J., ignoring Kates's interruption, "as a matter of fact, unless you're going to file charges or suspend the Bill of Rights, I'm afraid my high-priced show-biz lawyer *will* get me off the hook. There's a bunch of stuff like unlawful confinement, habeas corpus, all of that. I can explain it when you're done trampling on it. Number two—" He held up two fingers and wiggled them for Kates so he wouldn't lose count. "I don't have a clue who this guy Belcher is, and I make it a rule never to kill strangers."

R.J. stood up and leaned into Kates's face. "And number three, lieutenant, you can cut the crap right now and tell me what I'm supposed to know about this, and what gives you the right to drag me down here in the middle of the night and keep me here without arrest and without a lawyer, or I'll sit in a cell and see you in Hell before I answer a question from either you or this low-grade moron you keep for a pet. So get polite, or read me my rights, or I'm done for the night, Freddy."

"First, you'll answer me one question," Kates said. "And I'll like your answer or I stick you in a cell with a fag bodybuilder until I remember to call your lawyer. Which might not be for a couple of days."

R.J. knew he'd do it, too—and maybe even get away with it. So he let out a big breath and nodded his head. "One question, Freddy. Then I start playing hardball, too."

Kates nodded. R.J. had never noticed before how small and beady his eyes were. They were gleaming now. Kates looked like he was about to drool. "Where were you last night?"

"It's still last night now, Freddy," R.J. told him. "Can you pin it down a little better?"

"Yeah, I can pin it down, Fontaine. Let's say where were you between the hours of ten and one?"

R.J. frowned. This wasn't going to be very good. "I was home, Freddy. Mostly in bed."

The beady little eyes got brighter. "In bed alone?"

"That's right, Freddy. Sorry to disappoint you."

"Can you prove it?"

"That's three questions, Lieutenant. But just to show I'm cooperating— No, I can't prove it. No phone calls, no deliveries, no chance acquaintances dropping by for badminton. Just me. Stop drooling for Christ's sake."

"This just gets better," stuck in Boggs. He was leaning in the doorway trying to make his face a copy of Kates's, and more than halfway succeeding. "Shall I book him?"

"Not yet," said Kates. "I think we should just hold him for a while."

"Now look, I've done my duty," R.J. said. "I haven't even threatened to sue you two-bit sleazy bastards. I'm a good citizen, okay? Now it's your turn. Arrest me or let me go. So what's gonna be, Freddy? Miranda or The Flesh Man?"

"What the hell is The Flesh Man?" Boggs wanted to know.

R.J. grinned at him. "My dog-bite lawyer. He always gets his pound of flesh. He doesn't win cases—he just makes such a pain-in-the-ass of himself that the cases never go to trial. And I'm going to end up owning that ugly damn suit and everything else you've got."

Kates snarled and shook out a cigarette. "I got enough to hold you," he said through a cloud of smoke. "I can get a judge who agrees with me."

"Then read me my rights and shove me in a cell," R.J. said. "I'm sick of you, I'm sick of King Kong over there, and I'm through cooperating."

Kates bit a piece off the filter of his cigarette and spat it on the floor beside R.J.'s foot. He glanced up at Boggs. Boggs shrugged. Kates dropped his cigarette on the floor. "You can go. But we're not done with you. Keep yourself available for questioning—"

"Sure, Freddy," R.J. said tiredly.

"—or by Christ I *will* toss you in the can and lose the key. You hear me, Fontaine?"

"I hear you. And next time you come for me, you better

have some paper, Freddy." R.J. stood up and leaned into Kates's face. "Or you're going to find yourself in the same cell, sport. Do you hear *me?*"

But Kates just glared at him. "Get him out of here, Boggs," he said, and Boggs obligingly grabbed R.J.'s arm and led him out the door.

Boggs didn't offer him a ride home, not that R.J. expected him to. Still, he was plenty ticked off at being dragged down here in the middle of the night and then just dumped on the cold sidewalk.

Worse, he still had no idea what the whole thing was about. He knew that given half a chance of getting away with it, Kates would frame him for anything handy. He was that kind of cop. He wanted his cases to be on the books as solved, and he didn't care if he got the wrong guy as long as a jury might buy it.

And on top of that, he didn't like R.J. Never had. There weren't that many rules Kates bothered with, but he would bend any that he had to to get at R.J.

And he had something this time. Otherwise he wouldn't have let R.J. go like that. If he was just fishing for something, he'd keep R.J., make him sweat, hope something dropped out. He was sure of himself this time, too sure. He was hoping R.J. really was guilty, and that was a big difference from just hoping somebody else in the media or on a jury might believe it. He really thinks he's got me, R.J. thought.

But who the fuck is Murray Belcher?

CHAPTER 8

The headline read MURRAY BELCHER SLAIN.

It wasn't a big headline, just a squib on page four. Three short columns, no picture. But the way it looked made it sound like everybody would know who Murray Belcher was.

"It's a goddamned conspiracy," R.J. grumbled, slapping the newspaper against the counter.

"Oh, yeah? Then it's gonna cost you extra, my man," Hookshot said over the rim of a cup of coffee. He slurped noisily, just because he knew the sound would bother R.J.

Wallace Steigler, known as Hookshot, was one of R.J.'s closest friends and, outside of Bertelli and Henry Portillo, one of the only people in the world R.J. could really trust. Maybe because, like R.J., he had a couple of different strands of his background pulling at him.

Hookshot was a Jewish black man, the product of a brief marriage between an Israeli officer serving at the U.N. and a Harlem beauty queen. His father had been killed by terrorists when young Wallace was a month old. Fifteen years later,

Hookshot, a promising high school basketball star, lost his right hand by being on the wrong piece of turf at the wrong time. He wore a gleaming steel hook in its place and ran a newsstand in midtown Manhattan.

The stand was a drop for discreet individuals on both sides of the law and an unofficial intelligence center for anybody who had the price and could persuade Hookshot they needed to know. Most of the hot items were gathered by Hookshot's army of prepubescent street kids. He usually called them the Mini-mensch, and they were all over Manhattan on their skateboards and Rollerblades.

"I got expenses, you know," Hookshot was saying.

R.J. ignored him and read the article.

Well-known West Coast attorney Murray Belcher was found dead in his suite at a midtown hotel, an apparent victim of poisoning.

"Poison!" said R.J. "Jesus Christ, they really think I would *poison* somebody?"

"Never," said Hookshot. "Only if the car bomb failed."

R.J. read on.

Belcher, whose practice was limited to only one client lately, Andromeda Pictures, was in town to—

"Son-of-a-bitch!" R.J. shouted. An elderly lady reaching in for a *Times* gave him a frosty look down her nose. "*That* Murray Belcher!" He remembered the little rat with his slicked-back hair and scruffy terrier attitude, threatening him at the door of Janine Wright's suite. "Shut up, Murray," she had said maybe a half dozen times. And he hadn't put it together because she had never said, "Shut up, Murray Belcher, well-known West Coast attorney."

"Son-of-a-goddamn-bitch," he muttered one more time.

He finished reading about what a great guy Murray had been: tireless worker for charities, divorced father of three, on the board of this temple, that bank, right-hand man of Janine Wright in her meteoric rise to control of Andromeda.

Found dead by poisoning.

And now R.J. was ankle deep in sewage because somebody'd had the good sense to poison a Hollywood lawyer.

R.J. threw the paper down with disgust.

"Fifty cents," Hookshot said.

"Say what?" R.J. asked him.

Hookshot shrugged. "Ain't nobody gonna buy that paper now you messed it up. Fifty cents, man, and I throw in a doughnut." And he used his bright steel hook to flip open a box of a dozen he kept under the counter for his street kids.

R.J. laughed sourly. "Still the best offer I've had for a while." He threw down two quarters, grabbed the doughnut, and leaned against the kiosk while he ate.

The sun was coming up now, the dirty orange New York sunrise. It always seemed to make promises it wasn't going to keep. Today will be different, it said. But today never was.

"What else do you know about this?" R.J. asked his friend.

Hookshot shrugged and sipped again. "Just what's in the papers. And what's not. It's a little early yet for anything to be on the street." He smiled, his teeth gleaming in the dim light from the rising sun. "And anyway, ain't nobody else gives a shit about a dead Hollywood lawyer, 'cept you and the cops."

"All right, Hookshot. What's not in the papers?"

"Don't say what kind of poison. Usually mean they trying to stick somebody with it and they think they're close. Don't say what midtown hotel—"

"The Pierre," R.J. said. "In the Presidential Suite."

"Uh-huh. Which probably means they got a good idea who went in and out."

"Which means they got me," R.J. said with disgust.

"You were in there?"

"Yeah."

"And you knew this guy enough to kill him?"

"I just met him," R.J. said. "And that was enough."

Hookshot shook his head. "You in the shit this time, R.J."

R.J. dropped the last chunk of doughnut onto the counter. It tasted like cardboard. "Tell me about it," he said.

And being in the shit didn't stop there.

R.J. headed for Belle's apartment. It was close and he was so tired the extra twenty blocks to his own place were just too much to think about. But when he got there—

"Big trouble, Mr. Brooks," Tony the doorman told him. "There wasn't nothing I could do to stop them."

"Stop who, Tony?" R.J. said, his need for sleep making it all seem kind of far away.

Tony nodded as the door swung open. A black detective R.J. knew slightly came out, a cardboard box stuffed under one arm. "Them," Tony said. "He had a warrant and everything."

"What the—" R.J. stepped over to the detective. "Say, Jackson, what gives here?" He nodded at the open carton the cop was carrying. "That looks like my stuff in there."

"Used to be your stuff," Jackson said. "Evidence now." He pushed past R.J. toward his car, double-parked at the curb.

R.J. followed. "All right, let's see the paper, goddammit."

Jackson dropped the carton onto the trunk of his car. R.J. heard rattling inside, like from pill bottles. "Here you go, Mr. Brooks," Jackson said formally, holding out a piece of paper. It was a search warrant, all right. For the premises herein listed. Belle's apartment.

R.J. snarled and handed it back. "I'll need a receipt for that stuff in the box."

Jackson looked sour. "My shift ended four and a half hours ago, Brooks. How about a break?"

"A break!" R.J. demanded, outraged. "I got you goddamn storm troopers pounding on my door at three A.M., and when I try to go to bed, you're packing up my goddamned sheets, and now you want a break? Gimme the damn receipt, Jackson. And tell Kates if even one of you bastards bends the tiniest little rule I'm going to get my money's worth out of my ACLU membership and have him making license plates up the river."

Jackson made a face, but he made out the receipt, too, itemizing all the stuff he had taken from Belle's apartment. Mostly it was stuff from the medicine cabinet, which wasn't any big surprise. R.J. was a poisoner now, and he guessed that's where guys like him kept the tools of the trade. In the medicine chest, for Christ's sake. Sure. Pepto Bismol, aspirin, and cyanide.

"Here is your receipt, sir," Jackson said with savage formality. He tore off the sheet and handed it to R.J. "Here you go, sir. Thank you, sir. Please shove this directly up your ass, motherfucker sir."

"Thanks, Jackson. I suppose your pals are at my other place, and at my office?"

Jackson gave him a mean grin. "If it was up to me, man, we'd have a guy taking a dump with you. I don't like poison." He spat into the gutter about five inches from R.J.'s shoe. "Not something a *man* ought to do."

And he dumped the carton onto the backseat, got into his car, and drove away.

Jackson's pals were at R.J.'s apartment and office, of course. Tony had flagged down a cab for R.J. and he'd gone to his home first. He was too late there. The detectives were already gone. The place had been searched thoroughly in a professional manner—in other words, trashed. It would take R.J. two days to clean up.

Once again, his medicine chest had been cleaned out. Just when he really needed an aspirin.

He went downtown to his office. He was just in time to see Detective Epstein come out and put one of those damned cardboard boxes into a car double-parked at the curb. Unfortunately, Epstein saw him, too.

"Hey, Brooks!" Epstein shouted, waving him over.

"Warrant and receipt, goddammit," R.J. said, walking over to the skinny detective.

"Sure, of course, naturally. And you can come upstairs with me and open up your safe."

"Fuck you."

Epstein waved the warrant around. "The warrant says."

"Fuck the warrant, too. I've had it with this crap."

Epstein sighed and tucked the paper into R.J.'s coat. "Come on, Brooksy, it's legal and we're all tired here. The sooner you open up, the sooner we can all go home and go to bed."

R.J. fought it for a few more minutes, but there was really nothing he could do and in the end he went up to his office and opened up his safe. He hated like hell to watch Epstein poking through the stuff inside, carefully picking everything up and looking it over from all sides.

But it was finally over. Epstein didn't find any poison, as far as R.J. could tell. That should have made him feel better, but he was too tired and mad to think about feeling better. There was nothing he could do about it, short of sitting in a jail cell while his lawyer ran up a big fee. It made him feel helpless on top of the mad and the tired, but that was all part of the package. That's how it was when the cops got their teeth into you.

R.J. went home to bed, just hoping it would all go away soon. Before he snapped and punched out a cop. Kates, for instance. Or Boggs. It meant a reserved seat in prison, but the longer this went on, the better that trade-off was going to look.

R.J. was dragged down to Kates's office maybe a dozen times over the next two weeks. That didn't help his attitude, or his business. On the other hand, they always let him go afterward, which meant there was still some doubt in the tiny dark brains of Kates and Boggs. They were having fun playing with him, but they weren't ready or able to make it stick.

He still wasn't worried enough to solve it himself, and the

whole thing was starting to settle into an annoying noise in the background. Just like the mess that started it all, the business with the sequel to *As Time Goes By* and that brass-bound bitch Janine Wright.

Things were almost normal again for a day or two.

Of course, that was too good to last.

CHAPTER 9

I've had a job offer," Casey told him as they slipped into bed one night about two weeks after Boggs's visit, and R.J. knew by the casual, lighthearted, why-should-you-care way she said it, he wasn't going to like this much.

"What kind of a job?" he asked her, shifting his weight up onto one elbow and pulling the covers around him a little tighter.

"Associate producer," she said. She slid one hand along his chest in an absentminded way that made his heart pound.

"But you're already a full producer," R.J. said. "Why would you take a step down?"

Her hand slid lower. "It's not a step down. It's not TV."

"Oh," he said, already pretty distracted. "It's not TV."

"No."

"I thought you did TV."

She brushed her fingertips lightly down his stomach. "I did. But this is too good to let it go."

R.J.'s mouth was dry. "So what is it?"

"A movie." Her hand circled his hips, around back, and then softly coasted to the front again. "In Los Angeles," she said.

R.J. fell off his elbow. "What?"

"Associate producer on a feature is a step up from what I'm doing," she said, deliberately misunderstanding him. "A big step up."

"But it's in Los Angeles," he said, knowing how stupid that sounded.

Casey knew it, too. "That's where they make movies, R.J.," she said.

"But, but— It's three thousand miles away."

"I know," she said. "I saw a map once."

R.J. took a deep breath and pushed her hand away. "Tell me about this job."

She gave a half shrug, all she could manage lying down on her side like that. Her breasts shimmered and R.J. had trouble concentrating. "It's a major feature at a major studio. What's to tell? Professionally, it could really make me. It's what I've been wanting for ten years. I'd be a giant step closer to the top. Also, it's the only first-class production facility in the world where a woman can get a top job based on ability."

R.J.'s stomach had been slowly sinking. Now it lurched straight up in the air, did a double somersault, and smacked at his heart before flopping down like a soggy pancake. "What picture, Casey?" he asked, although he already knew the answer. "What studio?"

"Andromeda Studios," she said. "The sequel."

All the breath left him. He felt like he might never breath again. "Jesus Christ, Casey."

"It's my career, R.J. It has nothing to do with you."

"It damned well does have to do with me."

"R.J., it's my life. If I have a shot at improving it a friend won't stand in my way."

"But you know how I feel about that movie."

Now she came up on one elbow. "No, I don't. You haven't said a word to me. About that or anything else."

It was true. He had been churning the whole thing around in his guts, but he hadn't talked to her about how much it was bothering him. But still—

"Casey, wait a minute—"

"No, damn it, you wait. This isn't about you, it's about my career. This is what I've always wanted, R.J. If you had said anything to me about how much it bothered you it might have been different—"

"Casey, you were there. You heard what I said."

"To *me*, R.J. You never said anything to *me.*"

"I'm saying it now, Casey."

"Now is a little late, R.J."

He looked into her eyes. They were the same beautiful eyes they had always been, the ones he found it so easy to get lost in, but there was something new going on in there, something she wasn't saying because he was supposed to get it, and he didn't get it. He didn't get it at all.

"From what I said to the reporters you might have guessed what I thought about that goddamned sequel, Casey."

"Maybe I thought I shouldn't have to guess," she said.

R.J. felt the whole thing slipping away from him—as if he'd ever had a handle on it at all. "Listen," he said, "the only reason that goddamned harpy offered you a job is to get at me. You—"

"Really," said Casey, suddenly very cold. "So besides sleeping with you I'm just no damn good for anything, is that it?"

"Casey, goddammit—"

"Because I know it will surprise you, but there are plenty of people who think I'm pretty good at what I do."

R.J. took a deep breath and counted to ten. "Casey, I don't want to have this argument."

"Well then," she said.

"You are very goddamned good at what you do. I know

that, everybody knows that. But there's two things going on here. First, the timing on this job offer is kind of suspicious, don't you think? And second, there's the way I feel about this picture."

"The job offer was for me, R.J. I'm sorry about your feelings, I really am. I didn't think they were that overwhelming—"

"They're not over—"

"—and if I'd known, if you'd only told me, I would have considered that when I made my decision," she said.

"For Christ's sake, you sound like Rupert Murdoch making a hostile takeover bid."

"It doesn't have to be hostile, R.J. But this is a career decision that's about me."

"Isn't it a little bit about me, too, Casey?"

"Is it?" she asked, and they were both quiet for a minute. She seemed to be waiting for him to say something, but he was damned if he could think of what.

"R.J.," she said finally, "this was a very tough decision for me. You have to understand, I had to make it by myself, thinking about what was right for *me.*" She reached a hand out again, touching him. "But I did think about you. I thought that if I was there, working on this picture, I could help make sure it was done right. Because it's going to get done one way or another, you have to know that."

"I know that."

"That may be lying to myself," she admitted. "So I just had to make myself think *career.* And this is absolutely the best move I can make right now. Of course it might be a different story if—" She stopped suddenly, almost as if somebody had slapped a hand over her mouth.

"If what?" R.J. asked.

"Nothing," she said. And when he didn't say anything either, Casey slumped off to one side and R.J. stared at the ceiling for a while.

And they drifted off to uneasy sleep without making love.

In the week that followed, Casey seemed to be too busy getting ready for the coast to have much time for R.J. They got together twice, but it wasn't much more than a quick bite to eat and a few words on things that didn't matter.

And Thursday came, the day before Casey was supposed to leave, and R.J. had still had no chance to get things straight between them. And he hadn't really gotten anything straight in himself, either. All he knew was that he didn't want her to go, and he didn't want this awful goddamned travesty of a movie to happen, and now not only were they both happening, they were happening together, three thousand miles away, all wrapped up in one awful package.

So as R.J. sat in his office that Thursday morning he was feeling about as low and mean as a guy can feel. At least, that's what he thought until he decided to do something about it. And then he very quickly felt worse.

"Goddammit," R.J. said aloud.

Wanda stuck her head in. "I've been keeping track," she said. "I make a little mark on my scratch pad every time you say goddammit." She held up a piece of paper. "You're up to forty-nine."

"Wanda, goddammit—"

"Fifty," she said. "Do you want to look at the mail?"

"No," he said.

"Good. Because Reverend Lake has apparently made up with his wife and their lawyer wants to sue you."

"Sue me for what?"

Wanda gave him her best mean little smile. "Invasion of privacy."

"Put me down for fifty-one," R.J. told her. "Then just throw away the mail."

"You're the boss," she said.

"It's nice to think so."

Wanda swished out, leaving R.J. a lingering trace of perfume and a slightly better mood. Here he was, sitting here stewing instead of doing something. He was supposed to be a tough, active guy, and he was letting this damned L.A. Medusa and her dead lawyer ruin his life. "Like hell I will," he said aloud and, as he reached for the telephone, he added, "Goddammit."

"Fifty-two," said Wanda from the next room.

He had just made up his mind to do a little digging around into Janine Wright's background when the door swung open and Janine Wright's daughter came in.

For a long moment she just stood in the doorway, looking like she wasn't sure if gravity would work here. Then she finally took a hesitant step in. "Um," she said. "Mr., uh, Brooks?"

"Sure," R.J. said, glad to have a target for his bad mood. "And you must be, er, Miss, um, Wright."

The girl bit her lip but didn't say anything. For a moment R.J. felt bad about ribbing her. Then he remembered who she was. "What can I do for you, Miss Wright? Did you come to repossess my furniture? Steal my mail? Maybe just put red ants in the seat cushions? Or maybe sell me some poison?"

The kid bit her lip. "I don't think you should joke about that. It—Murray was a jerk, but nobody should have to die like that. All the twitching and throwing up and— It really isn't funny."

"Okay," R.J. said. "It wasn't funny. And neither is trying to pin it on me. Which your old lady is definitely trying."

She still didn't make any move to come in and sit down. Instead she stood up straight in the doorway. "I'm not my mother, Mr. Brooks. I don't like her any more than you do. Maybe even less."

"That doesn't seem possible," R.J. said. "I don't like her at all."

"You've only met her once," the girl said, and her face was twisted into a mask of bitterness. "Imagine what it would be like to see her every day, your whole life, and know that there's no way to escape, ever. And that . . . that there's maybe some of that awful woman in you. That someday you might end up—like that."

R.J. studied the girl. She seemed to be for real. She was upset, bitter. There was none of the brazen punk in her that she'd shown at the hotel. For no real reason R.J. found himself liking her a little bit. "Sit down, Miss Wright," he said. "How can I help you?"

She slid uncertainly into a chair. "Thank you. It's—I, um, actually. It's Kelley? Mary Kelley. Mother doesn't use Daddy's name, but I—would like to."

"All right. Miss Kelley. What's on your mind?"

She was having some trouble looking him in the eye. She looked at her hands as she talked, moving them around nervously. "First, um, I wanted to tell you?"

"Yes?"

"Ah, that Mother. You know. She's, um, I don't know. Been checking into you or—and now she's, um. Doing something? That would, you know. Really bother you?"

"Thanks for the warning," R.J. said, thinking about Casey. "She's already done it."

"Oh," said Mary.

"Was there something else?"

She looked up at him suddenly, and even though she almost immediately began to blush bright red, she held the look. "Yes," she said, and looked away.

"You want to tell me what it is?"

Mary looked out the window, still blushing. Okay, R.J. thought, give the kid a hand.

"How long are you going to be in town?" he asked her.

She answered without looking. "I—I'm not sure. Mother's already gone back to L.A. I told her— I said I was staying here for a while."

"Did you tell her why?"

Mary shook her head.

"Why not?"

A shrug.

"You doing anything she wouldn't want you to do, Miss Kelley?"

A nod this time.

"What is it?"

She finally looked at him. Her face was pinched, as if she had taken a bite of something that cut the inside of her mouth. "Can you find my father, Mr. Brooks?"

R.J. gave her a small smile. Points for effort. "I don't know. Is he lost, Miss Kelley?"

She looked away, then looked back. "Could we stop this, you know, Mr. Brooks, Miss Kelley stuff? It's really, you know. Like in one of those old movies?"

R.J. laughed. He was really starting to like this kid. She was showing spunk. She would have needed that to survive life with a mother like Janine Wright, but it was nice to see it out in the open. "Sure, Mary. Call me R.J. Tell me about your father."

She looked away again. "I haven't seen him since I was little. He was, um. In jail. Prison."

"What did he do?"

Her eyes snapped back to his. "Nothing. He was innocent. I mean, I don't think he did anything. I think Mother framed him. For drugs." She looked away. "I can't prove that. I just— She's so awful. She really would do anything if it, you know. Helped her in some way. Helped her get ahead."

"Where was your father last time you heard from him?"

"I haven't really heard from him. Mother got total custody, of course. Not that she gives a shit about me, but Daddy does, and she knew it would hurt him even more if he couldn't even send me a birthday card. So that's the way she had her lawyers set it up. So he can't even write to me." She looked at her hands again. "They sent him to the penitentiary. The one in Connecticut."

"Somers Penitentiary?"

"Yes, I think that's it."

"But he's out now."

"Yes. On parole."

"So he's still in Connecticut?"

She chewed on her lip. "I—think so. I mean, he likes it there and all, and . . . I mean where else would he go?"

"If he's still on parole, he probably has to stay in Connecticut. And you would like to find him?"

"Yes. I would."

He gave her a hard look. "Why haven't you tried to see him before this?"

She looked away. A tear glittered in the corner of her eye. "I know," she said. "I feel like a total—" She shrugged, letting him fill in the blank. "But I was just a kid, and I was in L.A. He was three thousand miles away, and in prison. You don't know what mother can be like."

"Yes, I do," R.J. said with a snort.

"I couldn't even leave the house. Let alone come all the way across the country, and—" She shook her head and kept looking away.

"All right, I get the picture." R.J. sighed. He was actually thinking about it, actually considering helping this kid. But hell, why not? If it had half a chance of infuriating Janine Wright, he'd pay for the privilege.

He gave the kid a grin. "All right, Mary. I'll take a look."

CHAPTER 10

That night, Casey's last night in town, R.J. tried one more time. He dressed up in his suit, the same one he had worn to his mother's funeral. Hell, it was his only suit. He braved the crosstown traffic at rush hour and picked Casey up at her office. He took her to a quiet place in the Village and fed her grouper with raspberry sauce, a $100 bottle of wine, hothouse asparagus with hollandaise sauce and peach cobbler.

Then he took her uptown to Belle's apartment, which he hadn't sold yet. It had a fireplace, and R.J. wanted a fireplace for what he had in mind.

R.J. led Casey into the apartment and sat her in front of the fire on one of Belle's elegant settees. He'd paid Tony, the doorman, forty bucks to light the fire and have the place ready. Tony, an ex-cop with a strong sense of romantic whimsy, had even put a spray of fresh roses on the table. They must have set him back at least forty bucks.

R.J. looked at Casey. She was watching the flames flicker. Her profile looked so perfect in the firelight it was almost like he could hear it shouting his name. She looked up and smiled and he sat beside her.

He'd gone to a lot of trouble to set the mood just right, and he'd thought for several days about the right thing to say and the way to say it, but when he sat down and took Casey's hand it all flew out of his head and what he said was, "I wish you didn't have to go."

And Casey looked at him, amusement showing in those cool blue eyes, and she said, "Well, I do have to go."

"Well, but I wish you didn't have to."

She patted his knee and let her hand rest there on his thigh.

"Are you going to give me your address out there?" he asked her and she pretended to look surprised.

"Do you want it?" she asked.

He nodded and put a hand on top of hers. "Yeah," he said. "I do."

She looked back at the fire and gave a very small shrug. "All right," she said. "I'll let you know. When I get settled."

"Thanks."

She began to move her hand on his thigh, just a slight, warm caress. "Now that you're rich, maybe you'll fly out and see me sometime. When I'm not too busy."

"Yeah. I could do that."

"Well," she said softly, "that might be nice."

It was the closest she had ever come to saying how she felt about him and R.J. melted. He leaned over and kissed her.

Afterward, R.J. thought it was maybe the cleanest, purest, best kiss he'd ever had in his life. None of that, though, explained how they ended up on the floor in front of the fire, with the flickering light playing off all the beautiful curves and hollows of Casey's body.

His suit was trashed, thrown all over the room, tangled up with panty hose and a high heel. At least one button on his only good dress shirt had popped off, and the silk tie his mother had given him would never be the same again.

None of that mattered. Their lovemaking was gentle and

crazed at the same time. There was a flavor of good-bye to it, and at the same time the discovery of something new between them.

And it was only after that, when Casey was asleep beside him, that R.J. remembered he hadn't had a chance to say any of the things he'd planned so carefully to tell Casey. He drifted off to sleep thinking he'd wake up early, make her a big breakfast, and tell her then.

But before he knew it morning was on them and it was late. They had to rush downstairs without breakfast, and R.J. stood shivering on the sidewalk in a bathrobe as Tony called a cab for Casey. He kissed her one time, a quick brush of his lips against her cheek, and she was gone, off into the morning traffic, to the airport, to California.

R.J. stood and watched until he couldn't see her cab anymore.

"Yo, hey, Mr. Brooks," he heard behind him. He turned. Tony was holding the door to the apartment building for him. "It's kinda cold this morning for how you're dressed," Tony told him. "Whyntcha get inside?"

"I kinda feel like standing here in the rain, Tony."

The doorman blinked at him, rubbing one large finger at the corner of his eye. "It ain't raining, Mr. Brooks."

R.J. looked down toward Central Park where the cab had disappeared. "Then I might as well come in," he said.

The day dragged on and R.J. couldn't seem to concentrate or get anything at all done. He went to the office and went through the motions, but by four o'clock he hadn't done anything except sign a few pieces of paper that Wanda shoved under his nose. He was glad he trusted Wanda so completely; he had no idea what any of the papers said. He might have been signing everything he owned over to her kid in Buffalo. It didn't seem to matter too much if he was.

R.J. knew he was supposed to be doing things—like finding Mary Kelley's father. That would probably be pretty easy. If only he could start feeling like doing it. If the guy was out on parole, he'd have a parole officer. The parole officer would know where Kelley was, had to know according to the law. So all he had to do was make a couple of phone calls.

It took him two and a half hours, but he finally made the first telephone call, to the Department of Corrections in Connecticut. He found out the name of Kelley's parole officer. Then he just stared at the name and number where he'd written it on the pad. It seemed like an awful lot of work to make another phone call. The last one had worn him out completely.

R.J. looked out the window. The day was cool but clear. The sky was blue. Casey was up in that sky somewhere. Trapped in a little metal tube at a great height, moving at a fantastic speed toward a terrible place.

Maybe she would hate California. Maybe she'd get fired. Probably not; she was too damn good. Maybe she'd quit. Up close Casey would see Janine Wright for what she was. Casey would never work for somebody like that. Never.

—Except she'd been working for Pike all this time and he wasn't much better, except that he was a man. At least Janine wouldn't "accidentally" grope her in the screening room. Casey wasn't exactly a feminist, but she wouldn't take shit from anybody, and she would probably like having a woman for a boss. Except Janine Wright could make Gloria Steinem long for a return to traditional values.

Sure. Casey would get off the plane, hate her job, miss him like hell, and be back by Monday morning, at the latest. Sure she would. And while he was waiting, R.J. could flap his arms and fly to the moon.

The day closed in on him. R.J. hadn't thought about Murray Belcher, Janine Wright's dead lawyer, for days. But now, for no reason, just to stop thinking about Casey, it was all he could think about. He thought of Mary Kelley's description of Murray's death. A bad way to go. Even a lawyer didn't deserve to go out like that. Even Janine Wright's lawyer.

R.J. half-expected Boggs to come for him, drag him away downtown for more of Kates's dull incompetent questions.

He would have welcomed it this once. Something to do, something to take his mind off things. But even Boggs stayed away and he was left to himself. Frankly, he didn't much like the company.

Finally fed up—with his office, with his inability to concentrate or do any work, with himself and everything else—R.J. stood up, kicking his chair across the room. He stomped into the outer office, fighting into his coat.

"Go home," he almost yelled to Wanda.

"Sure thing, boss," she said, careful not to put any expression in her voice or on her face.

Even as he slammed out of the office R.J. had to appreciate her just a little bit. By God, she even knew how to deal with him when he was like this.

He decided to walk home and felt a savage release in fighting through the crowds on the sidewalks. He went out of his way to bump into people a little harder than usual, hoping some idiot would be dumb enough to call him on it, to turn and snarl at him. Hoping to find somebody in a mood as bad as his, somebody who would be willing to stand and wing punches for a while.

But New Yorkers are used to the moods of other New Yorkers, and they gave him room on the sidewalk, barely glancing at him as he slammed through.

Five blocks from his apartment a door opened as he passed it and he stopped dead.

A smell came out at him, an old familiar smell, like the perfume an old girlfriend used to wear.

From inside he could hear a jukebox, some Michael Bolton tune wailing. Somebody laughed and a couple of other people joined in. They sounded happy.

R.J. looked in the open door as a fat, red-faced man brushed past him on his way out. There was a brace of neon signs inside, a warm glow in the room, the smell of beer and popcorn and happy people. R.J. wanted to go inside and have a drink, sing along with Bolton, swap stories with the comfortable-looking people inside; wanted it so bad all of a sudden his hand started to tremble.

It would serve her right, he thought. Serve her right if I got stinking drunk.

And he recognized that thought for what it was—the alcoholic trapped inside him, struggling to get out and take control again. Knew that thought for what it was and still stood there for a long moment, as the door swung slowly shut.

Then the rectangle of light on the pavement vanished. The music and laughter were cut off. The warm glow was gone and he was alone on a cold sidewalk. R.J. stuck his hands in his pockets, lowered his head, and turned away. But he could still feel the place pulling at him the last few blocks.

It was around seven by the time he got in to his apartment. His snotty cat, Ilsa, was perched on top of the answering machine, which meant there had been a call. R.J. stuck a plate of cat food on the linoleum by the refrigerator and Ilsa glided over to it and started smacking away.

Sure enough, the light was blinking. R.J. hit Play and in a moment Casey's voice filled the room.

"It's me," she said. "I didn't want to bother you at the office." That was just like her; work came first for Casey, and she hated like hell for anything to disturb her work. She assumed everybody else felt the same way.

"I'm here, I'm fine, the plane didn't crash. I'm staying at the Beverly Hilton until I get settled." A pause. "It's quite a place." Another pause. "Gotta go. Talk to you later." And then just line hum for a moment until the dial tone came back on and the machine hung up.

R.J. tried to imagine what her face had looked like when she spoke to him down the long wire. He couldn't. Maybe there had been some small touch of softness there around her mouth. Maybe a hint of nostalgia in her eyes. Most likely, though, just the same cool amusement.

He tried to picture her in the overstated tackiness of the Beverly Hilton. Compared to the Pierre, it was a fat drunk in a madras suit, Shriner's hat, and a tie with glowing red light-bulbs. Still, it was kind of tasteful by L.A. standards. It shouted money, but it was old money for Hollywood, at least thirty or forty years old. Maybe Casey would fit right in, with her ironic detachment.

R.J. almost smiled at the thought. But she had left no room number, no invitation to call back, and that took the smile out of him.

R.J. sat heavily in the chair beside the answering machine. Ilsa was still making smacking noises at her dish. I should probably eat something, too, R.J. thought.

But he wasn't hungry.

CHAPTER 11

R.J. ended up in a restaurant, anyway. Even though he wasn't hungry.

He sat beside the phone for ten or fifteen minutes. He re-placed Casey's message twice more, just to hear her voice. *Jesus, I've got it bad,* he told himself. He rewound the tape, drummed his fingers on the arm of the chair for a minute. R.J. knew he had to do something to break the mood or he would end up down in that warm-looking bar.

He hated like hell to think about going that way again. He'd lived inside a bottle too long, fought too hard to crawl out of it. If he had even one drink now— Well, he was sure he could quit again but it was hard, too hard to think about. Some people could tell their troubles to strangers over a glass of beer. For R.J. the stuff was poison.

Poison. That goddamned lawyer. Murray Goddamn Belcher. Without consciously thinking about it, R.J. realized he'd been turning the thing over in his mind. Something both-ered him. Who murdered a guy three thousand miles from home? Sure, German tourists got killed in Florida. But this was different. Poison.

That meant somebody hated the guy. Enough to kill him in a bad way. A sneaky way. Hated him enough to plan ahead and get poison and figure out how to get it to him—in a hotel room? Why not at home in L.A.? Easier to plan—and who knew Murray Belcher in New York?

R.J. didn't really know. Maybe it made sense. Maybe Murray had lots of enemies in New York. Maybe all over the country for Christ's sake. But it didn't add up.

Or maybe it did. R.J. didn't know enough to be sure.

For the first time, he wanted to.

R.J. picked up the phone and dialed Angelo Bertelli.

"Hiya, copper," he joked when Angelo picked up. "This is your favorite hard-boiled gumshoe."

"No kidding? Columbo, calling me? Hows about that!"

"I need a couple of hints on something, Angelo. You want some dinner?"

"Hey, I could do that. Say Ferrini's, half an hour?"

"I'll be there."

"*Ciao.*"

R.J. shrugged on his coat and headed out, feeling better. This wasn't really his problem, but doing something was better than sitting around stewing. Besides, if he was still the leading suspect after all this time, Kates was never going to solve this thing. And that meant R.J. was going to have it hanging over his head for the rest of his life.

Ferrini's was a cozy place down on Mulberry Street. Angelo liked it because Ferrini liked Angelo. And just incidentally they made the best marinara sauce in Manhattan. R.J. took a cab down to the restaurant. He was taking a lot of cabs lately. He wondered if that meant something. Maybe he was getting old. Maybe he was lonely, so lonely he needed to hear the surly Pakistani babble of a New York cabdriver.

Whatever. R.J. paid off the cabbie on the sidewalk in front of Ferrini's and went in.

It was a dim joint, depending mostly on candles for light. The decor was low key, homey. None of that chianti-bottle-with-a-candle-in-it crap, but real southern Italy home-style. Anyway, that's what Angelo said. R.J. hadn't been inside all that many southern Italian homes, so he couldn't say.

"Ah, Meesater Ehbrooks," Ferrini crooned as R.J. hit the door. *"Buona sera.* Meesater Angelo he's await." He beckoned toward the back. "Please?"

R.J. followed Ferrini to a table in the back, separated from the other tables by a small aisle leading to the kitchen. Angelo was already there, sipping a glass of Perroni beer. "R.J.!" he called out, and then to Ferrini, *"Agua minerale, per favore."* Ferrini bowed and smiled at Angelo and said something in Italian, too fast for R.J. Angelo said something back and made a hand gesture. Then Ferrini laughed and zipped off to the kitchen.

"You two weren't laughing at my haircut, were you?" R.J. said as he slid into a chair.

"Naw, that's a much louder laugh, and he brings out all the waiters to look. We was just laughing because we're Italian and we're talking." He shrugged. "It's a culture thing. Don't go getting paranoid on me, R.J."

"Tough to avoid." R.J. sighed. "Every time I turn around lately I bump into your buddy Boggs."

Bertelli shook his head. "I know, I know. Kates has this bee in his bonnet, and he can't get no honey from it, but he's afraid it'll sting him if he lets go." He spread his hands and shrugged. "Whaddya gonna do?"

"That's what I wanted to talk to you about," R.J. said. Angelo opened his mouth, then closed it again as Ferrini set a liter of chilled mineral water in a green bottle in front of R.J. *"Grazie,"* R.J. said.

"Prego," Ferrini murmured and quickly left the table.

"Angelo," R.J. said, unscrewing the cap of the bottle and pouring a glass full, "my ass is in a sling. I thought this might die down when Kates woke up, but he's still sleepwalking and it's getting on my nerves. He's still after me and it's a couple of weeks now. That means he's not going to let go, and since I didn't do it that means five years from now he'll still be trying to nail me for Murray Goddamn Belcher." He sipped the water. "So I figured maybe I should take a look at this thing."

Angelo blew out a big breath and shook his head. "R.J., you're like a brother to me," he started.

"Aw, cut the crap, Angelo, isn't that what the mob guys say before they pull the trigger?"

Bertelli pointed a finger at R.J. and dropped his thumb. "Goombah, if they found out I was feeding anything to the principal suspect in this case, my ass is grass."

"So I am still the principal suspect?"

"Bet your ass you are, R.J. And I shouldn't have told you that much. Sorry. I tried to steer the investigation another way, and now I'm not allowed near the case anymore." He shrugged again. "There's nobody else they like at all. Belcher is in town for like two days, nobody else raised their voice at him. Just you. They got you in the room with the guy, fighting with the guy, mad enough to do something, smart enough to know how—" Angelo shook his head. "Sonofabitch, the more I think about it, the more I like you for it, too."

"Knock it off, for Christ's sake, Angelo."

"Sorry, R.J. But they got enough to keep an eye on you, keep hassling you. They don't got enough to arrest you or they would've already." Bertelli wagged a finger at R.J. "Sometimes I think the L.T. don't like you much."

"No shit," R.J. snorted. "So what can you tell me?"

"I think I know how you did it," Bertelli said.

"Tell me. I forgot already."

"The poison was in the food, from room service."

"Then I am pretty good," R.J. said. "They run that hotel tighter than Fort Knox. How'd I manage it?"

"You are good, R.J. Very cute. Listen to this." He held up a finger and waved it in the air as he talked. "Waiter comes off the elevator with the cart. Turns the corner— Hey. Some asshole opened up the hall window. It's fucking freezing in here. So the waiter leaves the cart—the food might get cold, huh?—goes down the hall, maybe forty feet. Shuts the window, comes back to the cart, delivers it, goes back downstairs."

"The waiter checks out?"

Angelo nodded. "Cleaner than the Pope's ring finger. He's been working there twenty-six years. Deacon of his church, six kids—like they wrote the part for some old Perry Mason or something."

"All right," R.J. said. "Then it has to be the window."

"Bingo," said Bertelli. "So I get out there and I poke around on the fire escape. It's a tough climb, but it's doable. But there's no footprints. No bloody glove, no white Bronco, nothing. But he doesn't have to come in that way, it could be just a distraction. Whatever. I would bet the ranch that whoever it was came in, opened the window, went back down the hall, and hid around the corner. He waits for the waiter to go close the window, dumps in the poison, and he's outta there."

"What did he dump it in?"

"Plate of prosciutto."

R.J. frowned. "There were two other people in the suite—Janine Wright and her daughter, Mary."

"Yeah, I know. But Belcher ordered the prosciutto. Wright and the kid weren't even eating."

"But the killer wouldn't have to know that. He might have just been watching for a chance."

"And hoping he got the right one?"

"Maybe not caring which one he got."

Angelo made a face. "Sorry, R.J. I can't buy it. Poison is usually pretty personal."

"Sure. Like that stuff in the Tylenol bottles a few years back."

Angelo smiled. "That was some nut getting off on killing strangers. This is different."

"It's always different, Angelo. What else can you tell me?"

"I shouldn't have told you that much, R.J. Except you plied

me with liquor." He drained his beer glass and set it down. "I'll tell you this, though. First, there ain't much more to tell. And second—" He smiled again and his teeth shone in the candlelight. "—Kates wants you for this so bad he can taste it. Watch your ass, R.J."

And that was all R.J. could get out of him. They had their excellent dinner and talked about other things—the Knicks, local politics—but that was it. A small piece of R.J.'s mind stayed on the poisoning of Murray Belcher, and he went home full of marinara sauce and dissatisfaction.

Monday morning R.J. was not feeling a whole lot better, but at least he was starting to get used to feeling bad. He woke up early and as he stared into the shaving mirror, he told himself it was time to get a grip on himself. The face that looked back at him was slack, puffy, doughy-looking.

R.J. was no yuppie, but he hated to get soft. So he did his whole series of exercises—sit-ups, push-ups, crunches—and then ran a mile downtown and back again.

As always, getting his blood going like that made him feel alive, smart, ready for anything. He almost caught himself singing in the shower.

R.J. had a quick breakfast of a bagel and orange juice and headed for his office. For once he beat Wanda there by a good quarter of an hour. She came in a few minutes before nine and almost jumped out of her skin when she saw him.

"Jesus, boss," she said. "I thought you were a mugger."

"I may try that if business doesn't pick up," he told her. He set a cup of coffee on her desk. "Here you go."

Wanda eyed him suspiciously. "What's this?"

"It's coffee."

She still seemed scared to touch the mug. "You never make coffee."

"This morning I made coffee. Go ahead, drink the stuff."

She picked up the mug and took a careful sip, making a face right away. "My God, boss. Now I know why you never make coffee."

R.J. gave her a hurt look. "It's from imported beans," he said.

"If anybody on Ellis Island tasted this stuff, they'd deport it again," she told him.

"That shows how much you know. They haven't brought anybody through Ellis Island for years."

She sipped again and made an even worse face. "This stuff tastes plenty old enough."

But before he could fill up his lungs and hit her with a snappy comeback she flung a white paper bag at him. "It'll probably go down easier with one of these," she said.

R.J. opened up the bag. "Cinnamon rolls," he said. "Doll, I just promoted you to special executive assistant." He took a big bite and a sip of his own coffee. It tasted all right to him.

After the cinnamon roll, the coffee, and even the verbal sparring with Wanda, R.J. began to feel that this might not be a completely awful day. Okay, he was a murder suspect and Casey was gone. But life went on and he had a job to do.

A few minutes after nine he settled himself at his desk with more coffee—ignoring Wanda's looks—and dialed Kelley's parole officer in Connecticut.

They'd told him the party he wanted was an H. Gillam. After three rings, a bored-sounding woman answered. "Gillam," she said.

"My name is R. J. Brooks, Ms. Gillam," R.J. said, swallowing the last bite of cinnamon roll. "I'm a private investigator in Manhattan."

Ms. Gillam gave a long sigh. "Okay," she said.

Great, R.J. thought. Nine A.M., and it's attitude time already in Connecticut. But out loud he said, "I'm trying to confirm the whereabouts of a William Kelley." After a short pause with no response, he added, "I was hoping you could help me."

"Uh-huh," said Ms. Gillam.

R.J. began to think that maybe he was wrong, maybe this really would be a terrible day after all. He didn't know this woman from Adam and here she was pulling the Go-Ahead-Make-My-Day crap on him. R.J. was on the point of trying something cute, like asking for her supervisor's name, when all of a sudden Ms. Gillam giggled.

"Hello?" said R.J.

"I'm sorry," she said. "I tried to hold myself together, but this is just—" and she giggled again.

"What is?" R.J. asked. Hostility he could at least understand. It was one of the perks of his tough trade. But parole officers are supposed to be tough, too, and to have one giggle at him was disturbing. He didn't know what to think.

"What was he really like?" Ms. Gillam asked.

R.J.'s head was spinning. Maybe there was something wrong with the coffee, he thought. "What was *who* really like? Kelley?"

"No. You know," she said coyly.

"Uh, no. No, I don't know."

"Your *faa*-ther," she bleated.

Well, thought R.J., you never know where you're going to find one. He was only a little surprised that she had recognized him by his name alone. But it was happening more and more. As for the rest of it, well—

He'd been plagued by his father's fans his whole life, and the most he could say about them now was that it didn't bother him anymore. He'd gone through a phase where the mention of his father's name made R.J. furious, then fiercely protective, then paranoid, bitter, amused, and finally tolerant. R.J. knew who he was now, and he wasn't competing with his old man, and the only thing about the whole fan business he still found interesting was who turned out to be one. Like a Connecticut parole officer who was supposed to be tough.

"He was a great guy," R.J. said, giving her stock answer number seven, "but he drank too much."

"Maybe that was part of his greatness," Gillam offered.

"Sure," R.J. said. "Booze makes you smart, everybody knows that."

"Because he really was great," she went on, ignoring him. "The greatest. Unbelievable. But you know that. Whoo," she said with another giggle, "I can't believe I'm talking to you."

"I'm having some trouble with it myself."

"Because I have seen your picture in the papers over here and you look just like him, did you know that?"

"No, I never noticed that," R.J. said. It didn't matter; she just kept rolling.

"And I have always thought, whoo. That is one sexy man. Your father, I mean, not you."

"Yeah, I know. Not me."

She rattled on for another ten minutes. When she finally wound down, R.J. knew that her first name was Heidi, she was divorced with two kids, lived in Torrington, Connecticut, had a birth mark that you wouldn't hardly notice unless, you know; she went bowling with a church group on Wednesday nights, was paying for braces for both kids, and her car was in the shop again.

R.J. also managed to get out of her, finally, that William Kelley was also living in Torrington, in a small apartment over a block of shops downtown. He had a job as a clerk in a convenience store on the edge of town and seemed to be settling down into life outside prison about as well as could be expected. "He still says he's innocent," Ms. Gillam told R.J.

"You think he is?"

"Aw, they all say that. They're all innocent."

"Well, thanks for the information," R.J. said.

"No problem. Let me know if you get over this way. We could have lunch."

"Sure," said R.J., gritting his teeth. "Thanks again."

"I mean it," she said, but R.J. hung up before she could make dinner, or offer to do a tango for him with a rose in her teeth.

And there it was. Case solved. It was too easy. He had it all on a slip of paper in front of him: 713 Oak Street. R.J. had never lived in a town that had a street named Oak Street. Or if it did, the city fathers were just kidding. There were parts of Los Angeles that played some pretty cruel jokes with street names.

But Torrington, Connecticut, sounded like the kind of place that might really have an oak or two on Oak Street. A nice place to live. Nice place to raise a family, work, go to church, and serve out your parole.

Sure, Torrington. Maybe he'd retire there and raise dachshunds.

Meanwhile, he'd set up lunch with Mary Kelley. Give her the good news someplace nice.

CHAPTER 12

R.J. arranged to meet Mary Kelley at Ferrini's. He was starting to like the place, even without Angelo around. Besides, people from out of town almost never got down to that part of Manhattan. R.J. liked the area. It was naked New York, stripped of all pretense. It was pure city that might have been Calcutta or Hong Kong but somehow managed to be completely New York.

And Mary Kelley was young enough, and West Coast enough, to enjoy the kind of atmosphere the lower East Side had so much of. R.J. liked the thought of how she might react to the area. But he also told her to be sure to take a cab. She could afford it, and he didn't want any of the atmosphere to take a bite out of her.

A panhandler stopped R.J. outside the restaurant by shoving a hand under his nose, palm up. The guy had only part of one finger and that wasn't in good shape. His skin was blotchy and he was missing a piece of his nose, too. R.J. dropped a buck on the guy and backed away, trying not to breathe the same air.

The headwaiter was not Ferrini himself, who was only there at night. But he remembered R.J. as one of Angelo's friends and seated him with a good bit of ceremony. His English wasn't good, but he managed to let R.J. know that anybody who wasn't crazy would try the calamari.

R.J. had just finished a couple of breadsticks and a glass of *agua minerale* when Mary Kelley came in. She was breathless, her face flushed red in the cheeks, and she looked about as good as a client can look. Especially a client that young. The headwaiter showed her over to R.J.'s table, looking so pleased and proud R.J. was afraid the guy might fall out of his skin. He gave R.J. a number of beautiful little winks and bowed four times getting Mary into the chair.

"Mr. Broo—I mean, R.J., um—what?" Mary said, trailing off as the headwaiter said something in melodramatic Italian with a couple hundred hand signals in case Mary was deaf.

"I'm not sure," R.J. said, "but I think he wants to know if the beautiful lady would like a glass of vino."

She looked pleased, then uncertain. "Oh," she said. "I'm not sure. Would I? I mean, are you?"

"I don't drink," R.J. said, "but go ahead if you want to. It'll make this guy's day."

"You don't drink? But then— But don't you mind if I have wine, then?"

"Go ahead," R.J. said. "I like the smell."

"All right," she said, and turning to the headwaiter she added, *"Si, vino russo, per favore."*

The headwaiter's smile got so big it looked like it might stretch his face permanently. He bowed another three times and backed away, clapping his hands sharply and yelling for Giancarlo.

R.J. gave Mary a smile of his own. Not enough to cause any permanent damage. "Pretty good, kid."

"What? The Italian? That's nothing, I can just speak like a hundred words of it. I had an au pair from Udine. Uh, that's in northern Italy. It was when I was twelve." She frowned. "I had a lot of au pairs."

She looked shyly at the table. A napkin was folded elegantly onto her plate. She poked at the napkin. It fell over.

"Um," she said. "You said on the phone you had something to tell me . . . ?"

"I found your old man," R.J. told her. And the look on her face was all the payment R.J. wanted. It had been a long time since he'd made anybody that happy.

They had a pretty good lunch. The headwaiter and Giancarlo made sure of that. Mary looked so happy, and R.J. so smug, that the waiters were convinced that R.J. and Mary were in love, and Italian waiters are suckers for lovebirds. Always have been. Probably always would be.

They did try the calamari, and it was good. They munched away happily, talking about who they both knew, and places that had changed in Hollywood since R.J. had grown up there.

When the plates were cleared away R.J. sat back contented, liking this girl. "Anyway, kiddo, if you want me to I'll go over to Torrington and take a look—"

"Oh! No, that's— I think I'd like to surprise him, if— I mean, it's been an awfully long time."

"Suit yourself," he said, feeling full and almost happy. "Case closed."

"How much do I owe you?" she said, reaching for her purse and breaking his train of thought.

"What? Christ, you don't owe me anything."

She pulled out a slim leather checkbook with gold letters on the front. "I hired you to do a job and you did it. How much?"

"Listen, Mary, I didn't even break a sweat on this. Forget it."

"All right," she said. "Is five hundred enough?"

"Don't make me get tough," he told her. "I made two

phone calls. Give me a buck for the tolls and we'll call it square."

"But it's not like I'm even paying for it," Mary said. "It's my mother's money."

"That's the problem," R.J. told her. "I don't want to take her money. Not even for you, kitten."

"I'm afraid I'll have to insist."

R.J. leaned over the table, accidentally knocking over the bread sticks. "Listen, doll. Don't try the Hollywood Power Kitten act on me. I've seen that game, and I've played it out, a long time before you were born."

She blushed. "All right, R.J., but I—"

"No." He took her hand and patted it. "Not another word. Part of growing out of that West Coast spoiled movie-kid crap we both came from is learning to accept a favor. So learn." R.J. put her hand down and leaned back, smiling at Mary. "Anyway, I made two phone calls to find your old man, and I got to watch you make a fool out of two Italian waiters. That's payment in full."

She smiled back. "And you got to do something that might piss off my mother?"

He nodded. "You're learning, Mary. I don't do anything I don't want to do."

Coffee came, elegant little bone china cups filled with rich dark espresso. Perfect ribbons of lemon peel curled on one side of the saucer, and tiny silver spoons balanced them on the other side. Giancarlo placed a small plate of *biscotti* in the center of the table with six bows and one smug grin.

"Oh," Mary said. "But we didn't— I mean, I'm not sure I want any dessert."

"Relax, kid," R.J. told her. "You sure don't need to worry about calories." As she blushed, he added, "Besides, I think it's on the house. Their lovebird special."

"Their— Oh, you mean they think— Oh." She turned even redder and R.J. had to laugh. "I just feel funny taking advantage," she said, not looking at him.

"You want me to tell them we're not lovebirds?" he said, crunching into a *biscotti*.

Mary couldn't even answer; too busy blushing. She picked up one of the cookies to give herself something to do. It seemed to calm her down. After a minute or so she was back to normal.

R.J. admired her control. A lot. They had similar roots, coming from the same strange background. He had fought long and hard to break away from the life he had been born into, had come about as far away from it as a guy could. Now she was trying to take the same trip, showing the same stubborn pride, and he was glad to help her.

As he realized where his thoughts were taking him, he thought of Casey. She hadn't called him all weekend. Probably apartment hunting, too busy. He missed her a lot, but not as much while Mary was with him.

He shook it off. Christ, what was he thinking? Mary was just a kid. And he sure didn't want to trade Casey for Mary, no matter how cute the kid was.

Luckily, the headwaiter brought the bill over and knocked R.J. out of chasing down any of those thoughts. The guy gave a more formal bow this time and stuck his hand out toward R.J. He was holding a little hammered silver tray. The bill sat face down on the tray, on top of a doily.

"Oh," said Mary. "Wait, I'm paying for this."

The headwaiter ignored her, and so did R.J. One of the advantages of old-fashioned Italian elegance, R.J. thought as he handed the headwaiter his credit card. They're completely unliberated. Totally sexist piggy. I like this place.

The headwaiter marched back to the cash register with his nose in the air, after giving R.J. another massive wink.

"Damn it, R.J., I wanted to pay for this."

He leaned back and gave her a smug, well-fed shark smile. "Part of breaking away from your roots, Mary. You can't always get what you want."

"And part of it is learning to pay for what you get. I can pay my own way—"

"Forget it."

She licked her lips. "There must be some way I can thank you."

R.J. grinned. "You can get together with your father and enjoy it. That'll piss off your mother so much I'm bound to be happy."

CHAPTER 13

Casey called late that night. The phone ringing woke R.J. from a sleep so deep he didn't know where he was for a minute. There was the phone receiver held up to his face, but he couldn't be sure what that meant. Then he heard the voice humming down the wire.

"Wake up, R.J.," Casey said, with a voice like she was holding back a chuckle.

"Casey," he managed to croak.

"Did I catch you at a bad time? I can call back."

R.J. shoved the fog away. "No, damn it, wait a minute."

He could hear her chuckle softly. "That's my boy," she said. "As long as you're swearing, I know I have your attention."

"Have you found a place yet?"

"Yes. They've been very helpful at the studio. I saw five or six places today and I think I'll take one of them. It's nice."

"Where is it?"

She snorted a little. "You want to make sure it's in a safe

neighborhood? Relax. You have to drive way up this tiny road and then climb all these steps. There's not a mugger in the world in good enough shape to make it to the door."

"They don't have muggers in L.A., Casey. They have serial killers, and they all teach aerobics."

"Well," Casey said, "you'd like it anyway. It's got a great view. It's up at the top of, what is it called? Beechnut Canyon?"

"Beechwood," R.J. corrected. "You're right near the Hollywood sign."

"I can see it from the shower," she said. Then she laughed and R.J. felt his whole insides shift around at the sound. He tried to think of something to say to make her laugh again, but she didn't wait.

"Anyway," she said. "I'll probably move in tomorrow."

"You have a car?"

She didn't quite laugh this time, but it was close enough. "R.J., for God's sake, this is L.A. They won't let you off the airplane without a car." She paused, as if afraid to tell him. "It's a convertible," she finally admitted.

"For Christ's sake, Casey."

"I know," she said. "But I thought I should try for the full experience. I'm really going to *do* L.A."

"You want me to recommend a personal trainer, Casey? Send you a tanning machine?"

"I'll manage without," she said. "I don't think I'll have time. They're keeping me pretty busy."

R.J. went tight at the thought of what she was going to be busy doing—the sequel. He didn't say anything.

"We start shooting next week," Casey went on. "And, oh my God."

R.J. struggled for control and won. "What?"

"R.J., you wouldn't believe these people."

"Yes, I would. I told you."

She laughed. "I always thought you were exaggerating, but good lord. It's like a cartoon, like some kind of wild parody about Hollywood."

"It's always like that," he told her.

"Anyway, maybe it'll settle down when we start shooting."

"No, it won't. It gets worse, and so do the people. And don't go in to any of the star's trailers when you're on the set."

She laughed again. R.J.'s heart pounded. "I was on the set today, R.J. I saw those trailers." A long pause. "Oh. My. God," she said.

"You liked 'em, huh?"

"R.J., if you take a wicked, spoiled-rotten Cub Scout and show him a copy of *Playboy* from 1964 he might come up with one of these trailers."

"That's a pretty good description of a star actor," R.J. said. "A wicked, spoiled-rotten Cub Scout."

"Yes," Casey said, suddenly sounding cool again. "I met the star today. Alec Harris."

"Who?"

"You've never heard of Alec Harris, R.J.? Good lord, he was on TV practically forever, that lifeguard show."

"Holy shit," R.J. said. "That guy with no shirt? *He's* the fucking star?"

"Yes."

"Holy shit."

"It gets worse," she said. "The female lead is Maggie DeSoto."

R.J. had heard of her. He was stunned into silence. Maggie DeSoto had been a porn star. She crossed over into singing punk rock, and parlayed a couple of rock videos into a movie career. But her assets had stayed the same since the beginning. She could only act with her clothes off.

"They're—not exactly, um, anything like your parents, R.J.," Casey said apologetically.

"They're not even my species. Jesus Christ, Casey." It was worse than he had even imagined.

"And of course they hate each other," Casey said. The hidden laugh was back in her voice.

But all R.J. could manage was another feeble, "Jesus Christ."

As if she could tell how much R.J. was bothered, Casey let the conversation drift to an end. "Anyway, you need your beauty sleep. I'll call you when I have a phone. When I can," she said. "I guess it gets pretty busy now."

"Yeah," R.J. said. "It sure does." He felt drained, completely depressed—by her news of the casting and now by the fact that she was about to hang up. He wanted her more than ever, could almost feel her velvet skin under his hand, almost smell her hair. "Casey—"

"You take care of yourself, R.J. Keep your skirts dry."

"I will. And listen—"

"Bye," she said with a kissing sound. And she was gone.

R.J. found it impossible to get back to sleep. He didn't even try. He sat in bed for a long time, just staring into the darkness.

He missed her terribly. It was bad enough to lose Casey to the movies, to his new archenemy, Janine Wright. It was even worse when that movie happened to be this one, the brainless sequel to the only movie he really cared about. But now it looked like it was going far beyond worse. With those two actors in the parts, there was no way in the world this could turn out to be anything but the biggest stinker of all time.

Jesus H. Christ. That lifeguard guy playing his father's role? And a porn star in Belle's part? If Janine Wright had spent a year trying to come up with the two actors that would rip out R.J.'s guts in the worst way, she couldn't have done any better than those two.

R.J. was so mad he couldn't stay in bed. He flung off the covers and padded into the kitchen. Ilsa followed him, hoping for an early breakfast, but he ignored her.

R.J. poured himself a glass of orange juice and sat at the kitchen table, but the juice didn't taste right. After one sip he let it sit on the table.

A guy nobody would watch if he wore a shirt. A woman who could only act on her back.

Sure. This was going to be a deathless classic, all right. People would talk about it for fifty years. As the worst piece of garbage ever to come out of Hollywood. It would completely erase the original, cover it in sewage so nobody could look at his parents ever again without thinking of the lifeguard and the porn star.

And worst of all, R.J. had a sinking suspicion that Janine Wright knew what she was doing. That she was deliberately making the most malodorous piece of crap she could make, because she knew that would sell tickets. He was scared to death that this thing was going to be a hit, for all the same reasons that were making him sick to his stomach.

It explained why she was so pleased to have any negative publicity he might give her. Janine Wright's message was simple. People were stupid, pathetic jerks. Give them something awful and—if you *tell* them it's awful—they'll lap it up like ice cream.

R.J. would have given almost anything to prove her wrong, but he was pretty sure she was right.

R.J. went to work in the morning without any more sleep. He felt exhausted, without energy, but had been unable even to close his eyes. He walked all the way down to his office, stopping often along the way to stare at things for no apparent reason. A kid sitting on a bus bench, clearly stoned out of his skull. An old man leading an imaginary parade down the center of Broadway, traffic moving around him. Two hot-dog vendors in a fist fight, clobbering each other with mustard. A middle-aged matron yelling obscenities at a cop.

On a normal day these common sights and sounds of his city would have cheered R.J. This morning they just made him feel even more depressed. He saw all these people as future ticket-buyers to the sequel and he knew they outnumbered the sane, rational people who would stay away from something they knew was awful and stupid and pointless.

So when he finally trudged into his office—past the completely innocent smirk on Wanda's face, which he barely noticed—he was so dazed and depressed and tired that he had to stare for three or four long seconds before he recognized the man sitting in his chair.

The man was in his fifties, very good-looking in a hard-boiled way. His black hair was shot through with silver, a sharp contrast to his jet black mustache and dark, weathered skin. He wore a turquoise and hammered-silver belt buckle and had one foot in a hand-tooled boot crossed over his other leg.

"Uncle Hank!" R.J. blurted out. "What the hell are you doing here?"

Henry Portillo nodded. "Just the sort of elegant greeting I would expect from you. You never had two good manners to rub together, *hijo.*"

R.J. was not Portillo's *hijo*, and Uncle Hank was not R.J.'s uncle, either. The relationship was more complicated than that. Sometimes closer, sometimes worlds apart.

R.J. had been a kid adrift in Hollywood with two high-powered stars for mother and father, and nobody around to be parents. Portillo, a rising, young Mexican-American cop on the LAPD, had taken the boy under his wing. R.J. was grateful, but also knew that part of the reason Portillo had looked after him was because of his lifelong, unconfessed adoration of R.J.'s mother, screen legend Belle Fontaine.

"Well, then," R.J. said. *"Lo siento mucho, tío.* Take a chair, please. Here, please try mine, the other one is not soft enough. You want some coffee?"

"Did you make it?" the older man asked suspiciously.

"No, it's Wanda's."

"Then I would appreciate a cup of coffee, R.J."

R.J. got the coffee, and a cup for himself, and took it back to his inner office. He sat in the client chair and looked fondly at Portillo.

"I thought you were in L.A., Uncle Hank. What brings you to town?"

Portillo sipped the coffee. "Ah. Good. Keep that woman Wanda, she understands coffee. As usual, R.J., *you* bring me to town."

R.J. shook his head. "I don't get it."

Portillo pointed a hard, blunt finger at R.J. as if it were some kind of weapon. "I'm afraid you're in trouble again, *hijo*. And this time I don't know if I can bail you out."

CHAPTER 14

R.J. stared at Portillo again, for a good long time. "Okay, Uncle Hank," he finally said. "I know you wouldn't fly three thousand miles away from a decent plate of *huevos rancheros* for a practical joke. So I have to believe I'm in trouble in Los Angeles. Who did I kill? Another lawyer?"

Portillo shook his head. "This is not a joke, R.J."

"Then what is it? I'm living like a goddamned Boy Scout, Uncle Hank. I haven't even chewed a cigar in almost a week."

Portillo simply looked at him for a long moment. Then he shook his head as if disgusted at what he saw. "You look terrible," he said at last. "Have you given up sleeping?"

"I had a rough night," R.J. admitted. "What's that got to do with it?"

"When did you eat last?"

"Jesus Christ, Uncle Hank. You fly across the country, sneak in here and tell me I'm practically in prison, and now you come on like *mamacita*? What the hell gives?"

The older man sighed and pinched the bridge of his nose

with his fingers. "I worry, R.J. I see the way you crap away your life and I think it is maybe partly my fault."

R.J. laughed. "Why? Because you never taught me to play the violin? Come on, Uncle Hank. Spit it out. What the hell kind of trouble am I in?"

Portillo sighed again and shook his head. "I am here unofficially. The LAPD brass knows that I know you. They did not actually *ask* me to come. However, they did approve some extra sick leave for me. They know I am here."

"That's comforting," R.J. said. "Get to the point, okay?"

"The point, *hijo*, is that you have said some stupid things for the news cameras and now these things are coming home to roost."

"Uncle Hank, what the hell are you talking about?"

Portillo reached into a pocket of his houndstooth jacket and pulled out an envelope. From his breast pocket he took reading glasses, small half-lenses, and stuck them on his nose. He drew out a slip of paper and read. "I hope the goddamned animals responsible for this die a nasty death as soon as possible." Then he looked up at R.J. over the rims of his half-glasses. "Did you say those words, R.J.?"

"Fucking A," R.J. said. "Doesn't the LAPD have anything better to do? They run out of crime out there, Uncle Hank?"

"Did you?" Portillo insisted.

"Sure, I said it," R.J. snorted. "I meant it, too. And I still hope it. Especially that brass-plated bitch, Janine Wright. And if you're even half the man I think you are, you hope so, too."

Portillo watched R.J., then shook his head sadly. "All right, R.J.," he said. "All right." He put the glasses back in their case and the paper back in his pocket. He said nothing else.

"What?" R.J. said after a minute of puzzling silence. "That's it? You came all this way to ask me if I said that? I could have told you on the telephone."

"I needed to see your face when I asked you," Portillo said. "To see if you might have done this thing. I did not believe you could, but—" He shrugged.

"Well, did I do it? And what is it, anyway?"

"I don't know if you did it, R.J." he complained. "I don't think so. I hope not, but—" A shrug. "I can't always read you anymore. As for what it is—"

Portillo reached inside the envelope again. He unfolded a second sheet of paper and flipped it across the desk to R.J. Then he sighed and leaned the chair back, turning it to look out the window. "Someone is making death threats to the cast and crew of that movie and the studio is concerned."

"Jesus H. Christ," R.J. spat out, picking up the paper. He unfolded it and glanced down.

It was a photocopy of a note. Somebody had done the old cutout trick and pasted a bunch of words and letters together to spell out a message. It wasn't exactly a Valentine, either. It said:

Lawyers are dead, violence leaves me blue
But Stop The Sequel or I stop you.

"That's just the first one," Portillo said. "There was another one two days ago, which is why I came." He turned to face R.J. now. "The lab has not released it yet, but I am told it was more violent. They were both mailed from New York, both received by—" He hesitated. "—by the head of a studio, who persuaded the commissioner to take it seriously."

R.J. slammed the paper on the desk. "And did the head of the studio happen to mention my name?"

"Yes. But she didn't have to. R.J., your words made headlines in Hong Kong, Johannesburg, Buenos Aires, Bangkok— You got them one hell of a lot of publicity with that one." He sighed again. "Then, when Lieutenant Kates of the New York police contacts us about the death of Murray Belcher and tells us you are the main suspect—"

"That son-of-a-bitch," spat out R.J.

Portillo looked mildly curious. "Which one?"

"Both of 'em. So you think I killed the lawyer as a warning and then started sending notes?"

"I do not think any such thing, *hijo*," Portillo said with a hurt look.

"But you're getting a lot of pressure to act like you think it, right? Political pressure from a major contributor to city political campaigns—say, the head of a studio, for instance?"

Portillo sighed again. "Yes. You would not believe the amount of political pressure the head of a studio can apply nowadays." He pointed his finger at R.J. and dropped the thumb, pow. "I think you have made a very bad enemy there."

R.J. grinned, but it wasn't funny. "You're wrong about that. The fact is, she doesn't care if I stop breathing or win the lottery. But if she could get me arrested for threatening this picture it would generate one hell of a lot of publicity. Probably enough to make sure the goddamned thing is a hit."

Portillo shook his head. "And so Janine Wright threatened herself so she could blame you? That's a very obscure motive, R.J. I would have a hell of a time selling that one."

"I'm not saying she threatened herself, Uncle Hank. Have you ever met her?"

"I have had the pleasure," he said. "She is something of a dragon."

"She's the biggest goddamned bitch who ever lived," R.J. said, "And I've known some doozies. She wouldn't have to threaten herself. You'd have to take a number and stand in line to kill that woman. Hell, I'll bet she has a special In basket on her desk, just for death threats."

"That may be," said Portillo, "but we are taking this one seriously."

"So am I. What time is your return flight?"

Portillo blinked. "Seven A.M. tomorrow. Why?"

"I'm going back with you."

"That's not necessary right now, R.J."

"The hell it isn't," said R.J. "I'm sick of this, Uncle Hank. Three weeks I've been accused of poisoning a lawyer and now writing these damn notes. I've had it. If the only thing the cops in New York and L.A. can agree on is that I'm the kind of slimy coward who does that stuff then I'll just have to solve this my-self."

"*Hijo*—" Portillo said, but R.J. didn't let him speak.

"There's more," he told the older man, and his stomach lurched as he said it. "One of the cast and crew that's being threatened is Casey."

The flight was a long one. It stopped twice along the way and fought head winds the whole time. Portillo slept half the time but R.J. could not. He had not slept much the night before the flight, either, and that made two nights in a row.

R.J. was mad. It was not a kick-the-chair-and-say-dammit kind of mad, either. It was a slow, steady rage, a smoldering fury that made him grind his teeth and hiss a lot.

He was mad at Uncle Hank for suspecting him, even for a moment, of being the kind of pimple who would write anony-mous death threats. He was mad at the LAPD for being dumb enough to make Uncle Hank suspect him. And he was mad at Janine Wright, madder than he'd ever been at anyone else ever before. He hoped with all his heart that whoever was making the threats was really good, and that they would take out Janine Wright before R.J.'s plane landed.

And then he was mad at Casey, too, and that hurt the most. Because if your house needs painting and your lover is a house-painter, you ought to mention it to him. And Casey had not mentioned the death threats. Hadn't asked him to look into it. That was what he did, damn it, and she hadn't thought enough of him to tell him. She hadn't even thought their relationship was important enough that he would care if she was in dan-ger? If anything ever happened to Casey, if she somehow got in the way of a killer, just because she was involved in this god-damned farce—

R.J. ground his teeth again. He couldn't even think about what he'd do if that happened. Probably kill Janine Wright himself.

R.J. fumed about it until his jaw hurt. But there was nothing he could do until they landed, except snarl at the flight attendant, which he did.

They were somewhere over New Mexico when something completely unexpected happened: R.J. fell asleep.

He had been staring out the window and grinding his teeth, trying not to think about anything but the scenery, when somehow . . .

He was standing at the back of a huge room, more like a cave. There were hundreds of people in front of him and he couldn't see what they were looking at because they were standing so tight together, all in the way, but he knew there was a long dark box up at the front there and he knew what was in the box and he knew why they were all there.

It was Casey's funeral.

All the huge crowd were mourners, and they all had an official badge that let them get close enough to look down into the coffin and see Casey. And R.J. didn't have a badge and so he couldn't get close enough, no matter how hard he struggled and pushed to get up there.

And he struggled and pushed harder and harder, because he knew she wasn't dead, and if he could only get to her he could save her. But they wouldn't let him close and as he pushed harder a bunch of them grabbed his arms and pinned him.

"Who the hell are you?" they demanded.

"It's me, I'm R.J.," he said, trying to break free. He had to save her!

"What are you to her?" they demanded "Where's your badge?" And he saw now that they all had a word on their badges: MOTHER, FATHER, TEACHER, BEST FRIEND.

He struggled away from them, the way you struggle in a dream, with slow and weak movements that don't do anything. But he had to get to Casey! "Let me go! I can save her, let me go!"

"You can't save her. It's too late," they said, and started to shake him.

"I can save her! Please, let me through!"

But the crowd shook him and tossed him around like a beach ball.

"You can't get close without a badge," one of them told him and then tossed him high in the air. He could look down and see Casey in her coffin, so pale and still. Then the crowd grabbed him again.

"Please, I can save her, I'm R.J.!"

"R.J.!" the crowd changed. *"R.J.! R.J.! R.J.—!"* And as they chanted they were lowering the coffin into the endlessly deep, black hole—

"R.J.! For the love of God, will you please wake up?" Henry Portillo said, shaking R.J. by both arms. "We have landed."

R.J. blinked. His eyes were full of sand. It felt like his head was, too.

Around him on the plane the aisles were filling up. The people were starting to shove and whack one another with suitcases. It made R.J. homesick for Manhattan. He stretched and tried to come fully awake, but he couldn't stand up to stretch properly, and he was slow to shake off the cold lump of terror in his stomach the dream had left behind.

"We'll go over to the set later," Portillo said. "They are doing all studio interiors this week."

"L.A. is great," R.J. grumbled. "Even the cops know the movie jargon."

Portillo laughed. "Does that mean you don't want to stop at the studio, R.J.?"

R.J. shook his head. On top of the last shreds of the dream he felt a thrill of anticipation. In a little while he might actually see Casey. "No," he said. "Let's stop at the goddamn studio."

Portillo nodded. "I have some paperwork to catch up on first. I'll drop you at home to finish your nap, then come get you in a few hours."

CHAPTER 15

They arrived at Portillo's small house in the East Valley and carried their bags in. "You know where your room is, *hijo*," Portillo said, dumping his own garment bag onto the couch. "I will see you in a few hours."

R.J. watched him go, swallowed by memories. The old place hadn't changed much. Same furniture. Same slightly musty smell of leather, gun oil, and Mexican spices.

R.J. went down the short hall to the back of the house. Memories closed in on him in the dimness. This had once been his second home. After his father died and Belle had been too busy he had spent a lot of nights here, just because there was somebody here who gave a damn. It had made him laugh a lot of times over the years, the thought that an L.A. cop had more time to spare for him than his mother.

Well, that was all in the past. He'd worked it out and forgotten about it a long time ago. But the sight and smell of this hall could still bring some of it back.

R.J. pushed open the door to "his" room. And then he just stood in the doorway for a minute. He didn't know whether to laugh or cry. He even forgot that he was holding his suitcase.

The same tattered, quilted bedspread was on the bed. And over next to the window stood the same battered black bookcase. With a stack of his old books on it.

And his old baseball glove.

R.J. dropped his bag and picked up the glove and looked at it in the afternoon light coming through the glass. Just outside that window, in the backyard, he had learned how to throw a knuckle ball. How to catch the ball and whip it over to first. Had even practiced sliding in to home.

Until the maid at his house had complained about the ground-in dirt and grass stains. Then Belle had pulled one of her rare mother routines and told him to keep his damn pants clean. No more sliding.

R.J. sat on the bed and smiled. Because after that—

So many memories. Just from a kid's damn ball glove. Well, hell, maybe he was a murder suspect, and maybe Casey wouldn't talk to him, but this was a homecoming for him, too.

He closed his eyes, letting the memories wash over him. It was all too . . .

"Wake up, R.J.," came the voice, and R.J. was jolted out of a sleep so deep he wasn't sure what his name was. Henry Portillo was bending over him, shaking one shoulder with a hard hand.

"What time is it?" R.J. asked, slowly coming back to life.

Portillo straightened, shaking his head. "*Hijo*, you might as well ask, what year is it? I phoned twice from my office and you didn't hear."

R.J. sat up, his whole body creaking. "I guess I was really out of it."

Portillo cocked his head to one side. "Perhaps you are too tired to go to the studio . . . ?"

The thought of seeing Casey again sent a jolt through him and before he could even think of doing it he was standing. "I'm awake," he said, not too convincingly. "Let's go."

Portillo was amazed to see him jump up so fast, but they went out to the car, R.J. shaking his head to clear away the cobwebs.

Andromeda Studios was in a far corner of the San Fernando Valley. The main buildings had once been an aircraft assembly plant and the place still looked like somebody was making machines there. Machines, instead of movies. Which was kind of appropriate, because the way Andromeda made its movies was more industrial than artistic.

Andromeda had clawed its way up in town as the studio that made all the copies. If another studio had a hit movie about a German shepherd getting elected senator, six weeks later Andromeda had one out about a collie in the White House.

If Paramount bought a script about aliens who looked like vegetables, Andromeda dashed one out about space monsters who looked like fruit.

The movies were rushed, awful, and the concept of doing business that way was based on the idea that the public was pathetically dumb. But it worked. Andromeda spent almost nothing, paying starvation wages and ignoring all the unions. Then they flooded the video market with their cheap copies, and in a few short years, by a process that could only work in Hollywood, they'd become legitimate. They had no hits, nobody could remember one specific movie they'd made, but they had arrived; they were a major player.

And then, finally, the hits began to come. Three years ago they got their first Oscar. And in the last two years, Andromeda put three movies on the list of top ten in box-office receipts.

And the person who made all that happen was Janine Wright.

There were rumors now, Portillo told R.J., that Andromeda had moved too far too fast. They were stretched to the breaking point. They had to have a mega-hit on the order of *E.T.* or they were going belly-up. Without a few zillion bucks in quick cash transfusions, Janine would lose her studio.

It didn't look like much of a loss. As Portillo drove his car up to the gates, R.J. thought the place probably hadn't seen a coat of paint since the last time Howard Hughes dropped by. From the road it was shabby, seedy; the property looked as if it were abandoned and full of empty beer bottles and used condoms. Weeds grew up through the pavement.

Portillo slowed his big blue unmarked Chevrolet at the gate house. A uniformed young man with a clipboard stepped out of the hut and glanced into the car as Portillo rolled down the window.

"Hey, Lieutenant," he said cheerfully as he saw who was driving. "Whatcha got today?" He peered over at R.J.

"More of the same, John. I'm afraid we need to nose around the lot a little bit."

"No problem." The young man grinned and Scotch-taped a pass to their dashboard. "Visitor's Lot C please, lieutenant. Have a great day!" He gave them a huge smile and stepped back into the hut. A moment later the gate went up.

"Jesus Christ," R.J. said. "Does that guy simonize his teeth?"

"John is an actor," Portillo explained. "A nice boy. He has an audition next week for one of those cop shows. So he took his lunch break to study me, last week when I was out here."

"Yeah? What did he learn?"

Portillo gave R.J. a huge smile. It looked a lot like the gatekeeper's. "How to be nice, R.J. He learned to be nice. Picked it up right away. Twenty-some years, and you still haven't got it."

"I'm a slow learner," R.J. told him, returning the grin in spite of himself.

They pulled into a parking spot in a huge lot next to one of the hangars. R.J. got out of the car and stretched—and coughed. He looked at the mountains. They were only a few miles away, but they were barely visible through the thick haze of smog. I have a headache. So I guess I'm back, R.J. thought.

A Viking walked by talking to a Sumo wrestler. A moment later an attractive young woman in a harem suit rushed after them, saying things under her breath that would have made a sailor blush.

R.J. grinned again. He'd forgotten what a fun business this was. He'd never wanted to be an actor like his parents, but he'd played with the idea of doing something in the business, any-thing to keep him next to the high energy, odd sights, and twisted people. Luckily, he'd woken up in time to realize that it wasn't for him. It would have taken him only a couple of weeks before he started punching out some of the badly bent half-wits who ran the town.

Three guys in jeans and black T-shirts strolled slowly past, pushing an empty hand truck and sipping coffee as they went. R.J. knew what that meant. Andromeda was a union shop now.

"This way," Portillo said, pulling R.J.'s attention back to the hangar.

They went through a door with a red light above it. The light wasn't on, but it probably wouldn't have made any dif-ference. Uncle Hank had his cop face on. Nothing was going to slow him down right now.

Inside the hangar there were fifty or sixty people. About ten of them were racing around like headless chickens; mov-ing lights on the catwalk, sliding huge chunks of scenery around, rolling long black cables back and forth.

But most of the people were simply sitting or standing around. They were telling jokes, drinking coffee. A large clus-ter of actors, grips, gaffers, Teamsters, and carpenters sur-rounded a table covered with food—bagels, doughnuts, fruit, candy, juice, and coffee.

One woman was standing up on the set, all alone and ig-nored. R.J. recognized her: Maggie DeSoto. While the prepa-ration for shooting the scene went on, she simply stood in place. As R.J. watched she lifted her long skirt and absent-mindedly scratched her crotch. Nobody seemed to notice.

"Wait here," Portillo said. "I'll be right back."

He headed for a bearded man with a clipboard standing over beside the food table. R.J. turned back to stare at the set. It wasn't much. The inside of a cheesy European hotel room. Cracks painted on the walls. Glass shot out of the window. Maggie DeSoto turned and stared at R.J., her skirt still held up above her waist. A babble of voices took R.J.'s eyes away from Maggie's legs.

On the far side of Maggie a camera was set up. A group of people stood beside it, apparently having a Hollywood discussion. Nobody was throwing punches yet, but everybody was talking at the same time. With the lights in his face R.J. couldn't see much, but gradually he began to hear one voice calming down the others and taking over, telling them the way it was going to be and they had better learn to like it. It was a good voice; firm but not angry, controlled and tough but compassionate. It had a nice tone, good diction, a warm feeling to it.

Casey's voice.

Without thinking about it, R.J. found himself moving toward Casey. He walked straight across the set, dodging two gaffers and one chubby woman with big hair and a makeup kit who was powdering Maggie DeSoto. Maggie herself put a hand out to touch him and said, "Hey," as he walked by, giving him her version of a sexy smile, but he was focused on Casey's voice and hardly noticed.

And then he was there, standing behind her, almost close enough to smell her hair. He just stood and listened and looked at her. He could see a quarter profile, her neck, ear, and cheekbone.

For a moment it was enough. No matter what other reasons he'd thought he had, this was why he had come out here.

Casey was explaining to them that a certain scene was out

and that was all there was to it. She was listing the reasons; financial, artistic, time. The rest of the group didn't like it, but Casey was making them learn to live with it, telling them how to adjust.

"We're not curing cancer," she told them. "We're making a movie. And we're making it without this scene."

"Just the sort of Semitic bullshit I've come to expect from this silly lot of buggers," said a careful British voice.

"Trevor," Casey said with steel in her voice, "you don't have to like this. But you *do* have to go with it. Your alternative is over there," and she pointed to the door, locking eyes with the speaker, a scruffy, small white-haired man with the red nose of a hard drinker and the face of the world's meanest elf.

"Thank you, my dear," the elf said. "I shall take it under advisement. Bernard!" he yelled, turning away from Casey. "Is the fucking light ever going to be in place or shall I fetch a fucking candle?" And as he strolled away the group around the camera broke up and Casey turned around to face him.

R.J. wasn't sure what he was expecting, but he didn't get it. "R.J.," she said. She blinked and frowned, clearly shifting gears in her head, before giving him a quick hug. "Hi. What are you doing here?"

"I need to talk to you for a minute."

She shook her head. "I'm sorry, but I'm pretty busy right now. Can we talk later?"

"No," he said.

Casey sighed and pushed her hair off her forehead. "R.J., I really am glad to see you, but this is my job. I'm at work. I don't have time for personal stuff."

"Make some time," he said. "Did you know about the death threats?"

She blinked at him, gave her head a half shake. "Oh, Jesus," she said. "The goofy letter stuff? Is that why you're here?"

"Yeah, that's it."

She gave him a half smile, another shake of her head. "R.J., it's just a couple of stupid notes, bad rhymes. They're ridiculous."

"The cops don't think so. Neither do I."

She touched his face, a quick brush with one hand. "It's sweet of you to worry," she said, in a way that thanked him and made him feel clumsy at the same time. "But I can't take it seriously. I've got a job to do, and I don't have time for death threats." She touched his cheek with her lips, very quickly, and then stepped back. "Please. R.J. Let me talk to you later? I've got a million things going right now."

He put a hand on her arm. "Casey—" he said, but she pulled her arm away.

"This script thing is making me crazy," she said. "Please, I've got to get this under control. It's important."

"So is your life."

"R.J.," she said, with that same I'll-break-your-balls tone she had used on the elf, "I'd love to see you later, but right now I have a lot to do. This is my job. I'm at *work.*"

"You said that already."

"You can't just show up at my job and expect me to drop everything and have a nice chat, all right? I'll see you later." And she was off across the hangar and out the door at the far end.

R.J. watched her go, fighting down his feelings—anger with a touch of fear for her safety, shaken together with admiration at the way she was handling these Tinsel Town Turkeys—and him. And there was something else there, too, a softer feeling. Maybe he was just glad to see her. Even her back.

"There you are," Uncle Hank said at his elbow.

"Yeah. I think so." He turned to see a sour-looking guy with a goatee standing beside Portillo.

Portillo jerked his head at the sourpuss. "We're in trouble," Uncle Hank said. "Janine Wright wants us in her office right away."

CHAPTER 16

Janine Wright's office was on the top floor of the only building on the lot that wasn't a remodeled hangar. It wasn't much to look at, but it was a real building. It only had two floors, and Janine had herself a good-sized chunk of the second one.

Windows wrapped around two full walls of the office. On the other two walls there was enough brand-name modern art to start a pretty good little museum. A kumquat tree blossomed in a corner beside an L-shaped kid-leather sofa. In front of the sofa a coffee table stood on a Navajo rug. The coffee table looked to be a solid chunk of quartz crystal with a glass top. Except there were four or five live birds inside it, chirping miserably.

Janine herself sat behind a massive ebony desk in a high-backed black leather chair. The desk was a good twenty feet long and she sat right in the middle. Her hands were clasped in front of her, making what looked like one large fist, and she gave R.J. and Portillo a terrifying glare as they were shoved through her door. "Sort of like Christians getting pushed in with the lion," R.J. said to Portillo.

"What the fuck do you think you're doing here?" demanded Janine.

"Just doing my job, Ms. Wright," said Portillo mildly.

"Not you, greaseball. I mean that asshole. How dare you bring that son-of-a-bitch onto my lot? I told you he's trying to kill me!"

R.J. pulled away from Portillo and walked calmly across the wide floor to Janine Wright's desk. When he got there, he leaned slowly over and put one palm down on the ebony surface, just to the left of the blotter. Then he very carefully pushed sideways. The blotter, the solid marble pen holder, the telephone, the calendar, the In/Out basket, two large potted plants, and a huge stack of papers, printouts and scripts all slid the full width of the desk and onto the floor at the far side with a series of crashes, plops, thuds, bangs, and thumps. The trash can fell over and rolled back and forth in a quarter circle.

Then R.J. walked all the way back to the center of the desk and leaned in until his face was an inch from Janine Wright's.

"You stink," he said in a reasonable tone of voice. "There's nothing about you that anybody could possibly like or admire. You just stink. Nobody tells you that because they're afraid of you. Lieutenant Portillo doesn't tell you because it's part of his job to be polite, even to a scumbucket like you, because you are a scumbucket with political clout.

"But I don't care. I don't work here, I don't live here, and I don't give a good goddamn what goes on here. But I grew up here, and I know all about assholes like you and the crap you do to everybody around you because you think you can get away with it. Well, you can't get away with it with me. You can't buy me, threaten me, or persuade me to do jack shit I don't want to do. So don't pull any of your horseshit with me, lady. I'll shove it right back down your throat."

R.J. leaned in even closer. The tip of his nose touched hers. "And be polite to the lieutenant."

She frowned at him. He had to give her credit. She didn't even blink. But there was a little bit of uncertainty in her eyes now as she said, "Pick up my stuff."

"No." He moved back a few inches.

She frowned again, then looked beyond him to Henry Portillo. "Why did you bring him here—" Her eyes flicked to R.J., then back to Portillo. "—Lieutenant?"

"That's better," R.J. said, and stood up straight.

Portillo strolled across the big floor and stood beside R.J. "I brought him along," said Portillo, "because I believe he may be able to assist me in the course of my investigation."

Janine Wright stared at him. "Horseshit. He sent the fucking letters and you know it."

Portillo shook his head. "I don't know it. And you—"

She snorted. "Then explain *this!*" She held up an envelope. "He's not here in L.A. ten minutes and another one of the fucking things shows up in my mail! With an L.A. postmark! What about that, huh?"

Portillo's face was like an Aztec mask with two eyes carved from glittering gems. "May I see that, please?" He stepped forward and took the envelope. As he pulled the note out, R.J. leaned over his shoulder and read:

> *If you were just a little brighter*
> *you wouldn't need a brand new writer*
> *I can do this lots more times*
> *I got lots of tricks and rhymes*
> *STOP THE SEQUEL NOW*

Portillo folded the note and put it in his pocket. "Does this mean anything to you, Ms. Wright?"

"No. We're not looking for a new writer. Jason Levy has been on this project from day one. He's cheap and dependable."

"Then as far as you know—"

The door opened at the far end of the room. "Excuse me, Ms. Wright," said the sour little dork with the goatee. "A Detective Sergeant Brannigan is on the line." He managed to look even more disgusted as he nodded at Henry Portillo. "For the lieutenant."

"Tell him to go fuck himself," Wright snarled.

"I suggested something like that," said the goatee tartly. "But he said you would probably want to know about this, too."

"Know what?"

The goatee looked like he had a mouthful of rotten lemon. "Jason Levy is dead. Murdered."

———————●———————

Jason Levy's house was a small, neat wooden place stuck on a hillside in Coldwater Canyon. It had two bedrooms, one bathroom, a small carport, and probably cost a half-million bucks.

Jason Levy was waiting for them on the floor of the living room. He was a Cool Guy. You could tell he had thought so. He was about thirty and had an expensive shaggy haircut, an expensive leather jacket, and a pair of expensive silk pants. And right now, somebody had half-hacked off his head with a pair of expensive, walnut-handled scissors. They had left the scissors stuck into Levy's neck. What was left of it. As if they thought they might come back later and finish the job.

R.J. had seen uglier deaths. He just couldn't remember when. He turned away, moving to join Portillo over by the window.

A window had clearly been forced open: its screen was bent and flung on the floor. Portillo was looking carefully at the scratch marks on the window frame. Standing beside him was Detective Sergeant Brannigan, a large doughy guy with long sideburns.

"I gotta tell you, Sarge," Brannigan was saying. "If you don't got the note, I woulda said maybe we check this guy out for gay." He nodded at Levy's body. "The scissors and all. Looks like what ya call homosexual rage."

Brannigan said it like he wanted Portillo to pat him on the head, tell him he was a good boy. Instead, Portillo just glanced at him, and then turned to R.J. "What do you think?"

R.J. shook his head. "The script must be worse than I thought," he said. "That's one of the meanest edits I've ever seen."

"Meaner than poison?" Portillo asked softly.

R.J. glanced over his shoulder at the nearly headless body of Jason Levy. "Yeah," he said. "Meaner than poison." He looked back at Portillo. "You connecting the two of them? Officially?"

"Officially? Not yet. Too much paper work. In my own mind, however—" He shrugged. "You can only believe in coincidence so far, hey?"

"Jeez, lookit this," Brannigan said, and for a moment R.J. thought he was just p.o.'d at being ignored. But when he and Portillo turned, they saw Brannigan leaning out the window, looking down at the side of the house. Portillo leaned out.

"Well," he said after a moment, and turned to Brannigan. "Get them." Brannigan disappeared out the window, squeezing his doughy bulk through quickly for such a big guy.

"What?" R.J. asked.

"Don't touch them," Portillo said out the window.

"Don't worry," came Brannigan's strained reply. A moment later his hand came up, holding a Ziploc bag with a pair of black-framed reading glasses in it.

"They're not Levy's," R.J. said. "They're too cheap looking. And he was too young—those are the kind of cheaters a middle-aged guy would wear."

"Maybe the gardener dropped 'em," Brannigan offered, struggling back through the window. "Except there's no garden down there. Nothing but dirt and a eucalyptus tree." He brushed himself off. "They were wedged into the support beam," he told R.J. "The beams that hold up the house. Right where you'd have to climb to reach this window. So if a guy had them in his pocket—"

"Good work, Detective," Portillo cut him off. "Very good." Brannigan looked so pleased he didn't seem to mind when Portillo turned away from him again. "There's some kind of serial number on the frame," he said to R.J.

R.J. glanced at the black plastic frames. They looked like the kind of cheap reading glasses anybody might wear—anybody who was a little broke and not too picky. The odds against this being a real clue, dropped by a killer, were long—but it did happen. Still, R.J.'s money was on the gardener.

"Hey, Lieutenant, you in there?" R.J. turned to see a heavy-set woman with round glasses peering in the front door.

Portillo waved her in. "Come on in, Gilbert." To R.J. he added, "Crime Scene Unit. Let's get out of here. We'll just be in the way now."

They drove down the canyon and into the valley. R.J. turned it over in his head, trying to make the connections. It made sense that the two murders were connected—except that poisoners usually stayed with poison, slashers got their thrills using their blades. Somebody who did both—

It didn't make sense. But it was scary as hell.

Either the guy was a totally out-of-control maniac, or the kind of cold killer who killed for effect, picking his method like a flavor of the month. Either way, this wasn't going to be easy. Or fun.

"Did that note look like the others?" R.J. asked as they came off Coldwater Canyon and onto Ventura.

"I think so, yes," said Portillo absentmindedly. "The pasted-on letters look the same. It's a funny thing."

"What is?"

"In the previous notes, all the letters were cut from movie industry magazines."

"You mean the fan magazines?"

"No, that's the funny part. They are all from what you might call insider magazines. The ones all the executives have on their coffee tables and in their waiting rooms. Not too many people outside the business even know about them, but they sell a lot of copies here."

"So whoever is doing this is an insider."

Portillo shrugged. "Or wants us to think so, and is smart enough to know how."

R.J. laughed. "Sure. Or they really are an insider, and want us to think they're an *outsider* trying to *look* like an insider. Come on, Uncle Hank. Take the clue or you'll go nuts."

Portillo shook his head and sighed. "I have been on the LAPD for twenty-seven years, *hijo*. I am no longer able to go nuts. But I tend to think as you do. It's an insider. Motive is easier that way."

"Yeah. Janine Wright makes enemies the way other people make breakfast."

"True enough," Portillo said with a shrug. "Probably three quarters of this town hates her, and the other quarter is afraid of her but would like to hate her if they could."

"Uh-huh," said R.J. "Where do you fit?"

The older man turned and looked at R.J. with a huge smile. "If I have to arrest her, that would be okay," he said.

They arrived back at Uncle Hank's house and R.J. went back to his room, intending to unpack and think a little. But he had barely got his suitcase open when he heard the phone ring in the living room and, a moment later, a knock came on the door. "R.J.? The telephone is for you."

"Coming, Uncle Hank."

Nobody knew he was here, except Wanda. So it had to be important. He followed Portillo down the hall to the living room and picked up the receiver. "Hello, Wanda. Give me the good news first."

"Okay, boss. A Ms. Gillam from Connecticut Department of Corrections wants a word with you, and she didn't sound happy."

"That's the good news?"

"Yeah. I thought you should know that Mary Kelley kid has been calling all day, totally wigged out."

"Wigged out good? She found her old man?"

"Wigged out bad, boss," Wanda said. "She found where her old man *was*, but he's gone."

"What?"

"He took off. Skipped parole. Nobody knows where he is and there's hell to pay."

"Damn."

"You got that right."

CHAPTER 17

Wanda didn't have any more details. She gave R.J. the phone number where Mary Kelley could be reached and he called the kid.

"R. J. Brooks, Mary," he said when she picked up the phone.

"Oh, God," she said. "I went over there, it's such a miserable little place, and he's gone, and nobody knows where he is or why he suddenly just took off, except there's this woman, R.J., she says she's Daddy's parole officer, and she thinks I know where he is and now she's going to get me in trouble because I won't tell her where he is, except I don't *know* where he is, but she says I do because he was there until you started nosing around and she says she can have your license pulled—"

"Breathe, damn it!" R.J. growled down the wire.

"—and that it would be my fault if you— What?"

"I said breathe. I'm three thousand miles away and I can't slap you, but I'll hang up if I have to listen to any more hysterics."

"I—but I wasn't—"

"Yes, you were. Now take a deep breath and tell me what happened."

He could hear her take a breath. It was shakey, but it was deep, and when she spoke again her voice was a little steadier. "I went over there, to the, you know. The address you gave me."

"Sure, over in Tuffington."

"Torrington."

"Yeah, all right, Torrington. And your old man was gone."

"They said he hadn't showed up for work for two days and he had missed a meeting with that woman, his parole officer, which I guess is, you know, not a good thing."

"No, it's not."

"And she thinks he's skipped parole and it's our fault, yours and mine, and she says we could be in a lot of trouble."

"They always say that," R.J. said. "You get used to it. It doesn't mean much."

"And then I called your office and they said you were in California." She made it sound like he had betrayed her when she needed him most.

"I don't like it much, either. But that's where I am," he said. "What do you want me to do?"

"Oh," Mary said. She sounded surprised that he would ask her that. "Um. Can you find him? My father, I mean?"

"I know who you mean. I'll find him."

"Because that woman, the parole officer. She said the police had been looking for him and they couldn't find him."

"I don't have to take time out to write speeding tickets," R.J. said. "And I can walk past a doughnut when I need to. I'll find your old man, Mary."

It took another couple of minutes to calm her down, and then he had to let her know that it was okay, he didn't mind the job, it was what he did. But when he finally hung up she sounded a lot better than when she had called. R.J. wasn't sure why that should matter to him, but it did. He wanted her to have confidence in him. He liked the kid.

He dialed a New York number he knew pretty well.

"Broadway News," the smooth voice said on the other end.

"It's me, Hookshot."

"Hey! R.J.! Bubbe, where you been?"

"California," R.J. told him.

"Oh, man. I'm sorry to hear that."

"I need a favor, Hookshot."

Hookshot laughed, a rich, loud noise that was like a sound mosaic of his genes. " 'Course you need a favor, R.J. Why else you ever call me up?"

"Yeah, well, I don't read many of those fancy magazines you carry. Listen, I got an ex-con skipped parole. I need to find him."

"Shee-it, R.J. Ask me something hard sometime. Can't be that many ex-cons hiding out, can there? Not in New Fuckin' York?"

"It's not that bad. He's a white collar guy. Besides, he'll probably be over in Connecticut."

There was a pause, followed by a snort of disbelief. "Say *what?* The man is *where?*"

"Connecticut, Hookshot. It's not that far."

"The fuck it ain't. Someplace way the fuck out West, man. Still got Indians and shit out there."

"Hookshot, I might be stuck out here for a while. I can't do this."

Another pause. "Gonna cost you, man."

"Sure," R.J. said. "Why should this be different?"

R.J. always ended up paying for these favors. Not that Hookshot needed the money. He was rich. They both knew it, though Hookshot never admitted it. But like a lot of rich guys, Hookshot couldn't make himself spend a dime. And anyway, the money went to the street kids who sniffed out the information. Or if Hookshot did it himself, the money went to the kids, anyway. A new jacket, a pair of jeans, a decent meal.

R.J. didn't mind. It was just about his only charity. He gave

Hookshot what he knew about Kelley and said he'd call back in a few days.

"How long you going to be out there, R.J.?"

"I don't know. Until I catch some scumbag writing tough letters."

"Tough?" Hookshot cackled. "In Los Angeles?! Hee-hee, R.J., that's meshuggeneh. Don't get hurt."

"I'll try not to," he said. "Casey's out here."

Hookshot stopped laughing. "She in on this thing?"

"Yeah. The letters are all to the people at her new job."

Another pause. "You got Portillo with you on this?"

"Yeah."

"Okay, then. You let me know you need help, man."

"I will, Hookshot. Thanks."

"And R.J.! Don't be a schmuck! You stand in the doorway when you can, hear me?"

It made no sense. "What are you talking about?"

"Earthquakes, man. You got to stand in the doorway for an earthquake so the ceiling don't fall on your goddamn head."

R.J. laughed. One of the reasons he liked Hookshot was that the guy could always make him laugh. "I'll stay in the doorway, Hookshot."

"Do that. Don't do nothing meshugge, you hear me?"

R.J. hung up the phone feeling a lot better. Mary Kelley's problem didn't seem like much compared with what was going on out here, but he had said he would help her, and in his business you had to do what you said you would do. Maybe that's why he liked what he did. And maybe that's what he disliked so much about the movie business. It was just the opposite.

He stood up and followed his nose to the kitchen. Henry Portillo was up to his elbows in making dinner. From past experience R.J. knew it was an important ritual for the older man. So he stood well out of the way and watched, leaning against a counter and sniffing in the smells he remembered: onion, lime, green pepper, chiles. Something else.

He nodded at one of the pots on the stove. "Whatcha got going, Uncle Hank?"

"*Mole* sauce. With some chicken, rice, beans." He plopped four chicken breasts onto a tray and began sprinkling spices on them. "That was your office on the phone?"

"Yeah. Somebody skipped parole. Believe it or not, Janine Wright's ex. I'm finding him for the daughter."

Portillo grunted. "How long has he been missing?"

"Couple of days. Why?"

"Has New York made you stupid, *hijo?*"

R.J. stood up straight, annoyed. "What do you mean, Uncle Hank?"

Portillo turned to him, his finger pointed like a knife. "I mean, R.J., that tomorrow morning you are going to go with me down to police headquarters to talk to my superiors, and you will have to answer some very tough questions. And it will go a lot easier if we can tell them there is someone out there who is a more likely suspect than you."

Portillo opened the oven and shoved in a tray with the chicken breasts.

"Someone like an ex-con ex-husband, for instance."

R.J. blinked. He had been thinking he had two separate problems. Now it looked like he had only one. "You're right, Uncle Hank," he admitted. "I'm getting stupid. I should have seen it a long time ago. You think Kelley is out here? In Los Angeles?"

Portillo grunted and slammed the oven door. "To me this makes more sense than assuming you are guilty, chico. The ex-husband is a logical suspect. Especially if we can establish that he has a good motive for hating Ms. Wright."

"He's got a great motive. He was married to her. That woman could push Gandhi into a fistfight." Portillo gave him a look. R.J. looked back, then snapped his fingers. "Wait a sec, I just remembered something. No, damn it, *two* somethings. His daughter said she thinks Janine framed him."

"That's good," Portillo said, leaning on the counter across from R.J. "What's the other thing?"

"The parole officer in Connecticut. She told me Kelley was still saying he was innocent."

Portillo frowned and nodded. "I like it. This is a very good-looking suspect, R.J. I think I should phone this in." He winked. "You may be off the hook, *hijo.*"

He left the room and in a moment R.J. could hear him talking on the telephone. R.J. closed his eyes, suddenly tired and feeling bad about what he would have to do. Sure, Mary, I found your old man. And then I put him in jail.

Aw, hell. This one was out of his hands. He had to find Kelley—not for Mary, but to keep Casey safe, and to keep his own ass out of jail. And just incidentally, to stop a few more murders. He could feel bad about it later.

He stood up and went to the refrigerator for some soda.

He was going to talk to the cops in the morning. Get this all straightened out. Things would be simpler then.

CHAPTER 18

But things weren't any better the next morning. If anything, they were worse.

He'd called Casey late and gotten only her answering machine. The voice on the tape was a new Casey; crisper, impersonal, no warmth in it, nothing he could recognize beyond the mechanical sound of her voice. He wasn't sure he knew who it was.

He'd tried again. Same thing. Tried again. And again. Finally fell asleep next to the phone. Got woken up when the damn thing rang. And it wasn't even her, it was for Portillo. R.J. got up and handed the older man the phone and tottered off to bed.

He'd been up early, still dead tired. But the jet lag wouldn't let him sleep beyond 6 A.M. He made coffee and sat drinking it, waiting for Uncle Hank to come out, not daring to cook breakfast. It was an important meal for Portillo, and he demanded the right to make his famous *huevos rancheros* for R.J. whenever he could.

R.J. wasn't hungry anyway, so he could wait. He was still feeling sore about missing Casey. She hadn't called back and he had spent too much time wondering what that meant. He had just decided for the ninth time that it didn't mean anything and he was being a jerk when Portillo came into the kitchen for breakfast.

He didn't say much, just nodded and got to work cooking. In just a few minutes he handed R.J. a large plate piled with eggs, salsa, and refried beans. He set a basket of warm tortillas in the center of the small kitchen table and the two of them piled into it.

The salsa was hot—Portillo paid R.J. the compliment of giving him the *real* stuff instead of his gringo salsa. After two bites the sweat was pouring off R.J. It was damn good, but it was hard work to get it down without shouting. But if nothing else, it cleared the cobwebs from R.J.'s head.

When they were done eating they got dressed and headed downtown. Getting downtown wasn't easy this time of day, but they made it, and in a little over an hour they were sitting side by side in front of a big desk at police headquarters.

Captain Davis was as big as his desk and his face looked a lot harder. He stared at R.J. for a long time. R.J. began to think the guy maybe thought he had X-ray vision or something. But what the hell, if the captain wanted to stare, it was his office. Let him stare.

Still, staring was something you could do alone. So R.J. took out the crossword puzzle from this morning's paper and started to work on it. He'd stuck it in his pocket on the theory that you should never go into a building with a waiting room unless you were ready to wait. With Davis still hitting him with both barrels, R.J. just flipped the paper open, took a pen from the captain's desk, and went to work.

The puzzle wasn't as good as the one in *The New York Times*, of course. They even got a few clues wrong, misspelled a word now and then.

But R.J. generally figured it out, and it made him feel a little superior. That was something he could use this morning.

"Did you teach him that, Lieutenant?" he heard the captain asking.

"No, sir," Portillo answered in a neutral voice.

"Well, I don't like it," the captain said.

Portillo had nothing to say to that.

"Put down that paper, Brooks," the captain commanded.

R.J. looked up blandly and raised an eyebrow. "Why? So I can get another staring lesson?"

"I'm talking to you, that's why."

R.J. shrugged. "I figured if you had something to say, you would have said it. I'm sorry, Captain, I didn't realize you were so tough. Go ahead, talk. Or if you want, stare some more."

Captain Davis turned purple. "You're in enough trouble already, sport. I might go a little easier on you if you cooperate."

R.J. tried his hardest to look surprised. "But Captain, I *am* cooperating. I've flown three thousand miles at my own expense to answer your questions. If you can't think of any that's not my problem." He folded the puzzle and stuck it back into his pocket. "If you want, I'll think up my own questions, and then answer 'em, too. You can go for coffee. I like it black, two sugars."

Captain Davis slammed his hand down on the desk. It sounded like a hand grenade going off. R.J. managed not to shout *eek* or dive under the furniture. But it was a close call.

"Portillo!" he bellowed. "Tell this fucking clown this is serious!"

"I think he heard you, Captain."

"I heard you," R.J. said. "But I might be more inclined to believe it's serious if you start to treat it that way instead of trying to prove what a hard-ass you are. So why don't I just admit you are really a hard-ass, this is serious, I'm in trouble, and then cut all the horseshit and do some business?"

Captain Davis thought of three or four things to say, all at the same time, but none of them came out so you could actually understand them. The first thing that came out that R.J. and Portillo could make out was, "Lieutenant Kates was right about you."

R.J. smirked. If Davis had been on the phone to Kates, R.J. understood where the staring business came from. "Kates has never been right about anything. But if you think he is, that explains a lot."

"He said you're the biggest pain in the ass in Manhattan."

R.J. grinned. "Well, that's a compliment coming from him. What else did he say?"

Now Davis grinned. It wasn't pretty. "He said he's been talking to the Connecticut State Troopers. And Connecticut has a body on their hands that might interest you."

R.J. could feel the skin rise up on the back of his neck. The only people he knew of who had gone to Connecticut were Mary Kelley and Hookshot. If either one had gone over to Torrington and something had happened— "Who is it?"

Davis leaned back, stretching his power play as long as he could. "Guy named William Kelley."

R.J. could hear Portillo hissing explosively. But R.J. didn't have enough breath to do it himself. His head was swimming. "Excuse me?" he finally managed to say.

Davis's grin got bigger and nastier. "Yeah, that's right. William Kelley. Died in a car crash. Your big alibi ran into a tree, hotshot." He leaned back and for the first time looked almost happy. "They've had him in the morgue for three days. Looking for next of kin. Then they got the wire from us asking about him. Small world, huh, Brooks?" He leaned forward and slammed his hand on the table again. "Now, goddammit, let's talk about a couple of murders, punk."

R.J. got over the shock of Kelley's death in a couple of minutes. But it was two and a half hours of sweat before he got away from Davis and his staring act. At least an hour and a half of it was pure meanness by Davis, hitting up against pure stubbornness by R.J. Toward the end, R.J. knew that Davis didn't think he had killed anybody or even written the damn letters, but he also knew that if Davis had a chance to stick him with it, he would.

In a way, R.J. sympathized with that. Davis was under a lot of pressure to stick somebody, anybody, and if he could make R.J. fit, well, that would take the pressure off. And because of who R.J. was it would mean a lot of media attention, which never hurt a cop's career.

But it also meant that Davis was more interested in covering his ass than finding the killer, and that wasn't good news. Casey's life was in danger here and R.J. didn't feel like taking the chance. There was too much at stake to depend on a clown like Davis. He would never find this guy, unless he saw him in the commissioner's back pocket while he was kissing it.

And that meant R.J. would have to do it.

With Kelley out of the picture as a suspect, R.J. would be starting all over again, back at square one. And the killer, whomever it was, was out here now, off R.J.'s home turf. That made it tougher. But there wasn't anybody else, and the stakes were too high—Casey's life was on the line.

First, though, he had to go back to New York. He wasn't looking forward to it. He hated funerals, but Mary Kelley was going to hate this one even more, and she would be there alone. She was his client, and he owed it to her to be there. An obligation like that came first, no matter how much every cell in his body was screaming at him to stay close to Casey and keep her safe.

But before any of that he still had to sit through Captain Davis's torture session. And it was a nasty shock when he realized that he was now the leading suspect for Jason Levy's murder, too.

He found out the hard way.

After some routine opening questions Davis leaned back and went into the staring routine again. A little smile flicked across his skinny lips and R.J. thought, Uh-oh, here it comes. He looked at Portillo, who shrugged.

"Coroner says Jason Levy was killed early yesterday afternoon," Davis said.

"All right," R.J. said.

"Where were you, Brooks?"

R.J. almost choked. "What? Where was I? For Christ's sake, Davis, you think I killed Levy?"

Davis just smiled. "We know from the notes what the motive was—stop this movie they're making over there at Andromeda. That sound like something you want to do? Yeah, I thought so. And we know that lawyer, Belcher, was killed for that same reason, at a time when you had motive, means, and opportunity. Just like you had for Jason Levy. So of course, we'd like to know where you were when Levy was killed, since the two deaths appear to be linked." His sick little smile got a lot bigger. The son-of-a-bitch was really getting off on this. "Where were you, Brooks?"

With a sick lurch to the stomach, R.J. knew they had him in a bad place. "I was at Lieutenant Portillo's house," he said, with no hope at all.

Davis played it out, the sadistic bastard. "Oh. Okay. I see. So naturally Lieutenant Portillo can vouch for you, then. Very good. Is that right, Lieutenant? The two of you were together, at your house?"

Portillo looked pale, whether from anger or something else, and R.J. could see his jaw muscles standing out. "I was down here," he said. "In my office."

Davis pretended to look surprised. "Down *here*—then you mean Brooks was at your house *alone?*"

"That's right."

Davis stared at R.J. again, raising his eyebrows, pretending he'd just discovered something. Just like a real investigator. "Well, Brooks," he said. "I'm sure somebody else can provide some corboration."

"It's cor-*rob*-boration, Captain."

The smile stayed, but there was a mean glitter in Davis's

eyes now. "I don't give a flying fart how you say it, Brooks. Do you have any?"

R.J. sighed. "No."

"Nothing at all? No UPS deliveries, no passing fire trucks, no telephone calls from U.S. senators? Nothing?"

"Nothing," R.J. said. "I fell asleep."

Davis shook his head. "Asleep. Well, well. You must be a sound sleeper then. Are you a sound sleeper, Brooks?" R.J. didn't answer. Why give the bastard the satisfaction. "Because according to our records here, Lieutenant Portillo attempted to reach you by telephone two times at the approximate time of Jason Levy's murder and there was no answer." The smile dropped away and it was all triumphant snarl now. "How do you explain *that*, Mister Movie Star Fucking Brooks?"

R.J. couldn't explain it, of course. It sounded pretty feeble, even to him, and he knew it was true.

And for the next hour and a half Davis pounded away at it. The same questions over and over. The same veiled threats and cheap scare tactics. It didn't work on R.J.—he had nothing to say that he hadn't said already and the Gestapo-style bullying just didn't work on a guy who'd had it from experts.

It wasn't getting them anywhere, and it sure wasn't closing in on the killer. It was pure ticket-punching. Davis was making sure he could show that he had personally spent a good long time grilling the leading suspect.

Finally R.J. had enough.

Davis had asked him the same stupid question for the twelfth time and R.J. felt something pop inside. He'd felt it before. It meant he was in a kind of danger zone where he was going to do whatever he had to do and the hell with the consequences. It meant if he had to punch out a police captain to get some fresh air, that's what he would do.

R.J. stood up.

"Sit down, Brooks," Davis said. "I'm not done with you."

"Yes, you are."

"I said sit down!"

"Am I under arrest?"

"No."

R.J. took a step closer to Davis. "Are you going to charge me with anything?"

Davis licked his lips. "Not at present."

R.J. took another step, and another. He felt Portillo's hand on his arm, trying to hold him back, but he didn't care. "Am I a suspect in a capital case? Should I get a lawyer?"

"That won't be necessary at this time."

R.J. pulled away from Portillo's restraining hand and leaned right in over the desk. Davis tried to tough it out, but he was looking worried. "Then how would you describe my legal position at this moment, Captain?"

Davis twitched. He shot his eyes to Portillo, maybe looking for help, but he didn't find any there.

"You are voluntarily assisting the police in their investigation."

R.J. held the stare for a second. Let the bloated desk jockey squirm. There was nothing he could do. "Voluntarily," R.J. finally said.

"That's right."

R.J. stood up. "I just un-volunteered," he said. "If you're in charge of this investigation, I'm no longer assisting. You couldn't catch a cold in the flu ward."

"Damn it, Brooks—"

R.J. turned his back on Davis. "Uncle Hank, I'm out of here."

"All right, R.J."

"Portillo," Davis spluttered. "You'd damn well better make him stay—!"

Davis found himself looking into four ice cold eyes. "Captain," Portillo said gently. "If you are suggesting that I, as a sworn officer, unlawfully detain a citizen who has gone to great personal expense and inconvenience to assist us—"

"That's exactly what I'm suggesting, goddammit!"

Portillo nodded. "Then I'd like that in writing, please,

Captain." And he looked mildly at Davis, who made noises for a few seconds and finally gave up.

Davis hit his desk again. It didn't sound so loud this time. "You'll die a lieutenant, Portillo," he finally said.

Portillo stepped up and looked down at Davis. The captain probably outweighed Portillo by a hundred pounds and stood six inches taller, but Portillo filled the room and Davis looked small and insignificant. "Under the circumstances," Portillo said softly, "that will be a great satisfaction. Sir." And he looked down at Davis for a good long time to be sure he got the message.

Davis got it all right. He turned bright red. R.J. had to grin as he watched the captain squirm for control. He didn't find any.

"Will that be all, Captain?" Portillo asked him. And before he could answer, Portillo turned away. "Let's go, R.J."

They headed out of the building and into the parking garage without saying a word. But by the time they got to Portillo's car, R.J. was fighting back an attack of the giggles. As he climbed into the car, he lost the fight and started to laugh.

"Jesus Christ, Uncle Hank," he gasped.

Portillo stared at him with the same mild control he had used on the captain. R.J. lost it again. Portillo watched him laugh for a minute, shaking his head.

"R.J.," Portillo finally said. "This is not a laughing matter."

"I know it, Uncle Hank," R.J. said, still laughing, "but my God, you were great in there." R.J. pulled himself together. "I feel like a kid coming from the principal's office."

Portillo snorted and started the car. "Davis is not going to suspend you," he said. "He wants to put you in jail, and he no longer cares how. You have made a bad enemy, R.J."

"He'll have to take a number, Uncle Hank. Besides, he wasn't any friend of mine when I walked in. He's getting chummy with Kates by long distance."

But Portillo just shook his head. "We blew it, *hijo*."

They drove in silence for a few minutes, until the car nosed up the on-ramp onto the freeway. R.J.'s laughter left him quickly. Uncle Hank was right. There really wasn't anything funny about this. They had blown it. Given half a chance he could have gotten off the hook with the law. But he'd gotten no chance and had twisted himself more firmly on the hook than ever before.

He was just a step or two away from a jail cell, at a time when Casey's life might depend on him being free and finding a killer. Now he had to move that much faster—catch the killer before Davis or Kates nailed him for jaywalking—and he couldn't see any way to do it that didn't leave Casey exposed. He hated it like hell but there was no way around it. But first—

"I have to go back to New York," he finally said.

Portillo looked at him without expression. "I know that, R.J."

"Just for a couple of days. Then I'll be back. But—" He found it hard to say. Putting it in words made the danger more real somehow.

But Portillo understood. "I'll keep an eye on Casey. Have somebody watch her house, keep an officer on the set, and another in the offices. That's about all I can do."

R.J. nodded. It was probably more than he could have done himself, but it was not the kind of thing a guy should delegate. But he had to be there for Mary Kelley. She was a client, and that still meant something.

"Thanks, Uncle Hank," he said. He looked out the window of the car. The dry hills were almost visible through the smog. The traffic was moving bumper to bumper at sixty-five miles per hour. "I'd like to see Casey before I leave."

Portillo looked at R.J. again. "I know that, *hijo*. That's where we're headed."

CHAPTER 19

They got to the studio about twenty minutes later. The same young actor was working the gate and he let them in again with no problem.

It must have been union coffee-break time. The whole lot was swarming with people in jeans. They were lounging all over the place, leaning against cars, sitting on the pavement.

At the door to the soundstage a pair of Nazi storm troopers were yakking with a bearded Basque shepherd and a long-legged woman in a flamenco outfit. A guy in baggy pantaloons and a fez wandered by singing a Guns N' Roses tune.

R.J. and Portillo pushed through and into the hangar. The set this time was a basement room, steam pipes dripping onto ratty-looking crates. A dingy bed stood under a high window.

Maggie DeSoto was sitting on the bed under the lights, this time completely topless. Her breasts stood out unnaturally, an obvious silicone job. She had her legs crossed and was kicking the upper foot and smoking a cigarette. She looked bored, as if she was waiting for a bus to take her to the library. Except there were damned few people in the library dressed like that. Even in Los Angeles.

Once again there was a tense knot of people beside the camera. As R.J. approached them he could hear Trevor, the elfin director, speaking.

"—don't care if she pulls his balls off and dusts the room with them, I'll have him out of that great bloody Winnebago in five minutes or I'll bloody well sue his fucking agent!"

Casey was standing beside the elf, trying to calm him down. It wasn't working. He pushed her away and R.J. felt his blood coming to a boil, but Casey turned and saw him.

"R.J.!" she said with an actual smile. It was quick and strained, but it was a smile.

"Hi, Casey," he said. "Would you like this guy in six pieces or a full dozen?" The elf looked alarmed and quickly backed away.

Casey put a hand on R.J.'s arm. It felt good. "He's not the problem," she said, nodding at the rapidly retreating elf. "It's Alec."

"The no-shirt guy? What's his problem?"

Casey giggled. It was a sound so completely unlike her that R.J. just stared. "Apparently," she said, the giggle still just a half breath away, "Maggie DeSoto put her hand inside his pants during the love scene."

R.J. shook his head. "And?"

"And then she laughed and said something nobody else heard, and Alec stormed off the set and locked himself into his trailer. He says he won't come out again until Maggie is fired and replaced with somebody decent."

"Well then, great," R.J. said. "Let's take advantage and have some lunch. I need to talk to you."

Casey frowned and shook her head. "Do you know how much it's costing us for every hour this crew stands around doing nothing?"

"Well, hell, why throw good money after bad? Cancel the picture and let's get something to eat."

She ignored him, her eyes already roaming around the room, looking for something. "I can't leave the set until this is cleared up, R.J." Her eyes darted over to a bearded guy with a clipboard. "In fact, until Alec comes out of his trailer I'm going to be too busy to— Just a second, Bill," she said as the bearded guy walked past. She fell in step with him and they walked off, already deep in conversation.

R.J. fumed. So the guy got his crotch grabbed, and because of that, now Casey was too busy to talk. And because this was Hollywood, they would solve it by telephone, if at all, and it would take three days. Time he didn't have. He had a plane to catch.

It made him furious. He had to talk to Casey, let her know what was going on. Persuade her to keep a low profile and co-operate with the guys Henry Portillo would assign to her. And nobody was doing anything beyond high-powered fretting. Well, hell, there must be something he could do. He was from this town, from this life. He should be able to think of something.

But what? They sure as hell hadn't had this kind of problem when he was a kid. If anything like this had ever happened on the set of one of his father's pictures—not that it ever could have—his father probably would have—

It came to him just like that. He looked around the room. Casey was already on the cellular telephone, talking away a mile a minute. Portillo was talking to a cop over beside the food tables. The cop was practically at attention.

And on a chair beside Portillo, R.J. saw it.

Somebody had dumped a battered raincoat and a fedora on the chair. Wardrobe. Probably Alec Harris's costume. Based on the one R.J.'s dad had made famous.

R.J. stepped casually over and picked up the hat and coat. Portillo glanced at him. "R.J.," he said. It was part warning and part question.

R.J. ducked it with a reassuring smile. "I'll be right back, Uncle Hank," he said, and headed for the door.

Outside he shrugged into the coat as he walked toward the two big trailers. They had signs on the door. The one on the left said "ALEC HARRIS" and had a couple of gold stars around it. Just in case the poor slob forgot what he was supposed to be.

R.J. put on the fedora. It was a little tight but he jammed it down onto his head anyway. Let the pinhead son-of-a-bitch get it tightened again later.

The door was locked, so R.J. wrapped his fist in the hem of the raincoat and punched through the window set in the trailer's small door. He reached through, unlocked the door, and stepped up into the trailer, snapping up the collar of the raincoat.

"Jesus Christ," said a pained, delicate voice, "you can't come in here."

R.J. turned and saw Harris lounging on the king-size bed. R.J. tugged on the brim of the fedora. "Is this the trailer reserved for the male lead?" he asked, and he heard the star gasp.

"Oh, my God," Harris panted. "What are you doing here?"

"The question is," R.J. said, "what are *you* doing here? In the star's trailer?"

"Jesus, you look just like him!"

R.J. grinned at the stricken lifeguard. "I guess that's why they called me. They were having some problems with that other guy." R.J. sat in the big easy chair and put his feet up on the coffee table. "Who are you, pal?"

Harris was standing now, visibly trembling. "You even *sound* like him!" he moaned.

"I had a lot of practice. Say, I need some privacy before we start shooting." He nodded at the door. "Would you mind?"

Harris stumbled for the door, muttering to himself. "They can't *do* this. My agent said they wouldn't *dare*," he whimpered.

"Your agent steered you wrong," R.J. told him. "Maybe if you talked to the director—"

Harris snapped his fingers. "That's it! That's right, Trevor's got too much in the can already, he'll fight for me!" And he fell out the door and hurried away toward the set.

R.J. stood up and watched him go, grinning. "I'm a ba-a-a-a-ad boy," he said to himself.

R.J. gave it five minutes, just to be sure. Then he dropped the hat and coat on the bed and strolled back onto the set.

Alec Harris was already back in place, stretched out in fake passion with a still-bored Maggie DeSoto. She was looking across the set to the cop with Portillo and absentmindedly stroking Harris's butt as a gang of technicians bustled around them.

R.J. grinned. All was right with the world.

Casey was standing behind the camera. R.J. came up behind her and put a hand on her shoulder. "Casey," he said softly. "*Now* how about some lunch?"

CHAPTER 20

Casey took him to a swanky little place over in Studio City. It had a valet parking attendant who didn't speak English, a headwaiter with a bad accent, a wine list eight pages long, and an orchid in the center of each table.

A bodybuilder and a bimbo sat at the next table. The guy was wearing a sleeveless shirt and bulging out of it in all directions. The bimbo was doing some pretty nice bulging-out of her own. She was packed into a red sheath that hung off her like a coat of paint. The guy sneered at R.J. and turned away as the waiter handed Casey the menus.

R.J. didn't recognize anything on the menu except the Caesar Salad, and when that came he didn't recognize that, either. It was loaded with strange vegetables and what looked like sun-dried minnows. Julia Child would have fainted. But R.J. poked at it with an herbal breadstick and managed to get some of it down.

That was easier than getting through to Casey. She got up every two minutes when the pager in her purse went off. She apologized the first couple of times, but gave up after that and just made her phone calls. She tried to fill R.J. in about the complex negotiations she was neck-deep in as a way of explaining why she had to keep jumping up, but he lost her about the third time she mentioned gross points.

Finally the herbal breadstick snapped and so did R.J.'s patience.

"Casey," he said. She looked over the orchid at him. He met her look and held it for a minute. Jesus Christ, he thought, Who the hell is this? How can I feel this way about somebody playing that tired old Hollywood power game? But he did feel that way, and some of the irritation dropped away.

"Casey," he said again. "I have to go back to New York."

She nodded. "It's just as well. I'm really sorry, but I don't have time for anything but the job right now."

"I'll be back in a few days, a week, I don't know."

She frowned. "It's not going to be any better for me then." She shrugged. "I'm sorry, R.J. I don't mean to sound like this, but that's the way it is. You caught me offguard, showing up like this. I mean, I'd love to spend some time with you, but this job is important to me."

R.J. could feel himself getting cranky again. "More important than staying alive?"

Her lush lips grew thin and anger glittered in her eyes. "Aren't you being just a little melodramatic, R.J.?"

"No. There's a guy out there who has killed twice, and he's going to kill again."

"You don't know that."

"Yes, I do. I know it. Damn it, Casey, you talk about your job, but *this* is *my* job. I'm good at what I do, too."

"All right, R.J.," she said, a little softer. "But I still think you're overreacting. The police—"

"The police are half-wits. They think I did it. Jesus Christ, Casey, what do I have to say to get through to you? There's a homicidal maniac on your ass. For Christ's sake, just be careful. That's all I'm asking." She looked at him and gave a little nod.

R.J. took a deep breath and went on, not sure why this was so hard. "Uncle Hank is going to assign a couple of guys to keep an eye on you. Just cooperate with them until I get back, all right?"

"What does that mean, 'cooperate'?" she asked him. "Am I going to have a patrol car in the shower with me?"

"Christ, I hope not," R.J. said. "It's not going to be any big deal, Casey. Just a couple of guys watching out for you."

She gave him another of those looks. "What if I don't want anybody watching out for me?" she said.

R.J. blinked hard. "Excuse me?"

"You just assumed I would want protection. What if I don't?"

"Then you're nuts."

"That's very helpful, R.J. Very constructive."

R.J. shook his head. "I'm sorry. When did we slip into being constructive? What the hell, Casey, I'm trying to save your life. Not start a meaningful dialogue."

She nodded her head. Not like he was right, but like he had just said something that proved he was nuts. "That's good," she said. "Not much I can say to that, is there. Which is pretty much what you want, isn't it?"

"What I— Casey, what I want is to keep you from getting chopped into small pieces by a maniac."

"Why?"

He blinked. "Excuse me?"

She pursed her lips. "I guess I've been thinking, R.J. And I just wonder where we're going."

"We're not going anywhere if you're dead, Casey."

She brushed that away with the back of her hand. "We have two separate careers, and right now they're on opposite coasts. So I think it's a valid question, R.J. What am I to you?"

He felt his mouth open but nothing came out. Casey's

beeper went off again and she got up quickly, leaving R.J. with a bad case of dangling jaw.

She was gone for five minutes and R.J. used the time to re-group. A lot of slow, calm breaths, so he could get rid of the idea that he needed to smash some plates, break a little furniture, yell something that would wilt the orchid in the middle of the table. Because that wouldn't help this make sense, but it probably would close the door on Casey for good, the way she was talking now.

When Casey came back and sat down again, R.J. had managed to make himself look calm. "Why do you think you might not want protection, Casey?" he said.

She looked down at the table. She took a bite of her salad, maybe the third bite she'd taken. "I guess I'm at some kind of a crossroads, R.J. What they call a cusp out here."

"Christ, you're picking that crap up fast." It just slipped out, but lucky for him, she let it go.

"The last six months in New York, I felt like everything was closing in on me. The job was going nowhere, and my life in general—" She shrugged. "So when this chance came up, it felt like something I really needed to do."

"I'm not fighting that one, Casey," R.J. said wearily. "Do the damn job. Just give me a shot at keeping you alive while you do it, all right?"

"R.J., damn it, you're smothering me. I need a chance on my own. I can't just go back to being your girlfriend and grinding out TV, I *need* this. Don't you understand? I have to do this—on my own—or I'm not worth a damn. I have to do it without you here to fight all the hard battles for me. It makes me feel so little girly. Which I don't like. Why can't you fight your own battles for a change? Instead of mine. Because I have to make it here without you taking over when it gets a little tough."

"Murder is more than a little tough, Casey."

"It happens. I can deal with it. I'm asking you to understand."

"I don't understand, goddammit. All I want is to save your life and you're acting like that makes me Saddam Hussein."

The bodybuilder leaned over. "Can you folks keep it down?" he said, glaring at R.J. "We're trying to eat here."

"Keep trying, pal, I know you'll figure it out."

"Is that supposed to be funny?" he snarled. He put his hand over into Casey's plate and tipped it over, resting his knuckle on the table and looking at R.J. with a come-get-me sneer.

R.J. jammed his fork into the back of the bodybuilder's hand. "Yeah," he said. "It's hilarious. I'll explain it to you when you evolve out of the Stone Age." The bodybuilder stared at the fork sticking out of his hand and opened his mouth to scream, but only a whimper came out. He yanked back his hand and the bimbo pulled out the fork and wrapped a napkin around the wound.

R.J. turned back to Casey. She was standing up. "Casey—"

"That's exactly what I mean," she said. "You fight everybody's battles but your own."

And before he could figure that one out, she was gone.

R.J. shoveled some money onto the table without counting it and hurried out after her. He got out the door just in time to see the valet parking attendant close Casey's car door.

"Casey!" he yelled.

She put her car in gear and drove away.

R.J. stood and swore for a minute but it didn't bring her back. He decided he might as well go back in and call Uncle Hank for a lift. But as he turned around he ran right into a wall.

A wall of muscle.

"Say your prayers, asshole," the bodybuilder said, lifting a fist the size of a Thanksgiving turkey.

"Sure thing," R.J. said. He brought his hands together in front of his face and clasped them like he was about to pray. The bodybuilder hesitated for a second, trying to figure that one out.

The second was all R.J. needed. He jammed both hands

under the bodybuilder's chin. It took him right in the Adam's apple. While the guy was still making gagging noises, R.J. jammed his hands in again, right into the solar plexus.

The big guy had had enough. He bent double and fell to one knee. R.J. pulled back his foot, thinking about one last kick, but he was interrupted by a screeching noise as the bimbo raced over to protect her boy.

"Not his face! For God's sake, leave his face alone, you asshole, he has an audition this afternoon!" She crouched in front of him with her long red nails cocked, and R.J. stepped back. He wanted to laugh at the sight of the hulk with all the perfect-looking muscles, gasping in the arms of the fierce pin-up. But all the laughter he had was driving away down Ventura Boulevard in a rented convertible.

R.J. felt tired and sour and old. He turned away, went back inside, and called Henry Portillo for a ride.

While he was waiting he made another call. It rang until he was about to hang up. Then he heard the click on the far end and Mary Kelley picked it up.

"Hello?"

"Mary, it's me, R.J."

A pause. "Where are you?"

"Los Angeles."

Another pause. He heard her breathing. "R.J., they found Daddy. He's—dead."

"I know it, doll. I just heard."

"I—the funeral is tomorrow and it's— I don't know what . . ."

She broke off and took a few more breaths. R.J. could almost feel her fighting the tears. "I'm on my way, Mary. I'll be there tonight."

"I'm not coming home," she said.

"All right."

"No matter what Mother says." She put a bitter emphasis on the word *mother*. "So don't try to talk me into it."

"I wasn't going to," R.J. protested. "But why not? It'd be a lot easier on you for a while."

"Because *she* did this, I know she did."

"Did what, Mary?"

"She had him killed, R.J." And now the tears came. "I know she did, she had him killed, just when I was about to find him again."

R.J. let her cry for a minute while he thought about that. Janine Wright could get rid of an embarrassing past and a threatening future all at the same time. R.J. knew she wouldn't have any moral hesitation about knocking off anybody.

It was a good solution for Wright, and if it was true and he could prove it, it would solve a lot of R.J.'s problems, too. If Janine was in jail there would be no sequel.

The crying was getting worse. "Take it easy now, kid," he finally said.

"I know I'm right," Mary sobbed. "I know she did it."

"I'm not saying you're wrong," R.J. told her, and she got quiet for a minute, "but we'll never prove it if she finds out we think so."

"You . . . think we can prove it?"

"If she did it, I can prove it." He sounded too cocky, even to himself, but Mary didn't seem to mind. "We'll find something and we'll pin it on her, Mary. If that's what you want."

"I think— That's what I want," she sniffled. "I can pay you. Just— It will be with her money."

R.J. felt his face tighten into a grin. "That's the beauty part," he said.

CHAPTER 21

The flight back to New York was a lot worse than the one the way out had been. R.J. had too much to think about and nothing to do to keep him from thinking about it. And this time he didn't sleep. He just stared out the window while all the ugly suspicions churned around in his brain.

R.J. knew he should have been concentrating on a plan to corner Janine Wright. He should have been making lists of things to do, ways to connect her to her ex-husband's death, tricks to get to phone company records. Instead, he just sat and played over in his head that last scene with Casey.

He kept remembering what she had said, "What am I to you?" and trying to figure out what that meant. For Christ's sake, it should have been clear to her, should have been clear to anybody. He had been seeing her for over six months, hadn't even *looked* at anybody else in all that time. She knew that. Didn't that tell her something? Anything? What was he supposed to do, draw up a position paper and submit it to the head of her delegation?

What in the hell does she want from me?

And then he had another thought, even worse: What if she doesn't want anything from me?

He didn't even know for sure which end was up anymore.

He had thought all along that she wasn't going to hold him up for a ring. She was different. She was a strong, stubborn, independent woman and he was sure she didn't need that kind of talk, didn't *want* to hear it. Maybe he had been wrong. Maybe she wanted to talk about commitment. He had always thought it was a load of crap, and he had thought she felt the same way. They were together, there was nobody else, that was that.

Now he wasn't so sure. Maybe she thought they had gone past that and she needed to hear it from him. And maybe hearing it would be the last straw for her, make her think R.J. was trying to hold her down, trap her into something she couldn't walk away from. Goddammit, there had to be something else, something in between loneliness and uncertainty on the one hand and total commitment on the other.

But he landed in New York with no answers. Feeling sour and impatient, R.J. took a cab instead of the train. The driver took him for a tourist and tried to head for Long Beach. R.J. snarled at him to turn around, for Christ's sake, and the driver headed up toward the Triboro Bridge.

"What the hell are you doing?" R.J. asked.

"Very fast. Very scenery," the driver said in broken English. "Very nice."

"Very no," said R.J. "Midtown Tunnel."

The driver sulked the rest of the way into the city and up to the street in front of R.J.'s office, but he drove fast, so R.J. tipped him anyway. The driver took the tip, and then yelled a curse at him in Farsi as he drove away.

Stepping onto the sidewalk in front of his office, R.J. got thumped from behind by a large maniac pushing a rack of clothing. The guy glared at him and kept going. His back throbbed, but R.J. had to grin.

He was home.

Back in Manhattan, where he belonged.

No more palm trees, or low IQ sex kittens of either gender, no high-powered baby Hitlers in spike heels. Just plain, honest, hostile aggression.

The grin lasted all the way upstairs to his office. As he hit the door, Wanda started on him.

"Boss," she said, rising from her desk with a stack of papers. "Lieutenant Kates wants you in his office the moment you land."

"He blew it. I've been down over an hour now."

She ignored him. "A Captain Davis in L.A. says you'd better call him pronto, or else. I've got a slew of calls from reporters, and that poor Mary Kelley is practically going crazy from it all."

"Where's Mary Kelley staying?"

She held up an address on a slip of paper. "A friend's apartment on East Seventy-second."

R.J. grabbed the address and walked his garment bag into his office.

"R.J.," Wanda went on. "This is serious stuff, boss."

He unzipped the bag and took out his dark suit. "Sure it is. It's always serious. Otherwise I'd have to do something else."

He shook the suit out. It looked all right. He hadn't worn it since that last New York date with Casey. It would do.

He hung the suit on the coat rack behind the door and stepped over to his desk, grabbing the telephone and dialing as he sat.

Hookshot answered on the third ring. The only word R.J. could make out was "news."

"It's R.J.," he said.

"You owe me big-time, man," Hookshot said mournfully.

"For what?"

"Waste my time, chasing some dead guy's ass."

"I didn't know he was dead, Hookshot," R.J. said.

"Well, he is. They got him at some farm town over there. Torrington. Horses in the street and shit."

"Sure, I know," R.J. said. "They don't even take money. You probably had to pay for everything in corn."

"Cost me five bushels for lunch," Hookshot said, cackling.

"Sounds like a nice lunch," R.J. said. "Anyway, I guess that's all over, so thanks."

"Thanks don't cut it, man," Hookshot said.

"It never does," R.J. said. "I'll stop by and settle up when I have the time."

"What happened in L.A., R.J.?"

"It's not over. I have to go back. But first I got a funeral." He looked at his watch. "And I'm running out of time to make it."

"He'll wait, bubbe, believe me. That's 'bout all he's good at now."

"I gotta go, Hookshot."

"You look after that Casey, hear me?"

"Easier said than done," R.J. said as he hung up.

He changed quickly, listening to Wanda grumbling in the next room about being too old to look for a new job if her damn boss couldn't keep himself out of jail.

He straightened the tie—it was still a little frayed from when Casey had torn it off so fast—and stepped into the outer office again.

"Hold the fort, doll. I'll be with my client."

He headed back out the door again, leaving Wanda fluttering the stack of message forms and muttering, "But boss . . ."

Mary Kelley's friend had a place in one of those East Seventies brick high-rise buildings that had been chic in the sixties. The building had gone co-op maybe ten years ago. It wasn't chic anymore, but it was a lot easier to get a seat on the Supreme Court than it was to find a vacant apartment in the building.

R.J. managed to get past the front door without being arrested, and was soon knocking on a door on the twenty-sixth floor. The door opened a crack, chain visible across the gap, and a mean voice snarled at him. "Yes?"

"R.J. Brooks," he said as meekly as he knew how. "To see Ms. Kelley."

The door slammed shut. There was a long pause. R.J. had just about decided to knock again when the door opened again and Mary Kelley stood there looking like Barbie on a real bad day.

She looked frazzled. Her hair was dull and stringy, her makeup was smeared and blotched all over her puffy, pasty face, and she looked like she had lost ten pounds she couldn't afford to lose.

"R.J.?" she said in a voice worn down by crying.

"Yeah, it's me."

She looked at him. Her chin quivered, she sniffed, and then she was suddenly leaning against him, bawling uncontrollably. R.J. put an arm around her and just held on for a minute. Then he gently pulled away and led her inside.

Through it all Mary's friend stood watching without approval, her thick arms folded across an impressive chest. She had a pale face, pale close-set eyes, and her head was too small for her hairdo. As R.J. got Mary onto a bright yellow sofa and sat next to her, the friend made a loud *tsk*-ing sound and vanished down the hallway.

Mary lunged for a box of tissues. "Don't mind Roberta," she sniffled, "she's just being very protective."

"I don't mind," R.J. said. "How are you holding up, kid?"

"Oh, R.J." she said, and for a moment he thought she was going to do the fountain act again. But she recovered nicely and settled for a long, hard honk into a couple more tissues. "It just doesn't seem fair," she said after a while.

"It never is, Mary."

She shook her head. "But this is—I mean, I never actually had a mother, except in the biological sense. She just kept me around for a tax deduction. The only real *parent* I ever had was William—Dad. And I never really knew him. And now . . .

Now I never will," she said, and she was off into tears again, leaning against R.J. and shaking with grief.

R.J. let her go, patting her back, then stroking it, then finally just letting his hand rest on the small of her back, until she wound down.

When she did, he handed her the box of tissues again.

"I'm sorry," she said. "It's just—"

"I know it is," R.J. said. "Go ahead and cry."

But she sat up, holding a handful of soggy tissue. "No. I'm all right now." She gave her face a wipe and looked at the black streaks of mascara on the tissue. "I must look awful," she said.

"You look fine," R.J. lied. "Mary, if you're sure you're okay now, I need to know about the arrangements."

She blinked, but she held up. "I don't— I'm not sure. Roberta wrote everything down."

"Roberta?"

She nodded toward the hallway. "My friend."

R.J. stood up. "I'll talk to her."

He went down the short hallway. There were two doors along the hall. One stood open, showing a small room with a desk and a bed. A suitcase stood beside the bed. Guest room, occupied by Mary Kelley.

At the end of the hall, next to the bathroom, the second door was closed. R.J. knocked.

A moment later he got a repeat of the performance at the front door. The door opened a crack and Roberta stuck her face into the gap. "Yes?"

"Sorry to bother you. I need to know about the funeral arrangements."

She glared at him for a moment, then closed the door. Thirty seconds later she reopened it and shoved a piece of paper at him. "Here," she said. "You keep your goddamned paws *off* her." And she slammed the door.

R.J. was too stunned to do anything but stare at the door for two long minutes. Then he shook his head. He was too tired to laugh, but he sure felt like it. But instead, he just took the paper and headed back down the hall.

The funeral home was a place called Cooper & Schmidt's in Torrington. R.J. called them, found out they didn't have a limo. So he called around Manhattan and found a place that just happened to have one on short notice that, for a consideration, the guy was willing to drive over to the wilds of Connecticut.

He hung up the phone and looked over at Mary. She was still kind of huddled on the couch, but she looked like she might pull through after all. "If it's all right with Bob," he told her, "you might get yourself ready. The limo will be here in forty minutes."

"Limo?" she looked up. "Oh. I didn't— Are we really going to need a limo?"

He nodded. "I'm afraid it's de rigueur. You can't take a bus to a funeral, kid." He nodded down the hall. "Go put your face on."

She stood, a little unsteadily, and took a deep breath. He went over to her and held her shoulders. "It gets hard for a while, Mary," he told her. "But you can do it."

She sagged against him for a moment, took a ragged breath, then straightened. "Yes," she said. "I think I'll be all right." And with a real good try at a smile she turned and went down the hall.

CHAPTER 22

The ride to Torrington was a long one. Maybe it just seemed longer to R.J. It wasn't a lot of laughs being cooped up with a kid who couldn't stop crying longer than five minutes and a hostile woman who wouldn't talk to him.

At least they got there in time for the service. Without them it wouldn't have been much of a show. When they walked into the battered old funeral parlor, R.J. counted five people. One of them was the minister.

It was a closed coffin funeral. The pale oily guy from the funeral home who appeared at their elbow as they stepped in had explained that it was best that way. There was "significant burn damage" over most of the body. The face, he whispered to R.J., was not recognizable.

R.J. hated funerals. Even so, it seemed like he ended up going to an awful lot of them. Most of all he hated closed coffin funerals. He just didn't see the point. The way he saw it, the whole idea of a funeral was to let everybody figure out that somebody really was dead. Let it sink in that the guy wasn't going to show up for dinner anymore.

With the lid down, that didn't happen. People stood around and sniveled over the lid of a cheap pine box and for all anybody knew Salmon Rushdie could be hiding out inside, playing gin rummy with Elvis.

But if the undertaker thought the burns were that bad, there was no point in an open lid. It was supposed to be a way to say good-bye, not a horror show.

So he sat through the short, generic service. It was clear that the minister had no clue who or what was in the box. He rambled on for a while and then stopped without really coming to an ending. Then the handful of people sitting in the cheap folding chairs stood up and gawked at one another.

A white-haired couple oozed over to Mary and stood talking. R.J. gathered that they had known the Kelleys in some happier time long ago. He caught a couple of stock words of condolence and a phrase or two like, "Never believed he did it," and "He always said so, and we believed him."

The woman patted Mary's hand. "He was so big and strong, and yet so gentle. Such a sweet man."

The man chimed in with, "Of course you never really knew him, did you, dear?"

R.J. was about to step over and get rid of the oldsters before Mary decked them when Roberta steered the kid safely away. So R.J. turned away, trying not to listen to the sympathetic babble in the room.

Just when R.J. was tuning it out and thinking about stepping outside, he felt a sharp tug on his elbow.

He turned around to stare at a stick figure of a guy with a ferret's face and a permanent stoop, the kind old secretaries get from leaning over the desk for fifty years.

This guy was only around fifty himself, but he had a paleness to him that said he had never been outside during the daytime. He was so pale he almost glowed.

"You're that private investigator," he said in a voice that was part wheeze and part whisper.

R.J. shook his elbow free. "That's right," he said.

The ferret nodded. "I thought that was you." And he just nodded, looking at R.J. through thick glasses.

"Yeah," R.J. finally said. "It was me. Is that all right?"

"Tryin' ta figger, is all," the guy rasped.

"Great. Good luck to you, sport," R.J. said, tired of whatever game the guy thought they were playing. He turned away.

A surprisingly strong grip on his arm stopped him and he turned back around again.

"Don't get steamed," the ferret said. "Just gimme a sec, is all."

"For what?"

Ferret nodded. "No choice. Gotta be you. Well—" He shrugged, nodded, shrugged. "All right. Okay. Pauly Aponti," he said, sticking out a pale, damp hand. R.J. could see strong tendons in it, but the grip was slack. "Well, okay, so what's this about, right?"

"Is this *about* something, Mr. Aponti?"

Aponti blinked. "Call me Pauly. Mister, that's my old man or something." He gasped quickly. R.J. realized it was supposed to be a laugh.

"Okay, Pauly. So?"

Pauly's eyes got even vaguer and shifted around the room. His voice lowered and his lips didn't move when he spoke. R.J. realized suddenly the man was an ex-con; the paleness, the trick of lowering the voice and not seeming to speak. These were all old jailbird tricks.

"What were you in for, Pauly?" R.J. said, riding his hunch.

The eyes clicked back to his, looking huge behind the thick lenses. "Forgery," he said softly. "Bearer bonds."

"And you knew Kelley?"

Pauly nodded carefully, as if he didn't want anyone to know he could move. "I knew Kelley pretty good," he whispered.

"Yeah, pretty good. I was in Somers with him. My cell mate."

The man broke off and carefully looked over the whole room before speaking again. "The thing is, he gave me something."

It was eery watching the guy speak without seeming to, and it was getting on R.J.'s nerves. "I'm glad to hear it," R.J. said through gritted teeth.

Now the ferret eyes caught R.J.'s. "Thing is, I should prolly give it to you."

R.J. looked across the room at Mary. Roberta was trying to soothe her after what the white-haired couple had said, but she wasn't having any luck. He was stuck in a tacky funeral parlor, at the funeral of someone he had never even met, and a weird ex-con was chewing off his damned ear.

"Or maybe I shouldn't," Pauly said. "I don't know."

"Listen," R.J. finally snarled. "I don't care if you give it to Dolly Parton. Just get it over with and get out of my face."

Pauly nodded like that made sense. "Thing is, Kelley said if anything should happen to him. Looks like something did. You get the picture."

Suddenly R.J. did. He got the picture loud and clear. Kelley must have suspected that Janine would try to get him. He'd left something behind with Pauly in case she succeeded.

"Give it here," R.J. said.

"Can't," Pauly told him softly. R.J. wanted to smack him. "Why not?"

"Gotta have your promise first. Cops don't get this, and it won't come back on me."

"Deal. Gimme."

"Here," Pauly said suddenly, thrusting an envelope at R.J. "No cops," he rasped, and then slid quietly away.

It was a cheap envelope with nothing on the front. No writing, no smudges, nothing. Just a plain, white envelope. It wasn't even sealed. Just had the flap tucked in.

R.J. shook his head and looked around him. Mary was okay. She was standing beside the coffin, looking down, saying good-bye, with Roberta running interference for her.

He turned back to the envelope in his hand and opened the flap. There were five or six pages folded together. He unfolded them and looked at the top.

To whom it may concern,
If you are reading this I am probably dead.
I know that sounds corny, but I've always wanted to say it.

R.J. laughed. He was standing at a funeral in a cheesy funeral parlor, reading a message from the stiff, but he laughed. This guy had a quirky sense of humor. R.J. was sorry he'd never met William Kelley.

I have some very good reasons to think my ex-wife, Janine Wright, is trying to kill me. What you're holding in your hands is proof that she succeeded.

No, I can't prove—yet—that she is behind these attempts on my life. But I can finally prove that she framed me those many years ago. She sent me to prison for her crimes. She stole my life away from me, kept me from the love of my daughter, and if there is a Hell there is a special place in it made just for her.

I thought I had married a strong, ambitious woman. I found out too late what she really was. Ambitious, yes—to the point where I now know there is nothing she would not do to get what she wants. She has dealt in drugs and framed me for her crimes, taking away my life when it became inconvenient for her to have me around. God knows she has used her body when it would help. And now she has had me killed, literally this time, to keep all this from coming out.

Here are the few pieces of evidence I have managed to collect. A trained investigator should be able to make something out of this. I was never a drug dealer—God damn her twice, for saying I was, and for dealing in the filthy stuff herself to finance her brainless movies.

May God bless my daughter Mary.

And may He rot the black empty heart of Janine Wright,
the soulless monster who has now killed me twice.

There was a scrawl across the bottom of the page that probably said William Kelley.

R.J. looked at the other papers. They were photocopies of pages from a ledger. Any investigator nowadays had to be able to read financial records. It took R.J. only a few minutes to unravel what he was holding.

He gave a low whistle, then looked up, embarrassed. But no one appeared to have noticed. He looked down, flipped through the papers again.

What he had were pages from Janine's books, the financial records of her first movie, the one she had made after she sent her husband to prison. There was also a page of clippings from the local paper about Kelley's trial.

What the pages showed was that only a few weeks after his trial she had somehow gotten the large chunk of anonymous cash that let her begin shooting. Circled in red on one of the clippings was the date, and the sentence, "Police have never found any of the money Kelley is alleged to have made from the sale of the drugs," then an arrow drawn to the page of the ledger that showed the chunk of anonymous cash.

It was a pretty clear picture. She had sent him over, taken the money when the stink died down a little, and made herself a movie. The timing said it had to be deliberate. She didn't have enough time to get the movie ready between the trial's end and the movie's beginning.

Not unless she was already set to go. Not unless she had planned it, had deliberately framed Kelley in order to take the heat off her and make some money.

This wouldn't put her in jail, but Kelley was right. Any trained investigator could follow this trail, follow it all the way from the crummy funeral home in Torrington to a cozy cell at one of those country clubs the Feds set aside for executive tax frauds. Maybe she'd never do hard time for murder like she should, but she'd do time.

R.J. could put Janine Wright in prison.

He almost said *yahoo* out loud. At the last minute he remembered where he was and bit down on his lip. He looked around. Roberta was glaring at him from near the door, clearly ready to hustle Mary out and away.

R.J. shoved the papers into his inside pocket, dropped the ratty envelope into an ashtray, and buttoned his coat as he headed out the door.

CHAPTER 23

It was a long ride back, too. Roberta had taken over the whole business of comforting Mary. That was okay with R.J. He had some heavy thinking to do. It would have been easier without the sniffling and the sharp glares from Roberta. She had apparently decided that the whole thing was R.J.'s fault and didn't want him to forget it even for a second.

Still, R.J. managed to think. He had to get out from under a couple of murder charges, and that meant getting back to California. But he couldn't chase down Janine Wright's tax records from there, and he had to do that, too. He had said he would, and anyway he wanted to see her in the slammer.

Rooting for records was something Wanda could do. Probably do it better than he could, in fact. She was amazing with bureaucrats. Where R.J. would lose his temper and start yelling, she could drip honey or acid, whichever would work, and she got results he could only dream about.

Sure, Wanda was the answer for that. Give him a chance

to wrap up the other thing, find the killer. And just incidentally, while he was at it, keep Casey safe.

Casey. Jesus Christ. R.J. sighed.

In spite of everything else that was happening, R.J. couldn't keep his mind off Casey. She had always run hot and cold, driving him crazy. But now he didn't even know where to start, which end to pick up and look at. He only knew everything else was going to be a lot harder to do until he had figured out what Casey wanted. And whatever it was, he would find a way to want it, too.

But hell, first he had to keep her alive.

For the rest of the trip back to the city he tried to keep his thoughts on the killer. It worked for the most part. Mary would sob every now and then, and Roberta would murmur to her. Casey shoved her way into his thoughts every five or ten minutes, but he kept at it, adding up what he knew about the two murders.

Two killings, in two cities, with two very different MOs. The lawyer poisoned in Manhattan. The writer with his head hacked off in L.A. All they had in common was the sequel. Could it be two killers? It was almost fun to think about a secret organization dedicated to stopping the sequel. Guys in black hoods taking secret oaths in the basement, pricking their fingers and swearing on an upside-down Bible.

Sure, a secret society. And R.J. was really Doc Savage, cutting through the underworld like a bronze blade.

It had to be one killer. One guy, and R.J. tallied up what he knew about him.

He was smart—he'd figured the way into the Hotel Pierre, which was not easy. He was strong enough to climb up the outside of Levy's house, strong enough to overcome the writer and cut his head off with a pair of scissors. And he thought he was funny, with the cute rhymes in the letters he sent. The lettering said he was probably a show-biz insider.

It really wasn't much to go on. It's simple, R.J. thought.

Strong, funny, show-biz insider. . . . The killer is Joe Piscopo.

He needed something more, some angle that would give him a starting point. Otherwise . . . R.J. hated the thought, but he was getting the idea that the killer would do it again long before R.J. managed to figure out who he was. And he could kill everybody on both coasts, one at a time, before those goddamned paper-shuffling cops figured it out.

It was dark by the time they got back to the city. R.J. rode the limo to the door of Roberta's building and climbed out onto the sidewalk, holding the door for Mary. She was still crying, and Roberta still had an arm around her.

R.J. paid off the driver and walked Mary to the elevator, in spite of Roberta's glare.

"Listen, Mary," he told her. "I've got to get back to the coast."

She looked up at him with red eyes. "That's— You're not giving up?"

"No," he said. "I'm not giving up. I'll call you in a couple of days."

The bell clunked and the elevator arrived. R.J. patted the kid's arm. "You just take your time, and don't worry," he told her.

"All right," Mary sniffled. "But R.J.? You're going to get her, aren't you? You'll find something about Mother?"

"I just might," R.J. said. "Take care of yourself, kid."

R.J. left her there with Roberta. He was already on the sidewalk by the time the elevator doors slid shut.

He walked across town, taking the time to think. R.J. always thought better with New York in the background. But by the time he got to his apartment he hadn't come up with much new. What there was, Ilsa drove out of his head right away.

R.J. had a neighbor who fed the cat while he was away. He fed her again anyway, but Ilsa still went into a two-hour gymnastic routine, complaining that she was hungry, lonely, and bored, and where the hell had he been, anyway?

By the time he made himself a small steak and some broccoli from the freezer, the cat had calmed down. She went back to ignoring him, but from closer than usual.

After dinner, R.J. realized he was beat. Whether it was jet lag, or the funeral, or the combined weight of the last few days, he could barely keep his eyes open. So he didn't even try. He washed up the dishes and went to bed.

In the morning he barely dragged himself out of bed. A long hot shower, three cups of coffee and R.J. still didn't feel at the top of his form, but he thought he might manage to make it through the day. He threw on some clothes, buttoned his coat, and staggered off to his office. He needed to catch up on a little paperwork, and there was a direct flight back to L.A. in the afternoon.

"Boss!" Wanda yelled at him as he walked in.

"That's me," he admitted.

"The lieutenant has called four times this morning! You're to call him the second you're in!"

The lieutenant was Henry Portillo. Wanda had almost no respect for policemen. Lieutenant Kates was just Kates to her; Detective Boggs was Boggs or That Dumb Gorilla. But Uncle Hank she approved of, and as a mark of her approval, she called him by his rank.

R.J. grunted. If Uncle Hank had called four times, he wasn't just checking up. Something had happened. Maybe there's been a break in the case. Maybe they'd gotten lucky with the glasses they'd found at Levy's house.

"I'll call him in a minute. Let me go over this with you first."

"Boss, it's important enough to keep the lieutenant waiting?"

"If you'll pay attention, he won't have to wait long."

She stuck out her tongue, and R.J. pulled the papers Pauly Aponti had given him from his coat.

Wanda was fast. She caught on to what was there, and what needed to be done a lot quicker than R.J. had.

"No problem, boss," she told him, and R.J. put it out of his mind. Wanda would take care of it.

He turned back to the other thing, the reason Portillo had called. He hoped it was a break in the case, but it occurred to him as he sat in his chair and dialed Portillo's number that he had only been thinking about the situation from one side, the cop's side, where he usually worked. He was a suspect now, maybe *the* suspect, and a break in the case could just as easily mean he was headed for the slammer.

It was a good thought. It was right, too.

"R.J.," Portillo said when he picked up the phone, and R.J. knew from his tone that it was bad. "We have had another letter."

"Hell, Uncle Hank, I couldn't have done it. I'm in New York."

He could hear Portillo breathing out, attempting control. "Can you tell me *exactly* where you have been, *hijo*?"

"Sure. To my office, to a funeral, back to my office. That's it."

"And where was the funeral?"

"In Connecticut, Uncle Hank. Relax, nobody would ever go up there. A little place called Torrington."

There was a long silence on the line, very long.

"You there, Uncle Hank?"

"You had better come back at once, R.J.," Portillo said, and there was great weariness in his voice.

"I'm on my way," R.J. said. "What's up?"

"The new letter," Portillo said slowly, "was yet another death threat against the movie."

"I figured it would be. So?"

"So, *hijo*, it arrived this morning by Express Mail. And it was postmarked from Torrington, Connecticut."

CHAPTER 24

It felt to R.J. as if jet lag was finally catching up to him. He had kidded himself that he had ducked it by coming back to New York so soon after flying to L.A. But going back again, just like that, was too much for his system. He felt like hell, and he was starting to worry about something new.

Somebody was out to get him.

Oh, sure, he knew he had a cop on each coast who wanted to see him in prison and didn't care how it happened. And he'd made plenty of enemies in his life who would just as soon see him suffer if they could arrange it. This was something else, something more. Something that had trickled into his brain when he hung up the phone on Henry Portillo.

It had sprouted on the way to the airport, and during the long flight back to L.A. it had grown big enough to build a tree house in.

Somebody was out to get him.

Adding up all that had happened, capped with the letter postmarked from Torrington—it was just too much to be coincidence. Every time R.J. was in New York the killer was in New York. When R.J. was in L.A., so was the killer. It was okay to believe that it was all coincidental—up to a point. The last letter, from Torrington, had passed that point.

He didn't have any proof, but he was sure. Somebody was getting ready to kill again, and they wanted R.J. to take the fall for it.

It was almost funny. R.J. could even feel a small, savage laugh growing inside him. Very funny, he thought. I'm the only guy who can catch you, so you're working with the cops to put me away. Killer and cops on the same side. Har-de-har-har.

Sure. A real laugh-riot. Just keep chuckling and watching the bodies pile up. What was it they called it in the movie business? The Body Count. They said to have a big picture you had to have a big body count.

The sequel was shaping up to be a really big picture.

R.J. knew the body count was going to climb. It was going to keep climbing, because this guy was good at what he did. And if he turned out to be just as good at framing R.J., there wasn't going to be anybody around to stop him from killing again and again.

Henry Portillo might have been able to do it, but he was trapped by police politics, like a fly in a honey jar. He could buzz a little and beat his wings, but he wasn't going anywhere they didn't want him to go.

No, it was up to R.J. and he had to act fast. Before the killer got to somebody else—before R.J. ended up sitting on the wrong side of a set of bars.

This time R.J. didn't fall asleep on the plane. He kept working it over in his mind, the one question that could bring it all to an end: *Who? Who had enough stake in the sequel that they'd kill to stop it?* But there was no answer. With Kelley dead, it could be anybody. A stranger, one of Wright's discarded lovers, a film buff—anybody.

R.J. sat and ground his teeth together until he was on the ground in L.A. He got a headache, but no answer.

Henry Portillo was waiting for him. He looked tired, worn down. "I'm sorry, R.J." was his greeting. "You must come to see the captain right away."

"Captain Davis?"

Portillo nodded.

"Well, hell, Uncle Hank," R.J. said. "That makes me sorry, too."

Portillo had nothing to say to that. He just took R.J.'s arm and led him through the terminal. His big blue Chevy was parked at the curb, the red light showing on the dashboard.

"Get in," he said to R.J.

R.J. threw his bag in back and climbed into the front seat. Portillo nosed the car into traffic and headed for the freeway.

Portillo didn't say a word all the way downtown. He wove in and out of traffic at close to 100 miles per hour and they were in Captain Davis's office in half an hour.

Davis was behind his desk. When R.J. walked in, he leaned back and locked his hands behind his head. There was a smug sneer on his face. "Well, well," he said. He didn't offer R.J. a seat, but R.J. took one anyway. Portillo stood stiffly just inside the door. "Glad you could make it, Mr. Brooks."

"Cut the horseshit," R.J. said. "If you got something to say, say it and let me get back to work."

Davis raised an eyebrow. He was enjoying himself. R.J. didn't like that. If Davis was happy, it wasn't going to be good news for him. "Work?" Davis said. "What work is that, Mr. Brooks?"

"I know you have a tough time figuring this stuff out, Captain, but there's a killer out there, and he's going to kill again. And since nobody else seems interested in stopping him, I thought I might give it a try."

Davis nodded. "I see. So this killer is going to kill again. You feel sure of that, do you?"

"I know it. You would, too, if you'd take your head out of the commissioner's ass for five minutes."

Davis ignored that and R.J. knew he was in trouble. The

captain just looked at him with a secret little smile.

"But I do know it, Mr. Brooks. And I am doing something about it. I'm going to put the killer in jail." And he gave R.J. the biggest cat-ate-the-canary smile R.J. had ever seen.

R.J. felt his stomach do a triple gainer, double back-flip into a swan dive. "You know who it is?" he asked.

"Yes I do, Mr. Brooks." Davis was almost laughing now. He unlocked his hands and pointed a lazy finger at R.J. "It's you."

"Cut the crap," R.J. snarled. "You know damned well I didn't do it, and there's nothing to go on but your goddamned wish that I did it so you could look pretty in the papers."

"Is that what you think?" Davis said, still smiling.

"That's what I know," said R.J.

Davis reached into a drawer and pulled out a plastic evidence bag. "Know what this is?" he said softly.

"A bag. It has an envelope inside."

"Wrong, smart ass," Davis said through his teeth. The smile was gone now. "It's a one-way ticket to Folsom. With your name on it."

R.J.'s mind was blank. He had no idea what could be so damning about an envelope. "What the hell are you babbling about?"

"This is the envelope the latest death threat came in, Mr. Brooks."

"So?"

"It's postmarked Torrington, Connecticut. We know you were in Torrington at the time it was mailed."

"So were thirty-two thousand other people," R.J. said.

Davis's smile was the biggest, meanest thing R.J. had ever seen. "That's true," he said. "But none of them have your fingerprints." He dangled the baggy daintily over the desk. "This does."

A thousand things went through R.J.'s mind. The only one that made it out was "What?"

"Your fingerprints, Mr. Brooks," Davis said, as if he were talking to a four-year-old. "You made one small mistake this time. Your fingerprints are on this envelope. What happened? Did you leave your gloves in your other suit?"

R.J. looked at Portillo, who was standing up straight now. Portillo shook his head. "I didn't know, R.J."

"No, he didn't know," Davis said with a smirk. "The lab report just came back, and there's no doubt about it. A thumb print so clear it's like for a textbook or something. Plus an index finger and three partials. The lab says there's not the smallest doubt about it. It's you, Mr. Brooks. Your fingerprints."

He leaned forward and there was no more smiling or smirking. Now there was only mean-faced danger. "I've got you, buddy-boy. I've got you good. And if you think you're going to wiggle out of this one, *you're* the one with his head up his ass. This is just the start. It's enough to arrest you, but it's only the beginning."

R.J. noticed Davis's hand was trembling. He wants me bad, he thought. And he just might have me.

Davis leaned back again, took a deep breath and got control of himself again. "Know what they'll do to a movie star like you up at Folsom?"

"Sure," R.J. said. "Same thing you're doing to me now. But they'll probably be nicer about it."

But Davis just stared at him. "It's funny," he said. "Now that I've got you, your wise-ass attitude doesn't bother me anymore."

"Well, your dumb-ass one bothers the hell out of me. Have I got this right? You're arresting me for these murders?"

"In a few minutes. I'm having too much fun right now."

"I want my lawyer."

"Sure, Mr. Brooks. You'll get your lawyer. Not that it's gonna do you any good."

"We'll see about that. For starters, he can look into just how legal it is for you to interrogate me like this without him being here, and without you reading me my rights. Then we can move on to the good stuff, like whether you get to keep your job when I catch the *real* killer and let the whole damn world know what a brainless asshole you really are, Captain. Do you know what the press is going to do to a dumb, crooked, mean-spirited, butt-head cop like you?"

Davis clenched his jaw so hard R.J. thought he heard one of the caps crack. Then he nodded, just once.

"All right, Brooks," he said. "You have the right to remain silent—"

CHAPTER 25

Jail wasn't so bad. It was a lot nicer than the waiting area on the BMT. Fewer punks, too. Some of the guys were pretty nice, in fact, and R.J. found he had a lot in common with them. They were all innocent, for starters. A lot better company than Captain Davis. And some of them thought just as highly of Patrick Ewing as R.J. did.

Of course there was a couple of sour grapes guys who only wanted to talk about how great the Lakers used to be, but you had to expect that in an L.A. jail.

In fact, R.J. probably wouldn't have minded his stay in jail, not at all, if he hadn't been worried about Casey. Uncle Hank would have a couple of men keeping an eye on her, sure, but it wasn't the same as if he was watching her himself.

At least, he hoped it wasn't. After his last scene with her in the restaurant he wasn't so sure. For all he knew she could be shopping for a new boyfriend right now, and an L.A. cop might fit the bill just right. These guys weren't even real cops. Spent their off-duty time hanging out in juice bars at health clubs. Worrying about how tight their buns were.

Hell, maybe that's what Casey wanted. Maybe she'd gone native. Got to like driving around with the top down. Got used to the feeling of power. Developed a taste for avocados and sprouts in her salad.

R.J. had some time to think about Casey, and he did. Tried to think his way right into her head and figure out what was going on in there. Couldn't.

But he also thought about how his fingerprints got on that damn envelope. Davis wanted R.J. in jail more than he wanted to breathe, and he might bend a few rules to make it happen. But would he manufacture evidence? Coldly frame R.J. by planting his fingerprints on material evidence of first-degree murder?

R.J. didn't think so. For two reasons: First, it was hard to buy that any cop would do that. Maybe if he *knew* a suspect was really guilty and couldn't get him any other way—maybe. But not like this.

The second reason was that Henry Portillo worked with Davis. Portillo didn't like Davis, didn't approve of the way he worked, but he worked with him. He wouldn't if Davis was that dirty. Wouldn't come close to him. Henry was very funny about honor and that sort of stuff, very old-fashioned.

So Davis didn't plant it. It got there by itself. Also assuming the lab didn't screw up, and it really was his fingerprints on the envelope. That left only two answers.

Number one: R.J. was guilty. He was pretty sure he wasn't.

Number two: Somebody *else* was framing him.

That second one was a lot more interesting. It also started a whole string of other questions, like *who* and *why?*

There were no answers, nothing he could prove from inside jail, but after a day and a night in jail R.J. had narrowed it down a little. Because in the last week the only envelopes he had touched were in his office, going through his mail. Maybe somebody had gone through his trash, taken and reused an envelope he had handled?

It didn't seem likely, but there was no other possibility. He hadn't handled any other—

Hold on a second, R.J. thought.

A picture came to him, a memory of William Kelley's funeral. Pauly Aponti had handed him an envelope with evidence against Janine Wright. He had taken the stuff out and—

And what? What had he done with that envelope?

He had tossed it. He was sure. Hadn't even crumpled it. He had just dropped it into a standing ashtray by the door. Could he get the police lab to check it for traces of cigarette ash? Maybe. That kind of evidence would help a little, if he ended up in court.

But more important—who had taken it from the ashtray and used it to mail a death threat? Because envelopes were cheap, and the only reason to reuse that one was to put R.J. in jail. Who wanted that enough to frame him?

The quick answer was Pauly. He was an ex-con, which made him suspect. But why? What ax did Pauly have to grind? He had known Kelley, known him well enough that the dead man had trusted him with his last hope to get back at Janine.

They had been cellmates—had the relationship been even closer than that? Funny things happened in prison. Was Pauly getting a lover's revenge for the death of Kelley? Killing off the people close to Janine, and eventually Janine herself, to get revenge for Kelley's imprisonment and death?

But then why drag in R.J.? Why not just kill her and get it over with? It didn't make sense. Besides, he had seen Pauly, and the man didn't look strong enough to pull on his own jacket, let alone overpower Levy and snip his head off with scissors. And the killer was free to move around the country. Pauly was still on parole.

No. It had to be somebody else. But maybe with Pauly's help . . . ? That was a little easier to swallow. So Pauly, on instructions from someone else, sets him up with the envelope—

No, wait a second. There was no way he could be sure R.J. would toss the envelope. He might have just shoved it into his pocket—almost had, in fact. But when R.J. did toss it, Pauly noticed, decided to take advantage of it, snagged it for his Unknown Associate.

R.J. nodded. He was beginning to see some light at the end of this particular tunnel. Okay; Pauly was somebody's helper.

Whose?

R.J. began to arrange what he knew, and what he could guess, about the Unknown Associate.

Strong, clever, show-biz ties, R.J. already knew. But now he could add, with ties to Pauly. Which probably mean from Somers Penitentiary. Because before that, Pauly had no known ties to Janine Wright, or Hollywood. As far as R.J. knew. He could check that, but for now it was a good bet.

So figure also it was somebody inside Somers with Pauly. Not a guard or a social worker. Cons were funny about that stuff. They would pal around a little with a guard, but they'd never trust him. So it was another inmate. Someone Pauly liked and trusted, who was smart, strong, funny, and had show-biz ties.

William Kelley.

Which was impossible.

The guy was dead.

Wasn't he?

R.J. snorted. Drop it right there, buddy-boy, he told himself. That was a stupid idea. Just because Kelley fit all the clues that wasn't going to bring him back to life. He was as dead as you can get—R.J. had been to his funeral. Seen the casket.

A closed casket.

No way to tell who was inside.

No; this was just plain nuts. He'd been in jail just over twenty-four hours and he was already going stir-crazy. The cops had found and identified the body. They were satisfied it was Kelley's body. They were usually pretty good at that kind of thing, because they hated like hell to be wrong and look stupid.

So drop this dumbbell idea and bend the gray cells back into line, R.J. William Kelley was dead. So the killer was—

Hell, I don't know. Somebody else. Somebody who's as much like William Kelley as he can be without being William Kelley.

And there was an idea: If he had been really close to a brother, it might make sense for the brother to flip out over William's death and want revenge.

Except why hadn't this hypothetical ultra-close brother been at the funeral? Wouldn't it be natural for him to show up? And anyway no, damn it, that made no sense. Because the lawyer had been killed *before* Kelley's death.

When his own lawyer finally came to get him out, R.J. had ground the top layer of enamel off his teeth trying to think his way out of this mess, and he had gotten nowhere.

R.J.'s lawyer was a tall, silver-haired guy in a gray suit so soft you wanted to take a nap on it. "Mr. Brooks?" he said in a deep, smooth tone of voice.

"That's me," R.J. admitted.

He held out a hand. "The Flesh Man sent me. I'm Feldman. From Weiner, Belton, Nye and Feldman." He grinned at R.J. "You're sprung, gumshoe."

He must have seen R.J.'s look, because he immediately dropped the grin. "Sorry it took so long, Mr. Brooks," he said. "They didn't want to let you go at all, but we hit them with some fancy tap dancing, got the right judge to listen, and that was all she wrote."

"I appreciate it," R.J. said. "What was the gumshoe business?"

Feldman looked embarrassed. "Ah. Well. Um, actually, as you know, our firm represented your mother, and your father." He flashed a small smile. "Before my time, of course."

"Of course."

"Well, anyway, I was always a fan of your father's movies. And, ah—"

"Okay, I get it. It seemed like a natural."

"Yes, that's right. I hope you don't mind."

"Counselor," R.J. said, "get me out of this place, and you can even quote Rod McKuen."

CHAPTER 26

Henry Portillo was waiting outside the jail. He stood beside his big blue car, wearing a face that said nothing, while R.J. wrapped things up with Feldman.

"It is good to see you, R.J.," he said when R.J. finally walked over to him. But he said it so quietly, R.J. barely heard him.

"What's up, Uncle Hank?" R.J. asked him as they lunged into traffic.

Portillo would not meet his eye. "I am sorry, R.J.," he said. "I did what I could, but—" He shrugged. "That turned out to be nothing."

"You mean a couple of days in jail? Forget it. I've done worse time than that."

"I do not mean jail. There is something else."

R.J. looked hard at Portillo. The quietness now seemed to be apology, even shame.

Portillo finally looked over to R.J.—a quick look, since they were in traffic, but he connected.

"What?"

"Captain Davis found out that I had men assigned to watch Casey. He said that since you were guilty we could save the overtime by just watching you."

"He pulled the guys watching her? To save *money?*"

Portillo nodded. "I'm afraid so."

R.J. shivered. Casey was alone, unguarded, and the killer was ready to strike again. "That son-of-a-bitch."

"He was a good cop once," Portillo said, and shrugged. "He got bit by a political bug. Now all he thinks about is making chief."

"If anything happens to Casey—"

"Don't say it, R.J." Portillo said, cutting him off. "Making threats is what got you into this trouble to begin with."

R.J. took a deep breath and shut up. Portillo was right. Besides, the important thing was to find a way to keep Casey safe. It wouldn't be easy, since she was probably still mad at him.

But he had to do it. Somehow, he had to keep her safe.

He thought about throwing himself on her mercy, but he couldn't be sure she had any right now. And he played with the idea, too, that if he just hung around her, and the cops hung around him, she'd be as safe as she could be. But he was pretty sure she wouldn't go for that, either.

Whatever he did, he had to talk to her first. Try to patch things up a little. If he could do that, he could persuade her to be careful, to accept a little protection.

And if he could do *that*—then catching the killer ought to be relatively easy.

Still, he had to try.

"Uncle Hank—" he started.

"No," Portillo said.

R.J. blinked. "No, what?"

"No, we are not going to go to the studio."

"How did you know I was going to ask that?"

Portillo gave him a pitying look. "R.J., not only did I know that, Captain Davis knew it, Janine Wright knew it—everybody remotely connected to the case knew that you would want to go right to the studio. And we are not going there."

"Why not?"

"Because whatever I might think, Janine Wright has made up her mind about you and she does not want you on the lot. And Captain Davis happens to agree with her."

R.J. tried every argument he could think of. Nothing worked. Not only was Portillo's mind made up, but he had orders—in writing—that he was not to allow R.J. on the Andromeda Studio lot.

Portillo would not look the other way. He would not take R.J. to get a rental car and leave him to try it on his own. He would not leave R.J. alone, knowing he'd find a way to get on the lot and see Casey.

"In fact," he said, with just a touch of his old amusement, "I plan to have you watched around the clock, R.J."

"What the hell does that mean?" R.J. growled, knowing Portillo was having a joke at his expense, but without a clue as to what was so funny.

"You will see," Portillo said. And that was all he would say.

R.J. swore and fumed and threatened, but that was it.

After another ten minutes of weaving through the heavy traffic, Portillo pulled his car into the parking lot of a small Thai restaurant deep in the Valley.

R.J. looked at him. "I'm not hungry," he said, still sulking.

Portillo flashed a row of white teeth at him. "You will be, R.J."

They went inside. R.J. wondered why all these places seemed to be dim, with lots of wood. Thai people must have good eyesight. Must be from eating all the hot peppers, R.J. thought.

The waitress was dressed in one of those incredibly tight dresses that turned her walk into a cross between a sway and a tiptoe. She was expecting them and led them toward the back of the restaurant.

Almost at the end of the hall there was one of those private eating areas Thai restaurants sometimes have—a carved wooden screen wrapped around a table that was raised up a couple of steps. A pair of elegant and expensive wingtip shoes sat on the top step. R.J. could see the outline of a man's head inside the booth. Somebody waiting for them, obviously. Probably to watch R.J., as Portillo had said.

Great, R.J. thought. More cops.

And sure enough, when he kicked off his own shoes and climbed up, Angelo Bertelli was there, munching on an egg roll.

"Hey, goombah," he called out to R.J. He was dressed in a beautiful gray pinstripe suit with wide lapels, a soft pink shirt with gray stripes, and a loud silk tie with dinosaurs on it. His black hair was slicked back à la Pat Riley, and he looked like—Well, hell, R.J. thought. He looks like an Italian cop from New York. And from the way the waitress simpered at him, his charm worked out here just as well as at home.

"Angelo!"

"Geez, where youse been? I'm practically on the entrée."

"This L.A. traffic is a bitch," R.J. said, sliding into the seat opposite Bertelli. "Am I allowed to ask what the hell you're doing here? Or is that part of the surprise?"

"You may ask," said Portillo as he took his seat.

"Sure, go ahead," said Angelo, dipping the butt end of his egg roll into a pot of hot sauce.

"Okay. What the hell are you doing here, Angelo?"

"*Mmmpf,*" said Bertelli, mouth filled with egg roll. He swallowed and tried again. "The NYPD has decided to cooperate with the LAPD in a rare fit of good sense—which may have more to do with the fact that Lieutenant Kates and Captain Davis have fallen in love over the long-distance lines at the thought of sticking you away for twenty to life. And so, hey, goombah, here I am. To lee-aze."

"To what?"

"To lee-aze, R.J. I am a lee-aze-on officer.

"Kates and Davis, huh?"

Bertelli held up two fingers, crossed. "Like this. A real love feast. Soul mates. Charter members of the Let's Screw R.J. Club."

R.J. grinned. "And they picked you for the job, huh? That was smart."

"Yeah, well, far as I know, neither one of them boys is ever gonna join Mensa."

"Seriously, Angelo, how did you end up with this job?"

Angelo smirked. "You know the old story about the briar patch? 'Please, please, don't make me go to L.A. Lawsa mussy, I hates it out there.' And Kates thinks I'm too close to you anyhow, so he sends me as a punishment, because he figures I'm gonna help nail you."

"Are you?"

"Don't talk *stronzo*, R.J." Bertelli winked at Portillo. "That means *mierda*, Lieutenant."

"Thank you, Detective."

Bertelli turned back to R.J. "Buddy, I got my own list of suspects to check, and you're not on it."

"That's a first," R.J. snorted.

"Tell me about it." He held up a manilla folder with a stripe and the letters NYPD on the front. "And this stuff does not show up on the overtime reports, on account of it would be my ass if Kates found out I was working on something other than nailing you." He winked. "Which means, by the way, that you are definitely buying lunch."

R.J. laughed. "No problem. Have seconds. Order dessert. Hell, the only thing better than getting off the hook would be pissing off Kates and Davis by doing it. So Kates still wants me for it, huh?"

Now Bertelli laughed, which almost made him choke on another bite of egg roll. "Kates has got your picture on the front of the case file. With a little noose around it. He wants you so bad he'd trade in his pension to get you. But hey. You're paying for a lot of braces and a few years at college."

"Say what?"

"Yeah. So many of the guys have put in overtime trying to

nail you, it's practically doubled the budget for the year."

R.J. laughed. "My tax dollars at work, huh? Well, it's damned good to see you, Angelo."

The food started coming at that point. There was a spicy soup first. Angelo ate three bowls of it, sweating and swearing. Portillo ate his without any fuss at all. He liked Thai food, but to him, raised on a diet of Mexican peppers, there was nothing unusual about hot food.

So while Bertelli made a Broadway number out of eating, Portillo quietly finished and began to go through Angelo's folder, his crescent-shaped reading glasses stuck on the end of his nose.

And by the time coffee came and R.J. and Angelo had caught up a little bit, he was nodding and making notes on a small pad he pulled from his pocket.

"Got a hot one, Uncle Hank?" R.J. asked him.

Portillo looked up. "I believe so, yes. There are several interesting possibles here." He looked at Angelo, and his eyes were as hard and bright as the turquoise in his belt buckle. "Have Lieutenant Kates and Captain Davis seen any of these?"

Bertelli shrugged. "Kates knows about some of 'em. Like that Minch guy. He told me to drop it. I don't know if he told Davis."

Portillo shook his head. "This is unforgivable. To have these and not even check—this is simply bad police work. If I had seen this before, *hijo*—"

"All right, for God's sake," R.J. burst out. "I can't take any more of this. Just tell me, already."

"As Detective Bertelli says, there are several very strong leads," Portillo said. "Particularly this Ed Minch."

"Who the hell is Ed Minch?" R.J. asked, growing more irritated. They were both batting this thing around like a volleyball and he didn't have a clue.

Bertelli butted in. "Minch is editor of a small movie fan magazine. *SCREEN SCREAM.* They do nostalgia and hard-to-find old movies." Angelo winked at R.J. "Guess what's his favorite movie in the whole wide history of the world?"

"It wouldn't be *As Time Goes By*, would it?"

"Oh, but it would be, R.J. It definitely would. And if you think you wanted to shit a Buick when you heard about the sequel, you should read what Minch has had to say about it." Angelo waved a large hand at about half the room. "Threatens everybody. Wishes pain, suffering, and gooey death on anybody remotely connected to the thing." He pointed at R.J. "Including you, you traitorous, pig-nosed, dollar-sucking, fame-hungry whore."

"He called me that?"

Bertelli nodded, beaming. "Yup. And then he *really* warmed up on you. But the important thing is, he wanted Janine Wright dead, the director and stars dead, the writer dead—everybody."

"And," said Portillo, "it looks like he is getting his wish."

"And you really think he may have been acting as his own fairy godmother?"

"Who knows?" Bertelli shrugged. "Point is, nobody checked. And what they got on him is just as strong as what they got on you, buddy."

Portillo, looking down again at the folder, whistled. "I would say, stronger. Listen: 'This goes beyond box-office crime, the kind of sequel madness that has made contemporary film such a contemptible hodgepodge of vulgarity, violence, and stupidity. This is desecration, pure and simple, and should be treated the way true cultures have treated desecration down through the ages. With ritual murder. Decapitate the writer. Disembowel the director. Crucify the stars. And for Janine Wright, mega-mongoloid producer of this sick travesty—suspend her over a hot fire by fish hooks, and slowly cook her . . .' "

"Good stuff, huh?" said Bertelli, arching his eyebrow.

"Well, I can see that I have a lot in common with this guy," R.J. said. "What has he got against me?"

"He thinks you didn't yell loud enough," Bertelli said. "You were supposed to use the authority of your august lineage to bring down the temple around the bastards' ears."

"I can see how it might bother somebody when I didn't do that," R.J. said. "And what made Lieutenant Kates decide that this guy was not a suspect?"

Bertelli grinned. "Freedom of the press, R.J. Pure and simple. Gotta keep us thugs from coming down hard on a guy just for speaking his mind, *capish?*"

"Yeah, I *capish* that. Where is this Minch person?"

Bertelli shrugged. "Someplace called La Crescenta. Know where that is?"

Portillo nodded. "It is not far from Glendale. We can be there in half an hour."

R.J. turned sideways and reached for his shoes. "Let's be there," he said.

But as R.J. got one foot into a shoe, there was a trilling sound.

"My beeper," Portillo said. "Wait here for one minute." He slid into his own tassled loafers and headed for the telephone at the far end of the hall.

R.J. looked at Angelo, who shrugged and swallowed the last half glass of water, fanning his face with his other hand.

Portillo didn't keep them waiting long. Before R.J. even had his second shoe on, Portillo was back looking pale and grim. "There's another note," he said. "And this time it threatens Janine Wright's assistant."

R.J. felt all the blood slosh down to his feet. "Casey," he said hoarsely.

Portillo held out a hand and pulled R.J. to his feet. "That's right," he said. "Casey."

CHAPTER 27

I said stop it, you said no sir
Now I'm getting plenty closer.
If you'd like a Hollywood laugh
try shooting the sequel without any staff.
Stop the sequel—don't say no
or your assistant is next to go.

No matter how many times R.J. read the damned thing, it still said that. "Your assistant is next to go." He read the photocopy Henry had given him again anyway, trying to keep his hand from shaking.

It didn't change. The bright, cartoony cut-out letters. The goofy rhymes that didn't quite work. If there weren't already a couple of bodies lying around it would be hard to take it seriously.

But he took it plenty seriously. "Your assistant." This was Casey they were talking about.

Casey.

They'd made it to the studio in about five minutes, siren wailing. Portillo had agreed to let R.J. talk to Casey first. He needed a few minutes to call in reinforcements and talk to studio security.

Angelo Bertelli had taken off at a run for the main gate and then a check of the perimeter. He would call in by radio to have men posted at weak spots.

R.J. hurried along the hallway from Janine Wright's office, where he'd gotten the copy of the note, and then out into the sun. That bright California sun that made the whole movie business possible and made the rest of the country seem like a day job to a junkie. It made R.J. start a sweat as he ran across the lot, looking for Casey.

He found her coming out of the soundstage. She was talking on a cellular phone and scrabbling in her purse for a pen. She glanced at R.J. and turned her back, still talking.

R.J. reached around her and plucked the phone from her hand. "Ms. Wingate will have to call you back," he said into the receiver. He pushed the Stop button.

Casey was glaring at him, her hands on her hips. "You son-of-a-bitch," she said. "I've been waiting for that call for three days."

He handed her the note. "Let's hope you're still waiting in three more days," he said.

Still furious, she glanced at the note, opened her mouth. Looked up at him, then down at the note and read it quickly.

"Oh," she said.

"That's right," R.J. agreed.

"And this is for real?"

"Uncle Hank thinks it is."

She nodded. "All right. What do you want me to do?"

R.J. blinked, astonished. He had come expecting a fight, thinking he'd have to force her to accept protection whether she wanted it or not. And instead she accepted the whole situation calmly.

It must have shown on his face. She shook her head at him. "I'm not stupid, R.J.," she said. "And I'm not going to die for the glory of Andromeda Studios. If Henry Portillo says my life is in danger, I believe him. So what do I do?"

"Come with me," he said. "We're setting up a secured room for you. With a telephone and a fax, so you can work." She started walking toward the main office building. R.J. followed, trying to watch everywhere at once.

"What's wrong with my office?" she asked.

"We have to assume he knows it's your office. And there's a window. He could have it staked out. Site a sniper rifle through it from a hundred yards away. Toss a molotov cocktail through it. Plant a bomb on the outside. Throw—"

"All right, R.J., I get the idea. Windows are bad," she said. But she did not say it like the old Casey would have, with acid amusement. This was all acid. "Let me just get a few things from my office."

"No," R.J. said. "He could have something already set up—the other times he didn't send the note until he was ready to make his move."

"So I just sit in this converted broom closet and it's business as usual?"

"That's right."

They came to the front door of the office building. "And you're going to be lurking around the whole time?" she asked. R.J. couldn't quite read her tone, but it wasn't playful and it wasn't grateful. Maybe closer to scorn. And in spite of the way his heart was hammering and his whole mind was screaming at him to keep her alive, keep her safe no matter what, her tone hurt.

"That's right," he said. "Sorry for the inconvenience."

"I've worked under worse conditions," she said.

R.J. had never gone in for being a bodyguard. The real problem with it, as far as he was concerned, was that he didn't like a job where you only got one mistake in your whole career. Because when you make that one small goof as a bodyguard, your client is dead and probably you are, too. R.J. didn't like to fail. Not with those stakes.

Besides, it didn't really even take a mistake. If somebody

wants to kill you and they don't care what it costs, they're going to kill you. It was just that simple. You couldn't stop somebody who really meant business.

The only thing that gave R.J. any hope at all was that he didn't think Casey was the main target. The killer wanted to stay in business long enough to get the sequel off track. And that meant he wouldn't go all out to get Casey. So there was some chance of saving her.

So R.J. stuck with Casey, playing bodyguard. He sat in her small, improvised office, watching her make calls, get calls, send faxes, get faxes. He didn't think it looked as exciting as it sounded. Assistant producer. Whoopee. Sit in a closet, talk on the phone.

On the other hand, being a detective wasn't too exciting right now, either. Scary, yes. But damned little adventure to it. Sitting. Watching. Wondering where the hammer would fall. Wondering what else he might be doing that he wasn't.

Outside in the hall a couple of uniforms sat on folding chairs. One of them got up and patroled the hall at random intervals.

There were two more cops at the front door and more outside sweeping the lot.

There were even a couple of SWAT guys on the roof, flicking their cold eyes back and forth over what they would probably think of as their Field of Fire.

Casey was about as safe as they could make her.

And it wasn't enough. R.J. still felt the hair rise on his neck every time he heard a footstep in the hall. He was sure he was forgetting some basic precaution and it was making him nuts.

He sat there until seven o'clock at night like that, trying to figure what he'd forgotten and knowing he would never remember until it was too late. Somebody brought him a sandwich and some coffee. It still sat under his chair, untouched. The cops in the hall went home, replaced by the next shift. And R.J. sat.

Somewhere a pipe gurgled. A door opened and R.J. could

hear lush, romantic music. It was rising hysterically, the strings screaming something and the flutes yodeling back. The door slammed and he could only hear the pipe again.

He glanced over at Casey and felt an electric jolt as he saw that she was looking at him. Her head was tilted slightly to one side and her perfect eyebrows pulled together in a puzzled frown.

"What," he said, wondering what he'd done wrong.

"You," she said.

"What about me?"

She shook her head, left, then right, very slowly. "I can't figure you out," she said.

R.J. snorted. "I have the same problem."

"I mean it, R.J. You sit there with no expression on your face, like you could be waiting for a train or sitting at a funeral. And I watch you and wonder what you're feeling, or even *if* you're feeling."

"Oh, hell, Casey—" R.J. started, but she cut him off.

"But then every time there's a sound anywhere in the building your whole body gets tense, like you're about to grab a grizzly bear by the throat or something. And when that cop brought in the sandwich, you were in between me and him before the door even opened."

"I didn't know who was opening the door," R.J. said, confused. Where the hell was she going with this?

"You're protecting me," she said.

"Jesus H. Christ, Casey. What did you think I was doing?"

She smiled. There was still a hint of mean in it, but it was playful mean, and it was the nicest smile R.J. had seen in a long time. "I thought you were playing cops and robbers," she said. "I thought you were running some bullshit macho power trip on me. But if terrorists with Uzis and hand grenades had kicked in the door, you were ready to keep them away from me."

"I was ready to go down trying," R.J. said. "What the hell, Casey—"

"It doesn't matter," she said. "It was just something that occurred to me. You know."

He didn't know, but he nodded like he did.

"Could you shut the door tight, R.J.? I think I'd feel a lot safer."

Still totally baffled, R.J. got up and pushed the door tightly shut. When he turned around Casey was standing, kicking off her skirt behind the small desk.

"Uh . . . Casey—"

She shook her head and began to unbutton her blouse. "At least I know what you're thinking now," she said.

He started to ask her why that should be so important, but as the last wisp of her clothing hit the floor he realized the question could probably wait.

R.J. had shared wild passion with Casey plenty of times. But this time was different; gentle, almost introspective. Of course, the telephone still hit the floor, along with three file folders, as R.J. and Casey slid across the surface of the desk, joined together.

And afterward, it seemed to him that she held onto him just a little longer than usual, maybe with a trace more tenderness, a softness he had not seen from her before.

But once they had shrugged their clothes back on, she was quickly back to being all business. She straightened the desk, retrieved the telephone, and with one last smile for R.J., Casey dialed the phone and once more disappeared back into Mother Bell's Invisible Empire.

She worked steadily for several more hours and he did not catch her eye again. Finally, Casey hung up the phone for the last time. She glanced at him, maybe the third time she'd looked at him all day.

"I'm ready to go home," she said. "Do you have an armored car for me?"

"Stay put," R.J. said. "I'll have the car sent around." He stood up and felt his joints creak from the tense inactivity. He stepped into the hall and the cops there glanced up at him. "She's ready to go home," R.J. said.

"Oh, happy day," said the cop on the left, a stocky guy with a red mustache. He plucked his radio from his belt and passed the word as R.J. went back into Casey's office.

"Long day," R.J. said.

She shrugged. "There are a lot of those," she said. "But today was probably worse than most. Robert Brickel didn't come back from lunch."

"Oh, yeah? Who's Robert Brickel?"

"You know. That awful-looking guy with the goatee that works out of Janine's office. He's so flaky, I wonder why she puts up with him."

"He must know where some bodies are buried," R.J. said.

"He must. He's been late often enough, but to just take off the whole afternoon like that— He'd better have something good on Janine. He didn't even call in."

R.J. felt something run up his spine and back down again. It was a very small thing, very light-footed, and he frowned, waiting for it to take another run so he could see what it was. "Casey," he said as the thing tickled him again.

She glanced at him, one eyebrow raised.

"This guy, Robert Brickel. What's his job?"

She made a face. "Jesus, R.J., he's the hatchetman. He does all Janine's dirty work. Fires people. Runs the filing system. Keeps her schedule. Like that. Why?"

The little thing grew a few sizes and stuck around his throat. "Would it be fair to call Brickel Janine Wright's assistant?"

Casey's jaw dropped. "Oh my God," she said.

"Yeah. Mine too."

"Oh my God. Of course. Oh, R.J. what a bunch of jerks we are—"

But he was already stepping out and talking to the cop outside her door.

CHAPTER 28

They found Robert Brickel in the morgue with a John Doe tag on his toe. They were lucky to have found him at all. His body had been in the water at one of the large flood control dams in the Valley, the one out in the North Valley near the Foothill Freeway.

A party of Japanese tourists found him. They'd heard there were cranes living in the park around the dam. They'd come to photograph birds and had seen the body floating. They never found their cranes. But they'd taken some great pictures of the body. Then they had told their tour guide, bowing a lot. The tour guide had hissed and bowed back. Then he had called the consulate.

The consulate was unable to bow over the telephone, but his office called the cops, who fished the body out while the Japanese tourists took some more great pictures.

The cops didn't bow, either. But they did take some more pictures before they loaded the body onto the wagon and drove it to the morgue.

And at 3:00 A.M., R.J., Portillo, and Angelo Bertelli stood looking down at the body.

"That's him," R.J. said.

Portillo nodded. "Yes. I agree. I will tell the captain and he can arrange a formal identification." He turned away and left the large cold room for the telephone outside.

"Uncle Hank," R.J. said.

Portillo stopped and turned back, looking irritated. "Yes, R.J.?"

"You can tell Davis one more thing."

Portillo sighed with exasperation, as if he thought R.J. was going to suggest he tell Davis to jump up his own ass. "What's that?"

But R.J. gave him a big grin instead. He let the grin just hang there for a minute. It felt good, and he went with it until Portillo started to turn away again. "Uncle Hank? I didn't do this one."

Portillo stopped dead. "Say it again, *hijo?*"

"I said, I didn't do it. Couldn't have. I've been sitting in the middle of fifteen cops all day." He nodded at the body. "We know he was killed sometime this afternoon while I was warming a chair next to two uniforms. So unless they helped me carry the body, I didn't do it." R.J. felt the grin turn just a little mean, but he didn't care. "Tell Davis that."

The expression of annoyance dropped off Portillo's face and for a moment, his jaw just dangled. Then he slammed his mouth shut with a click you could hear across the room. "*Hijo de puta más grande en el mundo,*" he muttered. R.J. was impressed; Portillo had a puritanical attitude toward profanity. If he was using it himself, he must have been floored by what R.J. had said.

"Wish I could say that in Italian," Angelo said.

Portillo shook his head, and then he was smiling, too. He stepped back to R.J. and clapped him on the back. "I will tell Davis right now," he said with a wicked grin. "I have his home number." And he whirled away to the telephone.

R.J. and Bertelli watched him go, then turned back to the body on the slab.

"Ugly-looking guy," Angelo commented.

"The water didn't do much for his looks," R.J. said. "But he didn't start with much, either."

"The preliminary report says head wounds and/or drowning," Angelo said. "I'd give a shiny new nickel to know which. If he was killed at the dam, or someplace else—"

"It won't make any difference, Angelo. This killer is going to be one jump ahead of us. There won't be any witnesses, and there won't be any evidence that means a damn. We're going to have to either track him down or catch him in the act."

"What can I say, R.J. I like evidence."

"You have to. You're a cop."

Angelo went back to looking at the corpse, but R.J. felt like Bertelli was really looking at him out of the corner of his eyes. R.J. didn't care. He was feeling happier than he had in weeks. It looked like he was finally off the hook with the cops. After a minute, Angelo cleared his throat.

"So, um, R.J.," he said.

"Yeah, that's me."

"Uh, ahem."

R.J. looked at his friend. Normally, Angelo could talk to anybody about anything. "Something in your throat, Detective? Cold air in here getting to you?"

"Throat? No. Nothing like that."

"Then what?"

"Uh—"

"Angelo, for Christ's sake!"

"I was wondering about Casey," Angelo said in a rush.

"Oh." R.J.'s good mood drained out of him, almost as though Angelo's question had poked a hole in his chest. "Seems like you ask me that a lot."

"Yeah, well." Angelo shrugged. "Seems like it's, you know. There to ask. A lot."

"Maybe it is, at that." R.J. sighed. "What do you want to know?"

"You know. Where things stood wit you two. Hey, you don't have to say nothin' if you don't want."

"That's good," R.J. said. "Because I don't know what to say."

"Uh-huh."

"I mean, I thought this thing yesterday might give us a chance to talk. Get squared away, you know."

"So?"

"So she sits at the desk all day with a phone stuck to the side of her face. Says maybe two words at the end of the day, that's it."

"Nothin' meaningful, huh."

"Not to me. It's business on the phone, then she goes home with the two cops assigned to her. I don't even get a good night."

"On account of you were rushing around with this?" Angelo said, pointing his chin at the corpse.

"Yeah, maybe. No. I mean, I don't know. I don't think so."

Angelo nodded. "Uh-huh. And I should just pick my answer there, right?"

"Shit, Angelo, I would have found a way to say good night if it had been me."

"It ain't you, buddy. It's her. And she's got a whole different set of signals."

"What is that, some kind of Italian folk wisdom? I mean, what does that mean, a different set of signals?"

Angelo spread his hands. "I mean, this is why people talk, R.J. Because if somethin' don't get said, then what isn't said, and the *way* it isn't said, always means something different to everybody. Ain't no two people the same that way, know what I'm saying?"

"Not really, no."

"I mean, she don't say good night, and to you that's rejection, right?"

"That's right. What else could it be?"

"The fuck do I know, what else? It could mean, I'll see you later, so why bother to say good night now, huh?"

R.J. blinked. "You think she meant that?"

"Uh, not in this case, no. But you see what I'm saying?"

"Yeah, maybe. I guess so."

"I'm just saying you gotta talk to her, R.J. That's all."

"How can I talk to her when she's always on the phone?"

Angelo shrugged. "Call her."

"What. On the phone? Call her on the phone, Angelo?"

"Yeah, that's right."

"I'm sitting five feet from her all day and she doesn't say a word, why should she talk to me on the phone?"

"What do I know. She likes the phone. Call her up, R.J."

"Yeah. Maybe I'll do that, Angelo," R.J. said. He looked around the room, taking one last look at the body of Robert Brickel. "Let's get out of here."

They left the morgue and walked out to join Portillo. He was hanging up the telephone with a look on his face like he'd just won a long court case.

"Captain Davis wanted to be sure your whereabouts were accounted for," Portillo said. "Including your lunch break."

R.J. nodded. "He's a thorough guy. You have to admire that."

"I told him that a good cop must learn to live with conclusive proof." And Portillo smiled again. "He was not pleased. I woke him up."

"Goddamn that's great," Bertelli said, and he reached for the phone. "You've inspired me, Lieutenant. I'm gonna call Kates at home and tell him, too."

R.J. laughed. One of the lab techs looked up at him. Laughter was not a sound they heard much here at the morgue. R.J. didn't care. He hadn't heard it much himself lately, and it felt good.

"What's next, Uncle Hank?"

"I think we go to Detective Bertelli's list of suspects, R.J.

In fact, it has occurred to me—you remember this Minch person?"

"The guy that edits the film magazine. Yeah, I remember. What about him?"

"He lives in La Crescenta, R.J."

R.J. shrugged. "And?"

"And La Crescenta is just a few miles from where the body was found. Maybe three freeway exits."

"Damn."

"Yes. I think we have a new hot suspect."

CHAPTER 29

La Crescenta is maybe a thousand feet higher up than Glendale. Through the window of Portillo's car, R.J. noticed the smog thin out and then disappear as they climbed higher, driving up the freeway. They took an off-ramp and turned onto Foothill Boulevard, the main street in the area.

SCREEN SCREAM magazine had an office on Foothill Boulevard near a gas station and an Armenian grocery store.

"This is unofficial," Portillo said as he nosed the car into a spot in the cracked blacktop of the almost empty parking lot. "I had better wait here."

"I'm gonna go along," Bertelli said. "Unofficially."

R.J. glanced at Angelo, who shrugged. "That way, if this guy is it, I got a gun. Which you aren't licensed to pack out here. But hey—youse can do all the talking."

"Hell, butt in if you want, Angelo," R.J. said. "It's your lead." He opened the car's door. "I just hope we don't need your equalizer."

They didn't. But it was a near thing.

The office wasn't much. Just one small room with a big closet. The closet was bulging with back issues, clippings, stacks of newspapers. The office was equipped with a computer, a telephone, a VCR and monitor, and Ed Minch.

Ed Minch wasn't much more than a beard and an attitude. He could work three fingers on his right hand. His left hand was strapped to his wheelchair. So were his legs and his head.

Their suspect was a quadriplegic.

"What the fuck do *you* want, asshole?" Minch snarled as R.J. stutter-stepped to a surprised stop in the doorway.

R.J. shook his head and looked at Angelo, who shrugged. It was obvious from one look that Minch could not have committed the murders. Still, who knew that he might know about them?

R.J. had stopped in shock when he saw the wheelchair. Now he moved on into the room. "Are you Ed Minch?"

The head twitched slightly. There was a little *whee* noise and the chair spun to face R.J. "No. Ed Minch was a human being. I'm a roadkill that won't go away. What the fuck is it to *you* who I am?"

"I need to ask you a few questions." R.J. reached for one of his business cards. "My name is—"

"I know who you are, shit-for-brains. And I don't give a rat's ass what you need." The *whee* noise came again and the chair spun away, back to the monitor.

"Jesus Christ," Angelo said from his spot in the doorway. "Is this guy for real?"

The chair spun again, and then shot over to Angelo. R.J. had to jump back out of the way, or his toes would have been pulped.

"For real?" Minch said, coming to a stop practically in Angelo's pocket. "For *real*? You think somebody could make this up? You're stupider than star-boy here, and he's dumber than a brick."

R.J. stepped closer. "Minch, listen—"

Whee. The chair whipped around so quickly R.J. didn't

jump in time. The footrest banged him hard in the shins.

"What I'll *listen* to is your receding footsteps, Brooks. You and your pet dago monkey can just disappear. I have to work for a living. Not that this in any way resembles living." He gave a kind of cough that might have been some sort of laugh, and the chair lurched forward, straight at R.J.

R.J. jumped back again as the chair sped past him.

"Good reflexes," Minch said, "for somebody who couldn't find his ass using both hands."

"Goddammit," R.J. snarled, "people are dying, Minch."

"Our whole culture is dying, Brooks. Turning to shit, and we're all just shoveling flies at it. These people dying doesn't make a bit of difference either way. They're just foot soldiers. Pawns in the struggle to tear down two thousand years of Western civilization." He spun the chair again. As R.J. heard the *whee* he instinctively jumped back. "Besides," Minch said with acid sweetness, "there are worse things than death, you know."

He sat there in his motorized chair, unable to move except for one hand, and it occurred to R.J. that two large guys with a gun were helpless in front of him. The chair darted around as fast as this guy's mind. R.J. hadn't taken one normal step or finished one sentence since he hit the door.

"Part of the decline of Western civilization," R.J. said slowly, "comes from relaxing our moral values. And murder is not a moral thing, Minch."

The guy in the chair practically smiled. "Good! Wonderful! That was almost human thought! I'm astounded, Brooks. Listen! The sound of one hand clapping!" And he flopped his one half-good hand on the metal tray attached to the front of his chair.

"The point is, however," Minch said, lurching the chair closer to R.J. and looking up at him, "that this is not murder, but execution. *Justice.* It's a dying society kicking back at its own murderers. This is totally justified self-defense. Naturally it's too little too late— I'd like to see every studio in town running kneedeep in blood. Of course, I'd have to measure that with someone else's knee."

The chair lurched and R.J. jumped. Minch spun over to Angelo. "What about you, you dumb bag of bird droppings? Do you have any thoughts that didn't come from the wop version of *GQ?*"

Bertelli looked down at Minch. "I've got one," he said. "You might not like it much."

Minch made the coughing noise again and spun away. "Oh, you never know what I might like, Rocky. Go ahead and slug me, that may be the only way I can get off."

As Minch went zipping past, R.J. leaned forward. The batteries that powered the chair were perched on a shelf on the back side, about eight inches off the ground. R.J. yanked the power lead off the batteries' terminals and the chair groaned to a halt.

"Hey! You stupid son-of-a-bitch, what are you doing?"

R.J. grabbed the handles of the chair and turned Minch around to face them. "I'm leveling the playing field," he said. "We might be able to keep up with just your mouth."

"Not likely," Minch said. "Plug me back in, you scum-sucking Neanderthal orangutan."

"Not until you answer a couple of questions," R.J. said.

"Oh, this is great. This really is. Did you bring a sap? Besides the Guinea gorilla leaning in the doorway, I mean. We already know he's a total sap. You could get him to hold my hand down so I can't defend myself while you beat me."

"Minch. Shut up. Please?"

"Shut up. Sure, I'll shut up. Why the fuck shouldn't I shut up? All I have left is my voice, but the great R.J. Brooks wants me to shut up, so I'll shut up for the traitorous butt-licking son-of-a-bitch."

R.J. shook his head as if he could shake loose some of the poison pouring out of Minch. "What the hell have you got against me, anyway, Minch?"

"You could have stopped them and you didn't."

"I couldn't stop them. Anything I tried would just give them more publicity. Sell more tickets. Nobody can stop them."

"At least somebody is trying."

R.J. looked down into Minch's eyes. The light burning there was almost twice as bright as any R.J. had ever seen. But it wasn't burning clear. Minch was about a half step out of a straight jacket. Maybe being in the chair had done it to him. Maybe he'd always been like this. It didn't matter. The only thing they were going to get out of him was more of what they'd already had, and R.J. had had enough.

"All right, Minch," he said.

"All right? *ALL RIGHT?* It damn well isn't all right!" He waved his hand feebly. "You don't get it, do you, Brooks? I didn't think you would, but I was hoping. Well, there goes the optimist in me."

He gave his dry hacking little laugh again and lurched sideways. "*As Time Goes By* means something, Brooks. Something special, pure, *good*. Not just to me, but to all of us, our whole culture. Millions of people, all around the world. Because it stood for something. It was a rallying cry for the last great moral battleground—and the good guys *won*. It was important, goddammit—maybe one of five or six movies in history that are really *important*."

He slapped his hand on the tray. It was a feeble slap, but if the intention behind it counted for anything, it would have brought the building down. "And now those goddamned soulless leeches want to sodomize it! Like putting a Nike swoosh on the *Pietà*, for Christ's sake! Can't anybody else see that? See that it's wrong, beyond wrong, it's actually *EVIL!*"

He turned those burning eyes on R.J. again. "Can't you at least see that, Brooks?"

"I see it," R.J. said. "But you're right. You're an optimist. I'm not. You think you can save Western civilization by stopping this sequel. I don't believe that. I don't even think I can stop the sequel. But I can save a couple of lives if I stop this killer. Maybe that's not as much. It won't take the mustache off any Mona Lisas. But it's all I can do, Minch. So how about it? What can you tell me that might help?"

Minch stared at him for a long time. Then the light dimmed in his eyes and he flopped his head back down, away from R.J. "Go to hell," he said. "Get the fuck out of my office."

Feeling helpless, R.J. looked over at Angelo.

Bertelli shrugged. "Hey, what the fuck," he said. "Sometimes you just crap out."

"You ought to be used to it," Minch muttered. "Plug me in on your way out, huh?"

R.J. shook his head. But he reattached the wires to Minch's battery.

Then he headed for the door. He stopped in the doorway and looked back. But Minch was already wheeling back to the monitor and popping a tape in with practiced clumsiness.

As the sound came up—grand music mixed with explosions. R.J. closed the door behind him and walked down the five small steps behind Angelo, out into the bright sun of the parking lot.

CHAPTER 30

R.J. was busy the next few days. Still, he tried to call Casey a couple of times every day. She was always on another line. She left him a couple of messages with Portillo, but they never connected.

So R.J. tried to concentrate on catching the killer. There were other suspects. None of them seemed as promising going in as Minch had. Over the next few days, R.J. and Angelo checked them all out. And all of them fizzed out after only a couple of minutes of questioning.

There were people Janine had screwed over in personal and business matters, a lot of them. She left wounded bodies in her wake like a Sherman tank on a rampage. But most of the people in the business had that weird brand of Hollywood fatalism you only see in the industry.

Life goes on, they said. They'd shake their heads and say, Should have seen it coming. All part of the game. Besides, Janine's big now, and she can do what she wants. Anyway, can't afford to hold it against her. Some of these people, badly mauled by Janine Wright once, were doing business with her again.

Then there were the personal ones. There were a number of jilted lovers. But most of these, once they were sure no word would ever get back to Janine, admitted they were relieved when she broke things off. She was, apparently, a demanding and unrewarding lover.

Without exception, the people on the list would be happy to hear Janine Wright was dead. But all of them, like victims of a terrible beating, were too cowed to do anything about it.

By the end of the week the list was finished. Most of the interviews blended into one ugly sketch of Janine Wright. She was ruthless, dominating, vindictive, coarse, and almost evil. But they had known that. And no matter how much she seemed to deserve to be murdered, R.J. was no closer to finding who was killing those around her.

One interview stuck out in R.J.'s mind. He and Angelo, in a rental car paid for by the NYPD, had driven far out into the Valley to an address in Thousand Oaks. It turned out to be a retirement home.

The man they had come to see, Fred Goss, had known Janine Wright since her start. He had been her partner at first—it was Goss who had the experience in movies and had interested Janine in doing them. And then, when Janine Wright was on her way up, she had dumped him, cut him off without a nickel, and tossed him away like an old newspaper.

They knew all that before driving to Thousand Oaks. It seemed like a pretty good motive for murder, worth the hour's drive out the Golden State Freeway to see Goss. Until they pulled into the parking lot of Golden Hills Retirement Home.

R.J. put the car into a slot in the lot, but left the motor running. He turned to Angelo in the passenger seat beside him. "What do you think?" he asked.

Bertelli shrugged. "Who knew? So the guy is old. I've known lots of mean old guys."

"Mean enough to hack off Jason Levy's head?"

"Oh, yeah. Sure. They get brooding on something, it turns 'em all sour inside." He looked out the window. "Of course, this would have to be an exceptionally *strong* mean old man."

R.J. looked up the walkway to the home. A pair of nurses leaned against a doorway, keeping half an eye on a cluster of unmoving oldsters sitting in the sun. One of the nurses puffed on a cigarette. Still life with smoke.

"Well, hell," R.J. said. "We drove an hour to see this guy, and it's an hour back. We might as well talk to him."

"Uh-huh. And maybe they got a restroom in there, too."

R.J. laughed. "You drink red wine with lunch, Angelo, you have to plan your afternoon around pit stops."

Bertelli spread his hands. "Hey. It's all part of the price I pay for being Italian." He shrugged and ran a hand through his hair. "It's worth it."

They locked up the car and followed the arrow on a sign that said OFFICE. The office was cool, carpeted, and decorated in muted colors. There they found Ms. Helms, a cheerful woman of about forty-five, who had the look of an ex-hippie.

Ms. Helms was a member of the wonderful subspecies of California bureaucrat. She did her best to frustrate them and send them away without seeing Goss, but she did it so cheerfully, acting the whole time like a happy, helpful victim of regulations, that she clearly wanted R.J. and Bertelli to leave with a pleasant memory of a woman who just couldn't say yes, no matter how much she had wanted to.

Bertelli showed his badge. "Wow," said Ms. Helms. "New York, huh? What a great place. You are so lucky to live there." She flashed them a beautiful smile. "Of course, you're kind of out of your jurisdiction here. And California statutes are a little different. I can't let you see Mr. Goss without a court order. It would mean my job. Sorry, Detective."

"Call me Angelo," he said, with his best seductive smile.

She blinked, then blushed. "Angelo," she said.

R.J. sat on the urge to smile. Watching Angelo in action was always a treat. He had a big nose, and lord knows he didn't have a Fabio-style body. But something about him just seemed to radiate sexy charm.

He gave Ms. Helms both barrels. "You know, Ms. Helms—" he said it with a funny hesitation, like he wanted her first name but was too shy to ask.

"Julianne," she said with another blush.

"Julianne. Hey, that's a beautiful name, Julianne."

"Oh," she said, ". . . thank you."

"Julianne, you know we come like three thousand miles to see this guy?"

"Oh, I'm sorry," she said.

"Yeah, well, listen, don't be sorry. Just let us see him for ten minutes." He gave her his best wink. "Nobody has to know, and then we're outta here, huh?"

"Oh, no, I couldn't do that," she said.

Angelo looked at her like he couldn't believe she'd said that. "Excuse me? For ten minutes?"

"That would be totally against all our regulations."

"Ms. Helms—Julianne—we're the *good* guys here. Goss can maybe help us solve a couple of murders."

"I know," she said with a sweet, regretful smile. "I'm *really* sorry. I wish there was some *other* way I could help." And she actually reached across and patted Angelo's hand.

"Julianne. Ten minutes of easy talk—that's nothing. No matter how bad the guy is, ten minutes won't kill him."

"Oh," she said. "It's not a question of that. Mr. Goss is in excellent health. I simply can't let you visit him without either his consent or proper authorization."

"So how do I get proper authorization?"

She shook her head. "That's *really* a drag. You have all these forms to fill out and it takes about six weeks to get them approved."

"We don't got six weeks, Julianne. We got a couple hours, tops."

"Yeah. I'm really sorry. But . . ." She shrugged.

R.J. could see that Angelo was totally frustrated and about

to blow. He could also see that although Ms. Helms probably
would have gone home with Bertelli, she wasn't about to cave
in and let them see Goss. So he tapped Bertelli on the shoulder. "May I cut in?" he asked.

Angelo threw out his hands. "Be my guest."

"Ms. Helms," R.J. said. "My name is R.J. Brooks."

She squinted prettily at him. "You look kind of familiar,
too. Do I know you?"

"Some people say I look like my old man," he said.

She squealed. "Whoa! Of *course* you do! Whoa! No wonder you look familiar!" She frowned slightly. "What are you
doing with Angelo?"

"Angelo is a good friend of mine," R.J. said.

Julianne looked at Angelo, if possible, with even more approval. "Wow," she said. "And you really are— I mean *he* was
really your father?"

"That's right," R.J. said. "But listen, Julianne—"

"I know I have no right to ask you this," she said without
hearing him. "But I wonder—I mean, it would mean so much
to some of the wonderful old people here. Do you think—
Would you possibly consider . . . ?"

R.J. blinked. "Consider what?"

"Oh," she said, "I wouldn't even think about asking you
normally. But with the budget cuts lately, you know. Most of
the time they don't have anything except TV."

R.J. looked at Bertelli. He was looking back at R.J. with a
huge grin. "Do you have any idea what she's talking about?"
he asked Angelo.

"Yes, I do," Bertelli said. "You're gonna love it."

"It makes my flesh crawl when you say that, Angelo. Ms.
Helms," he said, turning back to her, "how about letting me
in on the secret here? What exactly do you want from me?"

She gave R.J. her most radiant smile. "It would be so easy,"
she said. "It would only take a few minutes."

"It might take an extra ten minutes," Angelo said, leaning
in as close to her as he could get with the lights on.

Julianne's eyes met Angelo's. "All right," she said.

And that's how R.J. found himself patting approximately forty wrinkled old hands, gazing into some seventy-nine rheumy old eyes—one old guy, a veteran, had an eye patch—and saying forty times, "Hey, how are you doing?"

About half of them just stared at him. Twelve of them thought he was his own old man, which was all right. Three thought he was their son come for a visit. One man thought R.J. was his wife.

But in spite of the fact that Angelo had shoved him into doing it, greatly against his will, R.J. found he didn't mind. Because the other half of the oldsters were glad to have somebody talk to them. Anybody. It didn't have to be the celebrity R.J. felt like he was imitating. Just somebody who looked like he gave a damn.

And when he was finished an hour later, R.J. was surprised to discover that he did give a damn, that he would have done it again even if he hadn't been forced into it.

Julianne Helms seemed satisfied with his performance, too.

"Mr. Goss is waiting for you," she said with a contented smile.

CHAPTER 31

Fred Goss was a cheerful, spry old bird. He didn't look like he needed the wheelchair he lounged in with his legs crossed. "They make me sit in this thing," he told R.J. in a voice that was dry, but surprisingly strong and cheerful. "They're afraid I'll slip on a cake of soap and sue them."

He shrugged, holding up two hands that looked knotted and strong. "What the hell. I couldn't afford to pay a lawyer a retainer. Who am I going to sue?"

"Janine Wright left you broke?" R.J. asked him. The old man shrugged.

"Yes, I guess so. I'm broke, anyway. Did Janine *leave* me broke? Well—If it wasn't her it would have been someone else, I suppose." He chuckled. "I guess I was just one of life's victims."

"Somebody did like that to me, I'd be pissed off," Angelo said. Goss glanced over at him with a raised eyebrow.

"Maybe you would be. Italian, by the look of you, hmm?"

Angelo grinned. "Yeah. Just lucky," he said.

Goss nodded. "I thought so. You people really go for the revenge thing. And you look it. As you get older you can tell. There's a great deal of truth to some of the things we no longer put up with. Racial types and so forth."

"Mr. Goss—," R.J. said.

"You can call me Fred. I mean no harm, but there are differences. You can tell. Spotted your friend for Italian the second he walked in." Goss frowned at R.J. "You're a little tougher to figure. More typical of the racial mongrels we're getting nowadays in this country. Can't keep the bloodlines separate anymore."

Angelo coughed to hide a laugh. R.J. shook his head, irritated. "I'm sure that's interesting, Fred. But we're here to talk about murder."

"Somebody finally got her, did they? Well, I'm not surprised. She's been begging for it for years. Any other business in the world and she would have been chopped into small pieces and fed to the dogs two decades ago."

"Nobody got to her. They've got to some people around her, and I think they're zeroing in on her."

"Well, let them," the old man said, totally unruffled.

"I can't do that, Fred."

"Why not? She paying you? I know it's not because you like her—nobody likes Janine Wright. No one ever has, except that poor fool she married." He shook his head and chuckled again. "By God, you can't tell the Irish a damn thing, can you?"

"You knew William Kelley?"

"Of course I knew him. I was in business with his wife. In bed with her, too."

R.J. glanced at Angelo. But Goss went happily on.

"Now, you have to know that didn't mean a thing. Everybody was in bed with Janine. That woman would sleep with the meter reader if it would get her a lower rate."

"And Kelley knew about that?"

Goss laughed. It was a dry sound, bleak and lifeless. For the first time he looked like an old man. "He figured it out eventually. My God, he'd have had to be deaf, dumb, blind, and stupid not to notice." The old man shook his head. "There was a scene. He was going to divorce her, leave her without a penny. Lord knows he had proof of infidelity. So she framed him."

R.J. blinked, thinking of the papers Pauly had given him. "Say that again?"

"She framed him. She set him up, blew the whistle, and had him sent away. So she got his money and he took the fall. And she made sure I was implicated so I wouldn't say a word about it." The old man's hand trembled slightly and he looked far beyond R.J. for a minute, before snapping back to the present and meeting R.J.'s eyes again.

"If anybody is trying to kill Janine Wright, it's Kelley. He's big—and my God, he was strong—and I imagine he's half crazy by now." Goss leaned forward and lowered his voice. "Let him do it. She deserves it, he's earned the right, paid for the crime ahead of time. Just let him do it. By Christ, I'd do it myself if I had the strength. The woman is evil, what she did to him. And me. To everybody. Let him kill her, Mr. Brooks. Please. Let him do it."

There was something in the old man's voice that was almost begging. As if he figured that he could get rid of his guilt if only Kelly killed Janine Wright. For a moment R.J. thought, *Why not?* But then he shook his head.

"I can't do that, Fred," he said. "Kelley is dead."

Goss looked at him for a moment, then straightened up and took a deep breath. Whatever had been eating him, he put it away again. He looked more like the strong, dry old man he had seemed to be when R.J. came in. "That's a shame," he said. "He was a nice man who got an ugly deal. Always smiling, great sense of humor. He deserved better."

"We all deserve better, Fred. But it's the Janine Wrights who get it."

Goss chuckled. "Maybe so. Still, it seems a shame."

"Can you think of anybody else who might have wanted to kill her?"

"Oh, sure. Dozens. Almost anybody would have wanted to kill her. But Kelley was the most likely."

And for five minutes he rattled off a list of people and their very good reasons for wanting to kill Janine Wright. Angelo wrote it all down, occasionally glancing up at Goss as if he couldn't really believe what he was hearing.

R.J. wasn't sure he could believe it, either. But when the list was done, he was even more sympathetic with Goss's plea. Janine Wright deserved to die if anybody did.

When Goss finally wound down, R.J. stood up to go. The old man looked up at him and shook his head. "You're sure he's dead?" he asked with just a hint of something old and still raw in his voice.

"I'm sure," R.J. said. "I was at the funeral."

"A shame," Goss said. "A very great shame."

They left him sitting there with his memories and regrets and walked out to their rented car.

CHAPTER 32

They took the hour-long drive back to L.A. and neither one of them had much to say. They were both hard guys in a tough profession, and neither one of them would admit that they were bothered by what was happening, but they were.

Janine Wright had left a trail of broken lives behind her like a tornado cutting through a trailer park. And she had done it without a second thought. She got no pleasure from it, she just did it, like you would swat at a fly. By reflex.

And now somebody was coming at her from the back trail and leaving dead bodies the same way. And although R.J. and Bertelli had both seen plenty of ugly death before, this time it all seemed uglier. While they were both trying to stop the killer, they were both secretly hoping they might be just a minute too late, because Janine Wright deserved to die. Especially after talking to somebody like Fred Goss.

They started to hit a little traffic around Encino and it slowed them down some. R.J. pulled into the lot of a coffee shop and parked the car. As R.J. slid into a booth, Angelo nodded toward the back. "I'll call Portillo and see what's up," he said.

R.J. nodded, already lost in the menu. "Yeah, okay. I'll order you coffee."

Angelo ambled off toward the restroom, where the phone was visible between two doors marked MEN and WOMEN. R.J. stared at the menu, but his thoughts were not on bacon and eggs.

The last few days had taken a lot out of him, more than he had realized until now, and he needed the coffee the waitress had brought over without asking. He felt like he was shut out all along the line. Couldn't figure out the simple things anymore. Like who was stalking Janine Wright. Like where the hell he stood with Casey.

Couldn't even figure out whether to order a burger or an omelet, or skip it altogether and just have coffee and a toasted bagel. Except L.A. bagels didn't taste right, so forget that. There—that was one thing he'd figured out. The rest ought to be easy now.

It was. It got a lot easier a moment later when Angelo came back to the table. "Let's go, goombah," he said, pulling out some money and throwing it onto the table. Something about his tone of voice made R.J. look up sharply.

"Go where? What's up, Angelo?"

Bertelli was already heading for the front door. "We got another one," he said over his shoulder. "At the studio this time."

R.J. got up and followed.

They arrived at the studio fifteen minutes later. The young kid with the smile was not at the gate. Instead, a large, crew-cut motorcycle cop blocked their way in and examined Bertelli's badge carefully before waving them on.

A cluster of official vehicles was already parked haphazardly by the main building. Angelo angled the car in sloppily. He got out and R.J. followed him into the building.

Portillo hadn't said who the victim was, and as they went

upstairs and down the hall toward Janine Wright's office R.J. felt an indecent flutter of hope. He didn't wish anybody dead, hardly. But if somebody had to die and they asked him for his choice—well, Janine Wright was right at the top of the list.

But as they opened Wright's office door and parted the crowd of cops bunched around the desk, R.J. quickly saw that his bad luck was holding. It wasn't Janine Wright.

It was Trevor, the sequel's director, the mean-faced little elf with the Limey accent.

He was lying on his back in the middle of the huge desk. He had a ball point pen rammed into each ear and each eye socket. A letter opener stuck out of his throat. One of those old-fashioned memo spikes was shoved into his chest.

The man's pants were missing. He lay there in florid boxer shorts, his hairy pink knees accenting the argyle socks pulled up so high.

A trail of blood led down the front of the desk and over to a pool on the floor.

And the oddest touch of all was that the desk was perfectly neat—except for the small corpse in the middle. The memos and printouts were still neatly stacked, the potted plants were undisturbed, the pencil jar was upright—although it was mostly empty now, its job of holding pens upright taken over by the elfin dead man.

The blood was still dripping down the front of the desk. It wasn't pretty and it wasn't funny, but it made R.J. wonder at the killer's weird sense of humor. He went over to where Portillo was talking to the technicians.

"Where's the note?" he asked when Portillo glanced up at him.

"So far there is none," Portillo said.

"So far . . . ?"

Portillo nodded. "Yes. I am thinking the same thing. Every time but this one the killer has made sure we have the note before we discover the body. This time, no note. Why?"

R.J. rubbed his chin. "Either the note is delayed— Or he didn't write one—"

Portillo smiled, a savage show of teeth. "Or he wrote the wrong one, *hijo.*"

"Excuse me?"

"The body is here, in Janine Wright's office. So let us say our note writer comes to kill Janine Wright, with a note prepared bragging about killing her."

"But Wright isn't here and this guy is. So the killer says what the hell, whacks this guy instead."

Portillo nodded. "Yes. Which means a couple of things, R.J. First, he's extremely confident—"

"Which we already knew."

"I suppose, yes."

"More important, Uncle Hank, it means he's wrapping up. He's ready to hit Janine Wright." R.J. returned the older man's version of a savage grin. "And that means we've got him."

There was a small clatter of footsteps and anxious voices behind them and they both turned.

Janine Wright was coming in, with Captain Davis hovering anxiously at her elbow.

"I promise you, Ms. Wright," the captain was saying. "Every resource of the department will be devoted to catching this sick individual. I will take personal responsibility and leave no stone unturned—"

"Cut the crap, Davis," Janine Wright said.

Davis stopped dead and R.J. thought he could see a small line of swear pop out on his forehead. "Excuse me?"

Wright turned on the captain, glaring. "First lesson of politics, Davis. Never shit a shitter." She turned away from Davis, leaving him gaping for air, and marched over to the crew from the coroner's office. "How soon can you get this garbage off my desk?" she barked.

Anybody who makes a living poking at dead bodies is likely to be hardened. The people who do it for the coroner, even more so. They pride themselves on the fact that they've seen everything, and can't be shaken. But the technician Wright barked at actually did a double take before answering.

"I would have said another fifteen minutes," the man answered. "But now I think we're going to have run a few more tests." And he gave her a polite smile and turned away.

R.J.'s attention was yanked away from that scene in mid-snicker when he suddenly heard Davis at his elbow, chewing on Portillo.

Captain Davis was not pleased. He was so unhappy that he forgot himself and let Portillo and R.J. see that he was unhappy. While it made R.J.'s day to see the big bastard squirm, it wasn't catching any killers, so the pleasure wasn't as deep as it might have been.

"I don't want to hear it," Davis said, looking like he might cry. "I want to see a killer behind bars." He glared around the room. "I at least want to know who it is."

"I'll accept your apology," R.J. said, turning to face Davis, and he got a lot of satisfaction out of seeing Davis's head swivel to face him, and the look of pure, powerless, meanness on the captain's face.

"You're not out of the woods yet, Brooks," he snarled.

"As a matter of fact, Captain, I am out of the woods. And if you don't get off my ass pronto—" R.J. leaned forward and tapped on Davis's chest to emphasize his words. "—I think you're going to find out just how good my lawyer is. Because he's going to hit you with so many law actions you're going to have to get a judge's order to take a pee."

Davis lost it. His face flushed bright red and he slammed his hands down on the desk. "All right, you smart-ass son-of-a-bitch," he hissed. "If you know so fucking much, suppose you just tell me who did it and I'll go pick him up!"

R.J. shook his head. "Can't do that. Sorry."

"Oh, you can't do that." The sarcasm was thick enough for a trowel. "You mean you haven't figured out who did it yet? Been too busy buffing your nails?"

"Sure. I know who did it," he said, and as he said it it occurred to him he *did*. Except . . . "The only problem is, he can't have done it, either."

"Why not?" Davis demanded.

R.J. sighed. "He has a perfect alibi," he said.

"I can crack any alibi I ever heard," Davis said.

"Not this one," R.J. told him. "The man is dead."

Davis just stared at him for a good long minute. Then he hissed out his breath and rolled his shoulders. R.J. could hear the knotted muscles cracking. He took a step toward R.J. and R.J. felt Portillo's hand on his elbow.

"Let's go, R.J.," Portillo said softly. "The captain has enough troubles right now."

R.J. stared at Davis for just a second longer, then let himself be dragged away.

Portillo walked R.J. down to the parking lot. "That's a very good alibi, R.J.," he said as they approached his car. "Unless you were just yanking the captain's chain."

"Wish I was, Uncle Hank."

Portillo nodded, opening his car door. "Dead men very rarely commit multiple murders."

R.J. sighed. "Yeah. Thing is, nobody else could possibly have done it."

They looked at each other across the blue roof of the car for a moment.

"Tell me," Portillo said.

CHAPTER 33

Casey was too busy to see him. She was on several long-distance lines at the same time, scrambling to bring in a new director to take over the picture.

R.J. sat in a small waiting area, next to a framed art gallery poster and a small end table stacked with old film industry magazines.

A few feet away stood a water cooler. It gurgled every time somebody walked past. After sitting for an hour and a half, R.J. was ready to gurgle himself.

He was trying to stay cool and understanding. He was working hard at respecting the fact that Casey was at work and had a job to do. He was also just about to go ballistic.

The new murder and his talk with Portillo had left him with a sense of urgency, and sitting here like some kid trying to pitch a screenplay to an important film producer was eating away at his nerves.

The killer had been using R.J. as a screen. Portillo had agreed that there was no doubt about it. All along, wherever

R.J. went, the killer had followed, building a mocking frame-up, leading on the cops, making them believe R.J. was guilty. Whatever his reasons, whether he had some secret grudge against R.J. or was just indulging his twisted sense of humor, the killer had been trying to stick it all on R.J.

That was over. The killer had slipped, and R.J. was in the clear. Portillo and R.J. were both sure that meant the killer was about to make a final run for his twisted goal line.

Before he did that, R.J. had to stop him. And before he could do *that*, he had to either put this stupid idea to rest or prove that dead men really do commit multiple murders.

And that meant leaving Casey in the line of fire one more time.

He couldn't do that, not without talking to her first. He had to make her see that her danger was real, that she had to take it seriously. And he had to make her see, too, that he was on her side, trying to understand what she wanted and support her in it.

But the longer he sat on the hideous molded-plastic-and-steel-frame chair with the secretaries smirking at him, the more his temper chewed up all the pretty things he wanted to say.

He had thought about simply pushing his way past the willowy USC boy Casey had guarding her door. The kid crouched behind a desk the size of a small car with a haircut that showed most of his skull and hid his eyes.

R.J. was pretty sure he could fold the kid up and stuff him in the trash can without wrinkling his suit coat. And he wanted to do just that, wanted it so badly his teeth hurt. Just put the kid in a drawer of that desk, slide into Casey's office, and un-plug her phone. Make her talk to him.

He was also sure that if he did that, it would be the last con-versation she ever had with him.

He sighed heavily and picked up a glossy year-old maga-zine. He tried to pretend for the fourth time that he really cared about one of last summer's sure-fire box-office hits that had never made it. He'd never heard of the movie, nor of its star.

He put the magazine down and picked up another. There was an article there he'd only skimmed twice, about why screenwriters never get the respect they deserve. It was written by a screenwriter. There were four mistakes in grammar in the opening paragraph.

He had just gotten to a carefully reasoned argument that screenwriters were more important than directors so they should get more money, when a cloud resembling some kind of fruit tree smell wrapped around him. He looked up.

The USC kid was standing there, probably looking at him from underneath all the hair. "She'll see you," he said.

R.J. stood. "Swish me in there," he said.

The kid stood his ground. "I know martial arts," he said.

"I don't care if you know Marshal Tito. Fly me in there, Tinkerbell."

For a minute the kid thought he was going to say something else. Then he changed his mind. He whipped away, his bangs flopping, and R.J. followed the gleaming, shaved back of his head a few feet down the hall and into Casey's office.

"Thanks, Bryan," Casey said, dismissing him. R.J. felt his head clouding over at the sound of her voice and he barely noticed Bryan leave. "Hello, R.J.," she said. "Quit gaping and sit down."

"Was I gaping?" he asked, swinging into a chair that made his back ache just to look at it. "I guess I wanted to remember you the way you were."

She tapped her fingers on the desk. "I don't have a lot of time," she said.

"No, you don't. So far everybody else close to Janine Wright is dead. It's a safe bet that you're in the line of fire."

She stared at him, then sighed. "You don't give up, do you?"

"It may be my only virtue," he said.

"So what am I supposed to do, R.J.? Lock myself in a bank

vault?" She shook her head. "I have a job to do. You may not approve of my job, and it may not be that important in the big picture but it's what I do, and I'm going to do it."

"Casey—"

"No, R.J., listen for a moment. Just listen."

He closed his mouth and took a deep breath. He looked across the desk at her. For the first time since she'd come out here she didn't look like she was hyperventilating. She was calm, centered, rational—she looked like Casey again. The sight made his heart hammer.

"I'm listening," he said with a tongue that was suddenly too thick.

"R.J., I'm sorry we blew up like that at lunch the other day. I think we both assumed some things we maybe shouldn't have."

He blinked. "Well, that's—"

She held up a hand to cut him off. "Let me finish. I appreciate your concern for my safety. I believe you when you say I may be in danger. But if I let this killer tell me what to do, I'm just giving in and letting a bully push me around. I won't do that."

"Casey," he said.

"No. I'll be careful, R.J., but I won't hide. And I can't have you following me around all day."

"I know that," he said. "But I can't let anything happen to you."

She shook her head. There was a slight smile on her face, but he couldn't tell what it meant. "That's not your job," she said.

"Yeah, it is. It's the only really important job I've got."

Her lips twitched, and now he could tell. It was a real smile. Not a big one, but the first she'd given him in a long time. "In that case," she said, "you need a life, sport."

"Look who's talking. Miss Power-Suit Executive."

"That's *Ms.* Power-Suit to you, ace."

"Yeah. Well— Maybe we both need a life."

"Uh-huh." And there was something hanging there in the air between them. R.J. couldn't tell what it was, but for a second it felt like the distance between them was shrinking and they were sort of sliding together without moving; then her telephone chirped and the thing between them, whatever it was, was gone.

Casey jerked up the phone. "I said no calls, Bryan."

R.J. could hear Bryan belting out some sad song through his nose. The kid's voice came through the receiver and through the wall at the same time, and he was obviously pretty worked up about something.

"Oh," Casey said. She sighed, raised an eyebrow at R.J., and shrugged. "All right. Patch him through."

She covered the phone with her hand. "I really am sorry, R.J. But I have to take this call."

He stood up. "Henry Portillo will have a couple of guys around. They won't be too obvious. But if they tell you to duck or run for it, do what they tell you."

"I will," she said.

He took a deep breath, looking at her sitting there. She was so beautiful, so composed. "And Casey—" he said.

But she was already gone. "Hello, Marvin," she was saying into the phone, diving back into her crisis.

He couldn't even remember what it was he had meant to say. He looked at her for a few more seconds. Then he turned and walked out.

CHAPTER **34**

He was on a plane again. It made him feel like he was stuck in some kind of weird dream where you try to fit things together and make them mean something, but you never quite manage. Besides, R.J. was wide awake. He was sure of that. Could tell by the pain in his back from the airline seat and the greasy rumble in his belly from the awful "snack." At least they didn't have the gall to call it a meal.

It seemed to R.J. that he had spent most of the last few years of his life on an airplane, slumping between coasts in increasing misery. And here he was again, headed back for New York, probably on a wild goose chase.

And probably this wild goose really was dead. All the experts agreed. Couldn't be anything else. Certified, identified and buried. The cops said it was him, the coroner said he was dead, and R.J. had been at his funeral.

So who the hell was he to buck the experts?

He had started this whole mess with one good suspect, and the idea that he would protect Casey and catch the killer. But he'd been spending all his time keeping the police off his ass and Casey didn't want his protection.

R.J. ground his teeth. He was beginning to hope it really was a dream. He was running as fast as he could, and still somehow sliding backward. Maybe he would wake up in his own bed, with Casey next to him, and go to work on some nice, simple multiple adultery. Something straightforward, obvious. Something he could take a picture of and then send somebody a bill.

Instead of this mess. Instead of Hollywood, and bad movies, and his parents' ghosts, and bad cops on both coasts. Instead of losing Casey to the nightmare factory.

Casey. Jesus Christ. Like this whole mess wasn't bad enough. Why did it always turn out that anything you were sure of bit you on the ass? The simple things always ended up being the most complicated. She was at least speaking to him again, but was that good or bad? What the hell did any of it mean? What the hell did she want from him? For that matter, what the hell did he want from her?

Well, whatever it was it could wait. It would have to wait. Because the killer wouldn't.

R.J. didn't manage to fall asleep on this flight. For once there was no kid barfing and squalling next to him, no fat hostile businessman kicking his seat. The plane landed only forty minutes late. Pretty good for the way these things went nowadays.

It was a clear evening in New York. It was still cold enough to make the city seem clean and R.J. caught a cab after only twenty minutes of watching his breath at the curb.

Ilsa pretended she was glad to see him until R.J. got food into her bowl, and then she ignored him completely. For himself R.J. made a frozen dinner that was only a little better than what they'd fed him on the plane. Then he called a rental place and reserved a car for the morning, took a long hot shower, and went to bed.

There was a state trooper barracks only a few miles outside Torrington. They weren't exactly happy to see him, but at least they weren't trying to frame him for murder and throw him in jail.

They made him wait an awfully long time, but R.J. didn't mind. That was just standard cop behavior. Besides, it gave him time to work through the *Times* crossword puzzle. When he was done with that he whipped through one in the local paper that somebody had left on a scarred end table in the waiting area. Then he read the sports, comics, and obits.

After almost two and a half hours there was a scuffle of feet and R.J. looked up. A big guy with a light-colored crewcut and a scar down one side of his face was looking down at him. His face was closed tight in that permanently neutral look the good cops get.

"Mr. Brooks?" the big guy rumbled.

"That's me."

The cop nodded. "Captain Schmidt. Come with me, please?"

R.J. followed Schmidt down a short hall to a small office at the back of the building.

"Have a seat, Mr. Brooks," the captain said, sliding his own large frame in behind the desk, very gracefully for a guy who had to be at least six-foot-four. "Now, what's this all about?"

R.J. took his license and a business card from his wallet and set them on the desk. Schmidt glanced at them and then fastened his eyes back on R.J.

"My client is the daughter of William Kelley. He was killed here recently. Car accident." Schmidt just nodded. "Captain," R.J. said, playing it the way he had decided might make sense and might even get some cooperation, "she hadn't seen her old man since she was just a kid. I located him a few days before he died, and he was dead before she could see him." He shrugged. "That's hard on a kid."

"Yes, it must be," Schmidt said, still neutral and patient. R.J. got the idea that it might take heavy earth-moving equipment to get any expression onto Schmidt's face.

"Captain, I'm sorry to bother you with this, but I hope you'll understand. She wants me to check into her father's death, make sure it really was an accident, and that everything is entirely kosher." He held up a hand, anticipating a protest from Schmidt that never came. "I'm sure it is—no reflection on anybody over here—she just asked me to look and be sure."

Schmidt still didn't say anything. He didn't even blink. R.J. had been sure he would have something to say, something defensive or derogatory. Cops hate to have anybody check up on them, and if it's a private investigator that's only one small step better than having Feds around.

But Captain Schmidt didn't look like he hated anything. Didn't look like he could. Just sat and stared at R.J. for a full two minutes while R.J. tried not to squirm, feeling like a kid sent to the principal's office for spitballing the teacher.

But R.J. managed to sit and not break into nervous giggles while Schmidt looked at him. Finally, just when R.J. was sure he had to say something, anything, to break that awful silence, Schmidt spoke.

"Bullshit," he said. His expression didn't change a bit.

"Excuse me, Captain?"

"I said 'bullshit,' Mr. Brooks."

"Oh," R.J. said, trying to recover, and finally giving up. "Why did you say 'bullshit,' Captain?"

"Because that's what you're feeding me," he said, and he went back to staring without moving.

R.J. took a deep breath, let it out, took another. "Captain—"

But Schmidt shook his head again. R.J. closed his mouth, shrugged, and thought, *Oh, what the hell* . . . "All right, hell," he said, "I think the guy might be alive. I'm sorry. I feel stupid about it. I know it's not possible. I know your men wouldn't have ID'd the body as Kelley unless they were sure it was him. But a whole lot of things I can't explain would start to make sense if he was alive somehow."

Captain Schmidt leaned back in his chair. His face still hadn't moved, but he looked a little more human. "Let's hear it," he said.

R.J. filled him in, giving him both barrels for fifteen minutes. When he was done, he thought it sounded pretty lame. But Schmidt's expression didn't change and R.J. couldn't make out what he might have thought of the whole thing.

Schmidt stared at him for another twenty seconds. Then he leaned forward and picked up the phone on his desk. "We had an automobile fatality last month. Last name Kelley, first name William. Bring me the file," he said, and hung up.

CHAPTER **35**

The Farmington River ran close to Torrington, close enough that William Kelley could burn up beside it without violating his parole.

Close to where R.J. stood, the river was relatively deep and wide. It bent through a stretch of countryside and a grassy bank came up to meet the road. There was no guard rail. Really didn't seem much need for one, with that slow, gentle slope down to the water from the road.

R.J. walked down from the road to a small stand of oaks and squinted back up. A young trooper named Bentt leaned against the car, his campaign hat tilted to keep the sun from his eyes. Schmidt had sent him with R.J. on the theory that, if anything came up, Schmidt wanted to hear it firsthand, fast.

R.J. had developed a respect for the captain. He seemed like a pretty good cop. In any case, R.J. wouldn't make the mistake of trying to con him again.

Bentt didn't seem too pleased with the whole thing. Kelley's death had been one of his first fatalities and he hated like hell the idea that anything might be wrong with his report. He wasn't actually sullen, but he wasn't anybody's idea of Officer Friendly, either.

The wreck had been hauled away already, but it was easy enough to see where it had happened. The tree that Kelley had hit was not going to make any more acorns. It was split and blackened. The grass around it was torn and burned. Other than that, there wasn't much to see.

R.J. walked back up to the car, where Bentt was trying to pretend he didn't care.

"Seen enough?" the young officer asked.

"How did it happen?"

Bentt stood straight. "Come here." He led R.J. over to the edge of the road about twenty yards behind where they had parked. "Here," he said, pointing down. "You can still see it."

R.J. looked where the young trooper was pointing. There was a set of skid marks on the pavement. "He lost control here?" R.J. asked.

Bentt looked pleased with himself for the first time. "No. That would be a different pattern, with the weight on the outside of the tire. From fishtailing. This," he said, squatting and pointing at the rubber marks, "shows the weight at the front. So he was braking."

"Braking? In the middle of the road, at high speed?"

"That's right."

"So something ran in front of the car, like a raccoon."

Bentt stood. "Something larger than a raccoon, Mr. Brooks." Bentt stepped out into the road and pointed. "Look at this one."

R.J. looked for traffic and saw none. He went to Bentt and, looking down, saw another tire track. It was fainter and seemed smaller, but there was no doubt about it. "Son of a bitch. What is it?"

Now Bentt looked positively smug. "Motorcycle. Big one. Probably a Harley, from the tread pattern." He walked back to the side of the road and R.J. followed. "The way I figured it, Kelley swerved to miss the bike, lost control, and hit the tree."

"You guys are pretty good," R.J. admitted. Bentt shrugged, but he was pretty happy with himself. "What was the bike doing at the time?"

Bentt smiled. "Fishtailing."

"Because the weight is on the outside of the skid mark."

"That's right."

"I don't suppose you had any luck finding the biker?"

Bentt looked scornful. "These guys ride the big ones around, they don't give a shit. Maybe he knows Kelley went off the road and died behind him, maybe he doesn't know. But he doesn't care, I guarantee you that. And he'll never tell us anything. Anyway, the most we could charge him with would be a traffic violation, which wouldn't stick."

"So you didn't look for him?"

Bentt stood almost at attention. He quivered a little, like he was fighting down the urge to take a swing. "Mr. Brooks. This was not one of your big-ticket homicides. It was a traffic accident."

Which meant that, as long as everything fit a certain pattern, and no powerfully connected citizens were expressing outrage over the death, there just wasn't enough manpower and overtime pay available to investigate this thoroughly.

R.J. nodded. It was the same everywhere. Cops see the same two or three crimes over and over, and they see a lot of them. So if one particular death looks like all the others, they're not going to bust their humps trying to prove it's something else. A case solved means there's time to solve another one.

And this one really seemed to fit the pattern. Kelley hits a tree, the car blows up and burns, he's dead. All one hundred percent normal. Except—

"How did you ID the body?"

Bentt twitched again, but he smiled this time. "There was only one body, Mr. Brooks. No big deal to ID it. It was in Kelley's car, carrying Kelley's ID, wearing Kelley's ring." He turned and started walking back toward the car. "There wasn't enough fingerprint left on the body to check, and I would have had a hell of a time getting DNA-testing approved."

R.J. followed the trooper, listening to a delicate little alarm bell ringing deep in his brain. "Just a second," he called after Bentt, and the trooper turned. "What was that about a ring?"

Bentt shrugged. "He was wearing a big gold ring on his right hand. Pretty distinctive, a skull with one small ruby for the eye."

"How do you know it was his ring?"

"We didn't guess. We're not Manhattan homicide up here, just some hick cops in the woods, but we try to be thorough."

"Yeah, I know. Sherlock Holmes with cows. What about the ring?"

Bentt gave R.J. a hard look for a moment, like he was trying to decide whether to be offended about the Sherlock Holmes crack. But he decided to let it go. "His pal identified it. Ring like that, very distinctive, there was no doubt about it."

"So you had his pal in to ID the body."

"There wasn't a lot of body left. It burned up, mostly. That's what I'm trying to tell you. His pal ID'd the effects."

"Was his pal's name Pauly Aponti?"

Bentt blinked. He looked uncertain for the first time. "That's right. Ex-cons don't have a lot of friends, except other ex-cons."

R.J. turned away and walked back down the bank to where the car had burned. What he had wasn't even an idea yet. There weren't enough details to call it that. But it was a lot stronger than a hunch.

His earlier doubts about Pauly began to bubble. If Pauly was in on framing R.J. with the envelope, the one with R.J.'s fingerprints, then he knew Kelley was alive. Which meant he was in on it, part of it somehow. How wasn't important, not right now.

What was important was that it was Pauly who had given

a positive identification of the body. And *that* means that it could be anybody in that coffin. It could even be William Kelley— But R.J. was more certain all the time that it was not.

So all right: Say it wasn't Kelley in the box. Then who was it? It was possible that Kelley and Pauly had gotten their hands on a generic body somewhere, but not too likely. Dead bodies are funny things; there's usually somebody keeping track of them. Somebody who notices when they disappear.

But the cops had pulled *somebody* from the wreck. Somebody with a gold skull ring. Somebody who had just happened to be here and Kelley had killed him? Or maybe somebody who wouldn't be badly missed, who had conveniently died on the spot?

Somebody like an outlaw biker . . . ?

R.J. turned to look at the river. A cold wind was whipping across it, slicing through his coat like it wasn't there. He tried to think like William Kelley. From the beginning the one thing that had bothered him was that, from the little he knew about Kelley, he didn't seem like a killer. It was hard to think that he was one, even now. But if it was the biker in the coffin, Kelley must have killed him.

Prison warps people. It had to have been hard on a gentle, educated guy, which Kelley was supposed to have been. He wouldn't want to go back.

Had it warped him enough that he would kill a stranger? A guy just riding past on a Harley?

People don't generally kill strangers. They kill their husbands, wives, sweethearts, parents, brothers, sisters, uncles, and aunts, not strangers.

But the biker was dead, had to be dead.

Wait a second, sport, R.J. told himself. Back up half a step. What if Kelley hit the biker accidentally, and the biker died? Kelley's on parole, the accident is his fault. All he can think is, if he calls the cops, he goes back to prison. He panics—he won't go back to Somers, no matter what.

So he puts the biker in his own car, runs it into the tree, torches it—

—And what? Walks away thinking he's free? And maybe a little unhinged from what he's done, figures he'll go for the whole salami? Starts stalking his ex-wife, the woman who put him in prison?

R.J. shook his head. It was a lot to hang on a bunch of guesses. He needed proof, something tangible, and there was only one way he was going to get it.

And he could just hear what Captain Schmidt was going to say about it.

CHAPTER 36

"S orry, Mr. Brooks. I need some proof."

"Captain, I'd love to oblige you," R.J. said, "but unless you'll drag the river there won't be any proof."

"What makes you so sure there's a motorcycle in the river?"

R.J. leaned forward. "There has to be. It's how the whole thing fits together."

Captain Schmidt frowned. "You think Kelley faked his death by putting the biker's body into the car with his own ID."

"That's right."

"And then he rolled the Harley into the river to hide the evidence, torched the car, and walked away. And had his former cell mate, Aponti, identify the effects."

"And when everybody thinks he's dead, he's free to kill off everybody connected to this sequel, and eventually his ex-wife."

"What's he got against this movie she's trying to make?"

R.J. shrugged. "Probably nothing. I think that's a smoke screen. His ex-wife is the target. She's vulnerable right now, overextended financially. If Kelley can stop the sequel, he stops her career. That's the only thing that might hurt her."

"So she suffers before he kills her."

"That's how I see it, Captain."

Schmidt's eyes hadn't moved off R.J.'s face the whole time. They didn't now, either. "Even if you're right, it's not exactly my problem."

"It's multiple murder, Captain. Four bodies so far. And he's not done yet."

Schmidt drummed his fingers on the desktop. He did it very lightly, but it was the first sign R.J. had seen that he actually had nerves. "Mr. Brooks. I think we have been pretty cooperative up until now."

"Very cooperative, Captain, and I appreciate it, but—"

"But there comes a point in time when asking for cooperation steps over the line and turns into being a pain in the ass." He pointed a huge, hard finger at R.J.'s nose. "You are standing on that line now, Mr. Brooks."

R.J. sighed. He had known this wasn't going to be easy. It was a hell of a thing to be right about. He'd take being wrong any day. "Captain, I admit it's a long shot. I'm telling you it is, so you know I'm leveling with you. But I'll bet my molars there's a motorcycle in the water there. And if there is, I've got proof of who's killing off half of Hollywood."

Schmidt shook his head and turned around in his swivel chair. He sat there facing the back wall for a minute. "I'm sorry," he finally said. "But I can't always do what I would like to do."

"Captain—" R.J. said wearily.

"I have to think about other factors. And dragging the river is going to cost me a full shift for five or six troopers." He turned back around to face R.J. "I can't justify it, and I can't fit it into the budget."

"I know I'm right about this," R.J. said.

Schmidt looked at him hard for a moment. "Are you willing to bet a little sweat on it?"

"Hell, yes," R.J. blurted without thinking.

And that's how R.J. found himself standing on the bank of the river the next morning, with a grappling hook on the end of a long line. A grappling hook provided by Captain Schmidt, in the spirit of cooperation.

R.J.'s fingers were already numb, and his shoulder was permanently cramped into a painful knot, from swinging the hook out into the water, hauling the line back, swinging it again.

A little too eager to bet a little sweat, he thought sourly. As if he could sweat when it was forty-five degrees, standing on a river bank with the wind blowing on him. Probably another twenty degrees colder when you figure in wind chill.

And the water, running down the rope and into his sleeves. R.J. had felt ice that was warmer. He'd probably catch pneumonia. But hell, look at the bright side. That would save Kelley the trouble of killing him.

Haul in. Swing the hook. Let it fly. Shake some of the water off. Repeat the whole thing.

The bottom was soft here, muddy. Which only added to the experience, since the hook came back covered with brown goo. Which of course dripped down R.J.'s sleeve. I'm freezing to death, R.J. thought bitterly, and I won't even get a funeral. I'll stink so bad they're going to leave me here for fertilizer.

But he kept swinging the hook.

The bike couldn't be far out. There was a stretch of only fifty yards or so where it had to be. Had to be.

Didn't it?

The hook stuck. R.J. grunted, felt the excitement swirl through him. He pulled hard, steadily, leaning all his weight into it—

—and saw a tree branch break surface fifteen feet out.

Swearing, he shook the line. No good: it was stuck tight, wedged into a space between branches.

He hauled in the branch, a nice big one. *At least I'm finally getting a good sweat going*, he thought.

He cleared the branch from the grappling hook and swung the line again. *This is getting old. What if I'm wrong?*

Don't even think about that. Just swing the line, let it fly, one more time. Swish, splash, pull it in, start again. Swish, splash, one more time. Swish, splash, clank.

Clank?

R.J.'s heart thundered. This had to be it. The hook had given out a clank that was clearly the sound of metal against metal. He pulled the line tight, leaned into it—

And fell onto his ass on the muddy river bank.

He stood up, not even trying to brush off the mud, and hauled in the line, noting carefully where the hook cut through the surface of the water. He threw just beyond that same spot again.

Clank.

There it was again, the same sound, no mistaking it.

R.J. slowly, carefully pulled the line tight. When he could lean away from it a little, he gave a couple of quick pulls, like he was setting the hook in a big fish.

The hook held.

Slowly, carefully, R.J. pulled. He pulled until the line was singing with tension and the drops of water flew off the taut rope. He pulled harder, pulled until his shoulders creaked and his neck crackled, until finally his foot slipped in the muck and he lay sprawled on the gooey bank again, sweating and swearing.

How much did a big motorcycle weigh?

More than R.J., that was clear. He couldn't budge the damned thing. That is, *if* the damned thing on the end of his grappling line was a big motorcycle. Or *the* big motorcycle.

So now what? If he let the tension off the line, he might lose the bike—if it was the bike. But he couldn't move it and he couldn't stand here forever.

R.J. glanced up the bank. His rental Buick was parked up on the shoulder, about two hundred feet away. He had about twenty-five feet of slack. He might as well have parked in California.

He looked around. The tree branch he had hauled out was lying on the bank about ten feet away. R.J. stepped over to it. The branch was just big enough to keep the line taut. He tied a clumsy bowline knot around the branch. He hadn't tied one for twenty-some years, since he was a Boy Scout. They had always told him that knowing knots would come in handy when he grew up. They just hadn't said how.

R.J. hurried up to the car, not really trusting his knot. He started the car and moved it gingerly down the bank. Up close to the road the earth was packed down, firm, and he had no trouble until he got closer to the river. There had already been one or two warmer spells and snow had melted and poured down to the river. Down there the ground was mushy from the run-off.

But R.J. found a patch of solid ground within reach of the rope. That was the important thing. He backed the car as close to the branch as he could get it safely, then spent a couple of bad minutes trying to untie his bowline without letting tension off the line.

His fingers were numb, stiff, and clumsy, and the rope was just as stiff. But he finally undid it and got a loop around the bumper, pulled it tight, and then, thinking what the hell, he tied another bowline.

He got back behind the wheel and just sat for a moment, turning the heater up to full blast and letting it blow onto his hands. He flexed the fingers, getting the feeling back into them.

Then he stuck his left hand on the wheel and turned in the seat to watch behind him. He put the car in gear and stepped down on the gas, giving it slow and steady pressure and watching the line. He knew the rope wouldn't break—it was half-inch nylon—but he wasn't so sure about his knot.

R.J. held his breath as the car eased forward a few inches. Something heaved under the surface of the river as the water churned and turned even darker. R.J. thought he saw a metallic flash, but it might have been just a reflection off the water.

Then the car's tires hit a slick spot and began to spin. The rope slackened a little. R.J. tried rocking the car, tapping the pedal in short bursts, but quickly gave it up when he saw that he wasn't going anywhere.

R.J. pushed the gear lever into Park and got out.

He grabbed up the dead branch he had hauled out and wedged it under the drive wheel. The branch was sure turning out to be handy. I should carry one with me from now on, he thought.

Back behind the wheel he gave the gas slow, steady pressure. The car moved forward over the slick spot. The tires kept gripping and he inched forward.

Now he was sure. It was no reflection from the water. He had hooked something shiny.

He moved forward slowly, steadily, until the something hit the shallows and broke water. Then it lurched and bumped up onto the bank and lay there while R.J. got out and went down to look at it.

It was a Harley-Davidson motorcycle.

Big one.

CHAPTER 37

The bike is registered to a member of the Devil Hoggs Motorcycle Club. His name is Burton Weisbrod," Trooper Bentt told R.J. "But nobody really knows that. They call him Jingo."

Bentt threw a folder on the desk of Schmidt's office. "His common-law wife reported him missing last week. She thought he was skipping out on child support."

"He is," R.J. said. "The hard way."

"I've talked to a judge," Captain Schmidt said, still without showing any emotion. "He's giving me a court order for an exhumation of the body of William Kelley." He nodded one time, at R.J. or at the folder. Maybe both. "I think we'll find it's Weisbrod."

"You're a good cop, Captain," R.J. said. "Think you can work a transfer to Manhattan Homicide?"

Schmidt shook his head and looked up at Brent. "Nope," he said. "I like the cows."

By the time R.J. got back to the city it was dark.

He turned in his rental car and took the opportunity to

walk the mile or so back to his apartment. New York was his city and he had missed it.

There were still crowds pushing through the streets. Going to dinner, or coming back from dinner. Trying to get in a few last-minute deals. Scrambling for a buck, hurrying to meet somebody. Hustling one last victory, for love or money, wrestling satisfaction from the city.

There was always an incredible energy in the city. Not in the California sense of *aura*, but real, literal energy. It made you feel clearheaded and tireless.

Just being here made R.J. walk faster, think harder, work a little quicker. It was why he had moved here and made it his home so many years ago. The way it made the blood pound through his veins— The first time he felt it, he couldn't believe he'd lived so long without that feeling. It was like realizing he'd been only half alive all those years.

Something emanated from the pavement, made everybody move a little faster. And in spring it got stronger, as if the melting slush was letting it out after five months of cold storage.

You almost didn't need to sleep if you lived in Manhattan.

R.J. didn't want to think about going back to California. It was like being forced to take a nap when you really wanted to play baseball.

But he was going back, he knew that. He had to stop Kelley. He didn't want to; Janine Wright had it coming, if anybody did. She'd taken away R.J.'s past with the sequel, and his future with Casey.

Whatever future that might be. He hadn't had time to think about what was going on between them, and he still didn't. But now, working his way along the Manhattan sidewalk, he wondered what he would do if he had to choose between Casey and New York.

It could happen. Whatever happened with the sequel, Casey had sipped from the big bottle of show biz. It was an addictive brew, R.J. knew. She might not want to come home.

She might decide to make her career there, in Hollywood, in a place and an occupation R.J. had left behind him forever. He'd had to leave it behind, or he knew he'd turn into something he wouldn't want to share a bus ride with.

So what if she stayed? What then? Could he tell her so long? No hard feelings? It's been swell, drop me a line sometime?

Could he say good-bye to her?

Could he say it to New York?

He didn't want to choose, wasn't sure he could. But it seemed like that was the way things generally shaped up. A month ago he'd been riding high and now—

A half second before the guy bumped into him R.J. noticed the smell. It was a cross between patchouli oil and a bus station urinal.

Then he was grunting from the impact of a shoulder in his chest and an elbow in his gut.

When he straightened up, he found an intense-looking bearded guy with matted hair, staring him down with hard, bright eyes. He was crusted over with dirt and something else that made the dirt look clean and wholesome. He looked like a walking scab.

"Now I've got your attention," the guy said, "are you ready to hear the word?" And he held up a Bible almost as crusty as he was.

"I've heard the word," R.J. said. "It's *syzygy.*"

The scab shook his head. A small clot of something fell off his head and onto his shoulder. It moved.

"Don't fight it," he said. "Open yourself and be free."

"I can't open yet," R.J. told him. "I'm still remodeling," R.J. pushed on past, shaking his head.

The guy started preaching anyway, and his voice followed R.J. for two blocks, rising and falling and flailing at the ears of all the people on the sidewalk. The people just shrugged him off, one or two nudging him a little harder than usual as they passed.

R.J. grinned and shook his head. For a moment or two he forgot all about Kelley and Casey and California, swept away again by another of those little surprises the city always threw at you.

How could he leave this place?

How could he go back to California, to that desert where nothing could live or grow?

He wasn't sure he could do it. He was like a junkie, and without the rush he got from Manhattan—

And Casey? Was it worth living here without her? She'd become part of what he loved about his city. In some ways, she represented the spirit of New York to R.J. Beautiful and classy and at the same time, kick-you-in-the-balls tough.

And if she stayed out there long enough, that would be gone, too. She would become somebody else. Somebody who made deals on a cellular phone from the driver's seat of a convertible.

That wasn't the Casey he knew. She didn't belong there, and neither did he.

Anyway, he had to go back, for a little while. He just wasn't going back alone.

Ilsa was glad to see him again. Or she said she was, until R.J. got a bowl of food down onto the floor for her. Then she let him know that she was deeply disappointed in his recent lack of character.

His apartment felt strangely dead after the cold of that Connecticut river bank and the hustling crowd in the street. He sat on the sofa for a second, just trying to collect himself. Then he picked up the phone and dialed.

"Hello, Bob," he said to the quietly hostile voice that answered. "I need to talk to Mary."

R.J. could hear the breath hiss out of Roberta. She didn't say anything, just hissed. But she put the phone down extra-hard and R.J. had to rub his ear to get the feeling back into it.

R.J. heard footsteps retreating, mumbling, then faster, lighter feet returning. In a moment Mary picked up.

"Hello? R.J.? Is it really you?" She sounded breathless. Maybe weary and older, too, but like she had hurried when she found out it was him.

"It's me," he said. "I need to talk to you."

"Is it—anything about mother?"

"No. But it's something I'd rather tell you to your face."

"Oh—I could meet you somewhere." She lowered her voice to something just above a whisper. "Roberta doesn't want you here."

"That's one of the things I want to talk to you about," R.J. said. "Have you eaten yet?"

CHAPTER 38

He met her at Ferrini's. He had started to think of it as *their* place, and anyway the kid knew where it was. Besides, there was no place like it in Los Angeles, and he was on his way back there, all too soon.

It was night, so Ferrini himself was at the door. He didn't sing arias when he saw them; after all, he was the owner, and he had a big mustache whose dignity he had to protect.

But he did give R.J. a small bow and a slight smile of recognition, and he led them himself to a good table.

R.J. let Ferrini seat Mary, using the time to study her. She still looked better than any other woman in the place, R.J. thought. But she had lost some weight, and she couldn't really afford to. There were bags under her eyes that her clumsy makeup couldn't hide. Even her hair was slightly off. It looked a little bit like a wig that didn't quite fit and wasn't properly cared for.

Mary glanced up and caught him staring. She blushed; even in the dim light R.J. could see the flush spread over her face.

He smiled. "You look good, kid," he told her.

She shook her head with a small, tight movement. "No, I don't. I look awful. But that's—" She fluttered a hand at him. "I feel like . . . I don't know. The walls close in on me in Roberta's apartment, but I can't do anything about it. I just sit there with the TV on, but I don't—I can't concentrate on anything and— Just . . . trapped."

"You need to get out of there. Get yourself to some place else, do something to get back together again."

"I don't— How? What?"

R.J. reached across the table and patted her hand. "I know it seems like you can't move or do anything. But you can. And when you do, you'll find that things will start to shape up again." He looked at her carefully before he went on. She seemed to be a little better. "I want you to come to California with me."

She jerked upright, nearly spilling her water glass. "That's— What do you mean? Back to mother?"

"No. Relax, I'm not shilling for your mother. You can stay as far away from her as you want. In fact, I recommend it. But something's come up and I want you there for it. I may need you there."

"What's come up? I can't— What kind of thing could I possibly help with?"

"I think your father's alive, Mary."

Mary blinked at him once. Then she fell out of her chair in a dead faint and hit the floor with a soft thump.

When a pretty girl faints in an Italian restaurant, the result is somewhere between a soap opera and a circus. For the next few minutes R.J. watched as everyone, from Ferrini himself to the cook on down to the busboy, raced around, calling out loudly and bringing dozens of glasses of water, cool wet cloths, small beakers of *grappa*—they even found some smelling salts somewhere.

And they all managed to find a moment to glare at R.J. with strong disapproval. After all, he must have done *something* to the poor girl.

In fact, the busboy, who was young and not too sophisti-
cated, mumbled, *"Bruto,"* as he cleared away the spilled water
glass.

R.J. took it all without worrying too much, once he was
sure that the kid was okay. He would find a quiet moment
someday soon and ask Angelo Bertelli to explain to Ferrini
what had happened. It would probably be good for a free glass
of wine next time he came in. Which he wouldn't drink. But
what the hell.

Either it wasn't much of a faint or Mary was a lot more re-
silient than any other fainter R.J. had ever seen. It was only ten
minutes later that she was propped up in her chair, sipping a
glass of *agua minerale.* She was still as pale as you can get unless you're in a vampire movie, but she was coping.

"All right," she said at last, taking in a big breath and closing her eyes for a second. "What's this about my father?"

R.J. looked at her carefully before speaking.

She shook her head slightly, just enough to toss back a small
wing of hair that had fallen across her face. "Relax," she said,
with a trace of her old toughness, "I'm not going to pull another flop on you."

"That's good," R.J. said. "From the looks I've been getting,
I'd say the staff here will put me under the end zone at the
Meadowlands if I make you faint again."

"My father," she said. "You said you think he might be . . .
alive?"

"Yeah. That's right. I could be wrong."

"But why do you think he is alive?"

She was starting to breathe a little too fast again and R.J.
put his hand across the table and grabbed her wrist. "Listen,"
he said. "This isn't all good news. In some ways it would be
better if all this was over and he was really dead."

She pulled her hand away and shook her head. "Dead is
never better," she said.

"Sure it is," he said. "If you want to remember a father who
was a sweet and caring man, an innocent victim of your awful

mother. Because if he's alive, he's a killer. A bad one. And he's getting ready to kill again."

"That doesn't matter. He's my father. If he's alive, I just want to see him."

R.J. looked at her across the table. Even in the dim light of the restaurant he could see something in her face he hadn't seen before. It was a look that said, as long as I get what I want, I don't care how high the bodies stack up. It was exactly the same thing he'd seen in her mother, Janine Wright.

He shook his head. It probably wasn't a great idea to tell her that. "All right, kid," he said instead. "But you might not like what you see."

"It doesn't matter," she repeated.

"Maybe it doesn't. How soon can you be ready to leave?"

She stood up. "I'm ready now."

CHAPTER **39**

It was just another plane ride.

R.J. had never noticed it before, but the flight attendants treated a man a lot different if he was flying with a woman. Especially if she was young and pretty. He'd probably failed to notice because he'd almost never flown with a woman before. Except Belle, years ago. And when he had been with her, nobody noticed him no matter what.

So it was different now. They still brought him the awful snack and offered to sell him earphones for the terrible movie. But the smiles were a little more mechanical. And they didn't give his seatbelt an extra tug to make sure it was snug.

And all because Mary was sitting there beside him. It was funny. Women put boundary markers out on their property to warn away other women. Even when it wasn't their property. More like planets and spheres of influence. R.J. was in Mary's orbit, and the flight attendant had to whirl away to check some other guy's seatbelt.

Not that Mary was doing anything. She sat straight up in

her chair for almost the whole flight. She would glance out the window every now and then, as if to be sure that the plane was still in the air and headed in the right direction. But that was it. She didn't eat her awful "snack." R.J. took her cookie.

She didn't talk. She didn't seem to want to do anything but get there.

In fact, for R.J. it was almost like flying alone. Except for the thing with the flight attendant.

Somewhere over the Rocky Mountains R.J. felt a soft, warm weight on his shoulder. Mary had fallen asleep. Her face had dropped down onto him. It was a pretty good face. In sleep a lot of the worry had slid off it and she looked like what she was again, a pretty kid.

R.J. had an impulse to touch that face, stroke it with his fingertips, brush away a strand of hair. But there was no strand of hair, and if he touched her face he might not stop there.

R.J. blinked. What the hell was he thinking? Was he *attracted* to this kid? Was he in male menopause, thinking about somebody young enough to be his daughter? Had his frustrations with Casey made him totally nuts?

Not that this was a bad package. Just that the idea of getting involved with anybody that age—she really was only a little older than his son, for Christ's sake!

Maybe that was it. Maybe he was just feeling a kind of fatherly affection. Sure, that was it. Probably fathers admire their daughters' legs all the time.

He realized that the last few times he had seen Mary there had been a subtle attraction working between them. He had laughed at Roberta's outburst, *Keep your hands off her,* but now he wondered. Had she seen something he hadn't? Was there something going on here? Was Mary aware of it—was she actually manipulating it? Christ, did *she* have a crush on *him?*

R.J. shook his head. This was rushing him from left field. Maybe he was losing his grip to let a thing like this surprise him. Whatever. He had more important things to worry about. When he'd quit drinking, and then quit smoking, he'd faced down temptation with a capital *T*. If he couldn't handle a kid with a crush at this stage in his life, he was hopeless.

But the rest of the trip his mind kept whirling between Casey, Mary, and Kelley. He couldn't keep them separated long enough to figure any of them out.

His arm fell asleep from the weight of Mary's head on the shoulder. He let them both sleep, and before long they were circling the airport and Mary was blinking herself awake.

Henry Portillo was waiting for them at the gate. He raised an eyebrow when he saw Mary and gave R.J. one of his significant looks.

Portillo had the idea that R.J. was some kind of smooth-talking satyr and R.J. had never been able to talk him out of it. Portillo, with his old-fashioned sense of what was proper, seemed to believe that R.J. spent all his waking hours chasing after anything in skirts.

Now, seeing R.J. arrive with a pretty young woman in tow, he simply gave a slight nod to himself as if to say, Naturally. And he gave R.J. that look.

But he was too much of a gentleman to say anything. He simply bowed an inch when he was and introduced and said, "Miss Kelley?"

Mary Kelley gave him a slight bow in return and the three of them headed down the long, bright hallway and out into the brown air of the Los Angeles afternoon.

Portillo didn't say much. He held the door for Mary and threw her suitcase into the trunk of his car, but he didn't speak until he was nosing the Chevy onto the Freeway.

"You said you had found what you were looking for, R.J.?" he finally asked.

"That's right. William Kelley is alive."

Portillo looked skeptical. "You are certain?"

R.J. shook his head. "I don't have a Polaroid of Kelley holding up today's *L.A. Times*, Uncle Hank. But I'm as sure as I can be, short of that.

"I found some proof that Kelley faked his own death. The

Connecticut troopers are getting an exhumation order to check the body. I think it's going to turn out that there's a biker named Jingo in Kelly's grave—"

"R.J.," Portillo interrupted, glancing at Mary Kelley.

"She's heard it, Uncle Hank," R.J. said.

"Even so—"

"I think you'll find she's tougher than she looks. Maybe tougher than you and me."

"Go ahead, R.J." Mary said. "I don't mind hearing it. The important thing to me is that my father might be alive. Whatever he may have done."

"See what I mean?" R.J. said.

Portillo sighed. "Go on," he said.

"Kelley killed this biker, probably by accident, and decided to use the body to fake his own death. That freed him up to get even with his ex-wife. So he had his buddy from Somers identify the body as his."

"Even if this is all true," Portillo said thoughtfully, "you are still a long way from proving that Kelley is the killer. And farther still from catching him."

R.J. grinned. "You always did look at things backward, Uncle Hank. I'm thinking that if I catch him at it, I'll know he's the killer."

Portillo snorted. "I think you have jet lag, R.J."

"It's a lot simpler than it sounds," R.J. said.

"It had better be. If I understand you, you are planning to set a trap for the killer?"

"You always were the only one who understood me, Uncle Hank."

"This is a dangerous man, R.J. So far he has made us all look like fools."

"This time will be different," R.J. said. "We'll be waiting for him. You, me, the LAPD—" he nodded at Mary "—and his daughter."

"No," said Portillo quickly.

"Yes," Mary told him.

He shook his head. "No. It is far too dangerous. He has not seen her for what, fifteen years? He may not know it's her."

"He'll know," Mary said.

"And you don't even know it's him," Portillo said stubbornly.

"I think it is—"

"You think it is, *hijo*, and you make a good case. But if you are wrong—if it is *not* Kelley—what kind of danger are you placing her in?"

"Extreme danger," R.J. said. "But I'm not wrong."

"R.J., no," Portillo said. "I can't allow it."

"Why not? This is the only way everybody gets what they want. I stay out of jail, you catch a killer, Mary gets to see her old man. I don't see a problem."

Portillo gave R.J. a disgusted look, but he said nothing more.

"Uncle Hank, I could really use your help on this."

Portillo let out three or four quarts of air through his teeth. "R.J., I do not like putting an innocent person in danger. I will not allow a plan that does so."

"If you help me swing this, she'll be surrounded by a hundred people. As many cops as you want. Nothing can possibly go wrong."

Portillo said nothing for a moment, then, "What did you have in mind?"

"A press release from the studio. We get them to announce they're shooting a new version of the airport scene from *As Time Goes By*."

"Oh, God, I *love* that scene," Mary gushed.

R.J. grinned. "Everybody loves that scene, kid. That's why I picked it. Maximum instant publicity. Everybody will be on hand for the shoot, from Janine Wright on down. And if I'm a killer trying to get to Janine Wright, I'll be there, too."

"It is too risky for Miss Kelley."

"Mr. Portillo—Lieutenant—you can't stop me," Mary said. "I don't take orders from you, or anyone else. It's private property, owned by my mother. And we're talking about my father, and I want to be there. I *will* be there."

"We will be there," R.J. repeated. "It's our best chance, and you know it, Uncle Hank. I can't do it unless you talk to Janine Wright and get her to go along with it."

Portillo clearly didn't like it. But in the end he gave in and agreed to help.

"I will speak to her," he said finally as he approached the intersection for the Santa Monica Freeway. "By the way, where am I going?"

"What do you mean?"

"I mean, where are you staying, Miss Kelley?" he asked.

"I don't— I hadn't thought— I mean, I don't know," she said, and a slow blush climbed into her cheeks.

"Forgive me if I do not offer my house," Portillo said carefully. "Although it would be a great pleasure, there is simply not enough room."

"I'll sleep on the couch," R.J. said.

A slight scowl crossed Portillo's brow. "R.J., I do not think—"

"I want her near me," R.J. said.

"I know perfectly well what you have in mind, R.J. I do not wish my house used for such a purpose."

R.J. snorted. "Relax, Uncle Hank. We're not looking for a place to play strip poker." He turned to Mary. "He thinks I'm hell on wheels with women. Ever since he caught me playing strip poker with Melissa Gallagher in the eighth grade." He shook his head. "She was winning, too."

"Oh," said Mary, still blushing furiously. "And he thought— I mean, it was . . . What happened?"

"Uncle Hank taught me to play poker," R.J. said.

"R.J.," Portillo said with a warning in his voice.

"Take it easy, Uncle Hank," R.J. said. "I'll be fine on the couch. Nothing is going to happen."

CHAPTER 40

In the middle of the night R.J. woke up with the sure feeling that he was not alone. He reached under the pillow for his gun before he realized he didn't have one. He wasn't at home; he was on the couch at Henry Portillo's house in the San Fernando Valley. And someone was very quietly, very carefully moving in on him.

And as he took a deep breath and prepared to whip his legs out of the blanket and into the attacker he caught a faint whiff of Obsession and a soft hand slid onto his hip.

He grabbed at the wrist, pulled—

—and a naked Mary Keller slid into his arms.

"Mary!" he hissed.

"Yes," she whispered back, wiggling closer to him and sliding her hand down his hip and around to his crotch.

R.J. tried to pull away but she held on. "What the hell are you doing?" he asked her.

She purred into his ear. "I thought it was obvious," she said.

"For Christ's sake, let go of me," he whispered.

"No," she said, and she bit his neck.

He put out a hand to move her away and came up with a handful of breast. She arched her back to press harder against his hand. "Damn it, kid—!"

"Stop calling me that!" she said. "Does this feel like a kid to you?"

"No," R.J. said, struggling to sit up. "But it acts like one." He managed to get out from under her and sit up awkwardly, but she still held on with one hand around his neck and the other—

He gently pulled the other hand away. "We have to talk, Mary," he said.

"Let's talk later," she suggested, again sliding as close to him as she could get. "Afterward."

"Now," he said.

"I know you want to, R.J." she said, and slid her hand back again to prove it.

"That's got nothing to do with it," he snarled, reaching to take her hand away again. His heart was pounding and his mouth was dry and yes, damn it, he *did* want to and she was holding proof of that in her hand.

He grabbed her wrist and moved her hand off him, but she just nestled down against his chest, placing her face against his shoulder. "Mmmm," she said.

R.J. stood up. The motion caused Mary to slide off him and onto the floor with a bump and in the dim light he could see her looking up at him. He pulled her to her feet, grabbed the blanket off the couch, and wrapped it around her. "What the hell has got into you, kid?" he asked.

She kicked him in the shin. "Stop calling me kid," she said. "You keep calling me that, and I'm not a kid. I'm a woman."

"I guess you are at that," R.J. admitted ruefully. "But you don't need to rape me to prove it."

"It wouldn't be rape if you'd cooperate," she said. "Why won't you?"

R.J. shook his head. He had been about to say that he couldn't, that he was committed to somebody else, and suddenly that made him wonder if that was true. And then he almost laughed out loud, because he was sitting in the dark with a beautiful naked girl, mooning about Casey.

"There's someone else," he said finally. "I think."

"What does that mean? You think? Shouldn't you be a little more sure than that before you say no to me?"

"It's complicated," he admitted. "We're kind of at a crossroads with each other right now." And he realized as he said it how true that was.

"I'm not asking you to marry me," Mary said. "Just—you know. For now. If it works out, great. If it doesn't, we've killed some time, right?"

"I can't," R.J. said.

"Because it's *wrong?*" she hissed at him.

"Yeah. For me, right now, it's wrong."

She sat there on the couch with the blanket draped around her. It didn't hide the fact that she was naked underneath it. It didn't hide the fact that she was feeling pretty blue, either.

"Well, *shit,*" she said, her head hanging down toward her knees.

"Damn it, ki—Mary, don't take it like that."

"How am I supposed to take it?"

"Listen," R.J. said, with as much kindness and firmness as he could manage. "I'm flattered as hell. You're a terrific-looking girl and I'm going to have to sit in a bucket of ice water for a week to get over this, but the answer is no. It would be great, but it's too complicated. I have to work out this other thing first. And besides, you're my client. I have a hard and fast rule—I almost never sleep with my client."

There was a rustle of cloth as the blanket moved and he felt a quick squeeze. "Hard, anyway," she said and stood up. The blanket slid to the floor and she stood in front of him again, naked and looking great that way.

"All right, R.J.," she said. "Just so you think about what you're turning down." And she slowly turned, making sure he saw all of her, and then slithered away down the hall.

"Believe me, I'm thinking," he muttered, and shook his head. Forget getting back to sleep. He'd be throbbing for hours. What the hell got into her? And for that matter, what the hell got into him, turning her down? Was he going crazy, or just getting old?

Maybe that was it. Senile dementia. Too much aluminum in his diet. He didn't eat enough fish and now his brain was shrinking. Hell, he'd never in his life turned down a tumble with a girl as good-looking as that. And whatever he'd said to her, he had slept with clients. Plenty of times. It was surprising how often they wanted to, figured it was part of the deal; after all, he was in a service industry.

He'd liked most of them a lot less than he liked Mary, too, so that had nothing to do with it. So what did it have to do with?

Casey?

Again, he'd never been particularly faithful in past relationships. Why stay single if you were going to get yourself trapped in something with all the disadvantages of marriage? "Seeing someone" didn't have to mean "*not* seeing someone else," and as far as he was concerned it never had.

Until now. Until Casey.

He hadn't thought about it, but he'd blurted it out and now he knew it was true. He was committed to Casey. Even though he had no idea if she was committed to him, he had said no to fooling around with Mary because he didn't want to put his relationship with Casey in any danger. He didn't even know if he had a relationship with her anymore, but didn't feel like taking the chance.

R.J. flopped back down on the couch with a groan. His brains were turning to mush, going soft on him, no matter how hard he was elsewhere.

And why did all of this have to come down on him right

now, when he needed to be especially sharp? How could he catch a killer with all this other stuff slamming into him? What was the old saying, about how it never rains unless it pours? In his case, it was pouring, and that wasn't water falling on him, either. It was pure, uncut raw sewage.

R.J. lay there for a long time, thinking about love and death. He never did get back to sleep.

CHAPTER **41**

It was bright and early when they rolled up to the gates of Andromeda Studios. R.J. wasn't feeling particularly bright, but he couldn't argue with the early part. He hadn't slept much the night before, thinking about what might happen today, and he hadn't slept at all the night before that, after his naked visitor had left him.

The encounter with Mary had left him in short temper for the meeting with Janine Wright, but luckily Portillo and Bertelli had been there to sweet-talk her—and to keep R.J.'s temper in check. He felt his bile rising just being in the same room with her.

But in the end she had agreed. Had to, really. There was no other way, and whatever she might say about bad publicity selling tickets, the body count was high enough now, even for her.

"Good morning, John," Portillo greeted the handsome young actor at the gate.

John flashed him a smile. "Hey, Lieutenant," he said. He glanced into the car and did a small double take when he saw

R.J. "Um, Lieutenant, I'm not supposed to let that guy on the lot."

"There's been a change in plans, John," Portillo told him. "I'm sure it's all right. They just forgot to update you."

The young actor still looked doubtful. "I don't know. It could mean my job."

Mary leaned over so John could see her. "It's really okay, Johnny," she said. "I kind of need him with me for protection."

"Muh-Mar—Miss Kelley?" the gatekeeper blurted, and to R.J.'s surprise the kid blushed. "Whu-when did . . . what are you . . . ?"

Mary gave him a sweet smile. "We're all supposed to be on the set. Mr. Brooks is working for me."

"I, I . . . um," John stammered. He was fire-engine red, and obviously so flustered by Mary that he couldn't find the floor with his foot.

"Please?" Mary said, and John lurched backward and stumbled for the button that opened the gate.

As the car moved forward onto the lot, R.J. snorted. "I think he likes you, Mary," he said.

She looked at him coolly. "Some people do," she said. "I don't know why you find that so strange." And she turned away and looked out the window.

Portillo gave R.J. a dark look. "Oh, brother," R.J. muttered to himself.

Since the incident on the couch two nights ago Mary had been a little distant, which R.J. guessed was only natural. He couldn't be sure since he'd never turned a woman down before, not when she was naked and in his arms, but he guessed this was how she might be expected to react.

Still, it was certainly putting a crimp in the working relationship. She hadn't said a word to him since, nothing more complicated than "Yes, no, pass the salt, please."

But what the hell. They were here, and there was a job to be done. And in a little while it would be over, one way or the other.

Portillo pulled into a parking spot next to a step van that was parked near the soundstage.

R.J. put a hand on Mary's shoulder and she stepped away from it. He shrugged. "Listen, Mary," he said. "Just keep your eyes open, and stay close to me."

"I'll try," she said, with a tone of voice that said it would be hard work to stay close to him.

R.J. ignored it. "My guess is, it's going to be a lot of waiting and maybe nothing happens. He knows we're waiting for him, but I think he's got to try, anyway. You'll be safe, there are twenty cops all over the soundstage, and another dozen studio security guys. And I'll be right there with you."

She gave him that tone of voice again. "Oh. Then I guess there's really nothing to worry about," she said, and she turned away and went in.

R.J. was beginning to wish he had just said fine, the hell with it, and let her have her way with him on the couch. He swore under his breath and followed her in.

Portillo went to check the perimeters and talk to his men. Mary quickly and pointedly found somebody she knew and went to stand and talk with them, leaving R.J. by himself.

All around the set, everything looked almost exactly the same. To R.J., it looked like the crew were even wearing the same T-shirts. The long row of food tables still stood along the wall, surrounded by casually grazing Teamsters, and the same three or four guys were still hustling at top speed while everyone else stood around in clusters, talking, and sipping coffee.

The set itself was completely different. The walls of the cheap hotel were gone and in their place was a smooth, featureless white screen. It folded around the stage with no visible seams or corners.

Three huge wind machines crouched in an arc around the set. Nosing in between them was the front end of an airplane, what looked like a DC-3. The nose and windshield were there, perched above the soundstage. Behind them was nothing, no tail section, no wings. The airplane was chopped off weirdly in accordance with movie-making logic; if the shot only shows the nose, you don't need the whole damn plane.

R.J. knew what the set-up meant. From the other machines and technicians standing around, R.J. could see they were all set to re-create the famous scene. Wind, rain, and heartache.

R.J. had seen the original maybe a hundred times. His mother and father facing each other on the runway, the wind and rain whipping around them, the fate of the world hanging in the balance, as they said good-bye. He still couldn't watch it without getting a lump in his throat, and he wasn't the only one. It was maybe the most famous movie scene of all time.

And there was the beach boy, standing next to the porn queen, in perfectly re-created costumes, getting ready to shoot that scene again. R.J. could hear the beach boy, repeating one of the lines over and over, in a bad imitation of his father's famous growl.

R.J. had no problem seeing in his head what they were trying to copy. His mother and father, eaten up by passion and now torn apart by a world gone crazy.

Like any kid he'd seen his dad unshaven and in his underwear, heard the two of them yelling things at each other—he knew they were human beings.

But they were the two perfect star-crossed lovers in this scene, too. And when he thought of them together, he thought of them standing there, holding hands and saying good-bye as the rain whipped at them.

It was his family portrait, damn it. And these half-baked clowns were cutting off the heads and sticking their own faces through the holes, smirking and gawking like two rubes at the fair.

And to make it worse, there was Casey on the other side, talking with the bearded guy who was always racing around with a clipboard.

Great, R.J. thought. Now the picture is complete. Mom,

Dad, and Casey. Three people who have yanked on my strings more than any others.

And standing next to Casey, looking bored and mean at the same time like a dozing rattle snake, was Janine Wright.

R.J. just looked. He felt like his guts had just gone twelve rounds with Mike Tyson.

Janine Wright had agreed to loiter on the set for a day and act as bait. Not because she really gave a damn, but she knew it was publicity, and she knew that for every clip she placed on the evening news she sold thousands of tickets to the movie.

So there she was, surrounded by a clump of photographers, looking around for somebody to disembowel and eat. And just maybe, somewhere nearby, somebody was looking at her the same way.

R.J. turned away and headed for the food table. A large silver coffee urn stood on one end. He went over and grabbed a cup. There was no point in trying to talk to Casey. And there was nothing for him to do except wait. So he sipped the coffee and did that, trying to keep an eye on Mary and not on the horrible mockery on the soundstage.

Six cups of coffee and two apples later he was still standing, waiting, and watching. R.J. felt like he would slosh if he moved. But his feet and his back were aching from just standing. And in spite of trying not to watch what was going on out on the soundstage he'd seen and heard enough to make him feel queasy.

So he talked himself into a short walk around the outside of the soundstage. Just to stretch for five minutes, check around, see if maybe Kelley was hiding behind an old piece of scenery or something. And mostly to get away from all of it before he bit a camera.

He stepped over to where Mary Kelley and a young guy in a salad bowl haircut were talking about something with an unlikely name that might have been a band from what they were saying.

"Excuse me," R.J. said. Mary turned cool blue eyes on him.

"Yes?" she said, the way you might talk to the gardener when your mouth was full of cucumber sandwich and petits fours.

"I'd like to step outside for a couple of minutes," R.J. said.

"Oh, please feel totally free," Mary replied. The bad haircut snickered.

"Thanks," R.J. said, and grabbed her by the arm just above the elbow.

"Hey!" Mary said as R.J. yanked her toward the door.

"Hey, yourself, your highness," he said. "I'm trying to keep an eye on you, and since you graciously granted me permission to leave the room, you're leaving the room with me."

"But I was just—"

"You were just being a pain in the ass. I understand. It's not a big deal, I have to work with pains in the ass every day. And you're too nice to be any good at it."

"Damn it, R.J.—" She tried to yank her arm away, but he held on tight.

"Damn it yourself. Listen, Mary, I'm sorry if I hurt your feelings. But people get their feelings hurt every day. It's part of what life is about. So get over it. You don't want me to call you 'kid' anymore, so stop acting like one."

She was quiet for a minute. At least she stopped struggling until they got close to the door. Then she sighed. "I guess it was—you know. Kind of funny."

"Only if it had happened to two other people," R.J. said. He let go of her elbow and turned to face her. "I said I was sorry. I mean that. You walked right into me when I was trying to figure out where I am with somebody else."

"Bad timing," she said. "The story of my life."

"Bad timing," R.J. agreed.

A guy dressed like a giant smirking blue lizard pushed past them behind Mary's back. The poor yutz was pushing a dolly with a couple of metal tanks on it. A fistful of balloons was draped over the handlebar.

R.J. shook his head. "Look at that if you want funny."

Mary turned and looked at the lizard's back. "Oh, God, not *him*. More publicity."

The Big Blue Lizard was one of the most famous characters on the tube right now. All over the country there were guys making a hard buck at kid's parties with the suit. This one obviously made balloon animals, too, with his tanks of helium.

R.J. almost chuckled. "This is probably the schmuck's biggest gig ever," he said.

"Maybe. But he's likely to get mugged here."

"What do you mean?"

She shrugged. "The rights to the character are owned by another studio. So somebody is probably having a joke at Mother's expense."

"The less funny she thinks it is, the better I like it," R.J. said, and they went out the door together.

Outside it was warm, the sun was shining, and R.J. supposed that birds were singing somewhere. Not on the Andromeda Studios lot. Not with Janine Wright on the set. The birds wouldn't dare.

They walked one time around the building, taking about fifteen minutes to do it, stretching, breathing deeply. It was a large building, a converted airplane hangar. Henry Portillo had stationed men at all the key points. They were dressed in jeans or overalls.

"Oh, my God," Mary giggled.

"What?"

"Those guys are trying so hard not to look like cops, you know what?"

"Yeah. It makes them look like cops."

They had a small laugh together, and most of the tension from their awkward encounter in the night was gone.

After a few more minutes R.J. had walked the kinks out of his back and neck.

"You ready to go back inside?" he asked Mary.

She sighed. "Yes. I guess so. I just—"

R.J. waited for her to finish the sentence. She didn't for a minute. Then she sighed again and squared her shoulders. "Mother hasn't even said hello to me. You know. Not that it matters, but—"

"But it matters."

"Yeah."

R.J. put a hand on her shoulder. "I've been there, Mary. But everybody loved my mother, and I couldn't even complain."

She smiled a little. It wasn't much, but it was better than a sigh. "You've had it rough, Brooks."

"You too, Kelley."

"Okay," she said. "Let's go back in and watch the Teamsters eat doughnuts."

The first thing R.J. noticed when they came back inside was how quiet it was inside. They must be shooting already, R.J. thought, and he peeked around to the set.

Between them and the soundstage were maybe fifteen people. And beyond them he could see another dozen and maybe fifteen more by the food tables.

And all of them were stretched out motionless on the floor.

CHAPTER 42

Kelley was here.

Had to be. There was no other explanation for a room full of people suddenly stretched out on the floor, and R.J. had no idea whether they were alive or—

Casey!

R.J. pushed Mary behind him, scanning the room for danger. Nothing. Nothing but a strange smell that made him dizzy. "Stay here," he snarled to Mary. "Prop the doors open," he added, and lurched quickly across the room to Casey.

Kelley. Somehow he had gotten in, slipped past all the security, and he was here, now, and somehow had even smuggled in something else, a way to put down a whole room full of people. But how?

If everybody knows what you look like and you want to get past them, cover your face.

Cover it with something that everybody expects to see anyway.

Something like a costume if you're on a movie set.

Something like a Big Blue Lizard costume . . . ?

Of course. It was simple, and R.J. felt pretty simple himself for not figuring it out sooner. He had known the lizard was out of place and thought it was a joke. He had forgotten Kelley's sense of humor.

It was a joke all right. But the laugh was on R.J. And he would be out of laughs for a long time if anything had happened to Casey.

R.J.'s head was pounding and he felt dizzy as he ran across the room to where he had seen her last. There was no way to tell whether everybody was dead or just unconscious from looking at them as he stumbled past. But no one was moving, not even a twitch.

And whatever had knocked these people out, there was still some hanging in the air. Not enough to drop him, but he felt it.

It didn't matter. He would have crawled on his belly the last twenty feet to get to Casey.

He knelt beside her and felt for a pulse. It was going strong, that beautiful big vein in her lovely neck throbbing with a steady beat. He lifted her eyelid. The eye was clear, the pupil reacted to the change in light, but there was nobody home. She was okay; that was all that mattered. He could leave her for a minute and concentrate on catching a maniac. Wherever he was. And as R.J. stood carefully, fighting the dizziness, he noticed for the first time.

Janine Wright was gone.

He had last seen her standing next to Casey. The cluster of photographers that had been following her around was still there, laid out in a fan shape. But the center of the fan was empty. Wright had been there. Now she was gone.

Where?

And even as he looked around, struggling against a creeping sleepiness from breathing the tainted air in here, he heard it: a soft, faint scraping sound. Not far away, but he couldn't quite place it in the huge hangar.

R.J. stepped softly across the room, trying to locate the sound. It came at regular intervals, a kind of—dragging?

Somebody dragging something heavy?

Like a body?

R.J. moved on, trying to keep the sound separate from the pounding in his head. He moved silently past the set. The two stars were stretched out in place. The makeup woman with the big hair was beside them.

The sound seemed closer now. R.J. went past the huge wind fans. At the foot of one was the dolly, draped with balloons, and two now-empty tanks. Whatever had been in the tanks, it wasn't helium. Kelley had opened the valves right behind the fan to make sure that everyone in the entire hangar got hit fast. It had worked.

The dragging sound was interrupted by a thump and then it stopped. R.J. moved around back of the screen.

There. Along the wall, maybe thirty feet away, there was a ladder built into the wall, leading up to the catwalk. And climbing the ladder, with the limp body of Janine Wright over one shoulder, was the Big Blue Lizard.

R.J. reflexively reached for his gun, but he wasn't carrying. Couldn't in California. He'd have to go it alone, without the comforting weight of his .357 in his hand, and with a steady throbbing between his ears that was making concentration very tough.

Kelley was up on the catwalk now, Janine Wright's body still over his shoulder. With the stuff in the air already making him light-headed, R.J. felt like he was watching some weird dream: a Big Blue Lizard carrying the woman away to its nest in the sky. And R.J. was on the ground, with both feet stuck in cement.

He shook it off and moved to the foot of the ladder.

He started up, slowly, finding that his head was gradually clearing. Either the stuff was dissipating or he was climbing above it. Didn't matter; either way, as long as he could remember how his hands and feet worked for another minute, he'd be okay.

R.J. made it to the catwalk and stood with his hand on the wall, swaying slightly. He took a deep breath and felt himself steady. Then he accidentally looked down. It seemed like a long way down to the floor. R.J. scrabbled at the wall for a handhold, momentarily dizzy again. He had never been bothered by heights, but then, he'd never been half off his nut from knock-out gas while chasing a maniac across a catwalk, either. And damn it, it *was* a long way down.

It didn't seem to be bothering Kelley. If the lizard knew he was being followed, that didn't seem to bother him, either. Of course, he was wearing the Big Blue Lizard mask. Maybe he couldn't see or hear R.J. But he was walking along the thin strip of metal with his ex-wife over his shoulder, apparently as carefree as if he were walking through the park to a Sunday picnic.

R.J. wasn't wearing a goofy, bulky blue suit, and he wasn't carrying 150 pounds of woman over his shoulder, either. But it was all he could do to follow Kelley and stay on the catwalk. The guy was impressive, no question.

Kelley was moving much faster than R.J. could manage. He was now about a hundred feet ahead, over a distant section of the hangar. There was another scene set up on the floor over there, R.J. didn't know what.

And now Kelley was stooping, dropping the motionless body of Janine Wright to the catwalk. R.J. felt it shiver slightly as she struck. He moved faster, aware that whatever Kelley had planned, Janine Wright was running out of time.

R.J. was seventy-five feet away. Kelley uncoiled a long rope from his other shoulder. He bent and began to tie it to Janine Wright's feet. A faint orange glow came up from below and lit the lizard's features.

Fifty feet away. Kelley finished the knots, yanked on them to make sure they would hold, and stood up with the far end of the rope in his hands.

Twenty-five feet. Kelley, holding tension on the rope, began to nudge the body off into the darkness below. Closer now, R.J. could see the glow underneath them was coming from a hole of some kind raised up off the floor. He didn't have any idea what the glow was, but it wouldn't be much fun for Janine Wright. And he couldn't get close enough in time.

Janine Wright was headed down toward that glowing hole.

"Hold it, Kelley!" he called. Kelley paused, looked up. "That's enough. Let her go."

He said something R.J. couldn't catch throughout the lizard mask.

R.J. shook his head. "Sorry. I'm sure it was a cute comeback, but I can't hear you through that thing. Now pull her up and take a step back."

Kelley didn't step back, but he did pause. And then he pulled the lizard head off. He dropped it off the catwalk and then took off the gas mask he was wearing under it. "I said," Kelley repeated, "that I don't think you really want me to let her go from this height." And he smiled. It was the gentle smile of a man making a small joke to help an awkward guest relax.

"You know what I mean," R.J. said. "Just ease her down to the floor."

"I wish I could. But I'm very sorry." Kelley shrugged and lowered the body another few feet.

"Kelley!" R.J. said, taking a step forward.

"Mr. Brooks—" Kelley said, and held up the end of the rope. R.J. got his drift and stood still. "I would very much like to help you out. I know I owe you a few favors for the trouble I caused you."

"You're goddamned right you owe me," R.J. said, thinking anything to keep him talking, just a little longer . . . "Why the hell did you frame me, you son-of-a-bitch?"

Kelley held up a hand, palm outward, and Janine bobbed upward on the end of the rope. The bastard is strong as hell, R.J. thought. "I really do apologize," Kelley said out loud.

"But when I saw what you said in the paper, I realized it made you a perfect suspect. A lightning rod. You'd take all the heat and leave me in the open to do what I wanted. I'm sorry, Brooks, really, and I'd like to make it up to you. But—" He smiled again. "Perhaps some other time? I'm kind of busy throwing my wife into a volcano at the moment."

"What the hell does that mean?"

"I know. It really sounds crazy, doesn't it? But remember, this is Hollywood. Crazy is the major industry." He nodded down at the source of the glow. "A model volcano. What they call a miniature. With real lava flow. Temperature's only a few hundred degrees, about as hot as a deep fry at a burger joint. But it should be enough for dear Janine. Funny that she should go this way. Kind of a sneak preview of her afterlife?"

He laughed. Not a crazed, wild-killer laugh, not at all. The laugh of a guy who had stubbed his toe and was making a joke out of it instead of complaining.

"You can't do this Kelley."

"Why not?" Kelley asked gently.

R.J. was stuck. He knew it was wrong, but the truth was, he didn't really want to stop Kelley, and he couldn't get close enough even if he did want to. But he couldn't let him do this, either. "It doesn't look good," R.J. said. "In my profession, I try to stop guys like you from doing things like this."

"In your profession," Kelley said with a slight chuckle. "Come on, Brooks. In your profession you might possibly take pictures of me doing this—especially if I take my pants off. But stop me? I don't think so. However, if you have your camera with you, I'd *love* to have a few shots to remember this moment. I'll pay your going rate, and honor is satisfied."

And he lowered the body another few feet.

"Kelley!" R.J. said, taking another few steps toward him.

"Brooks!" he said, mocking R.J.'s tone. "She started this and the only way I can finish it is like this. You must know that as well as I do. She *has* to die, Brooks. The sun will never shine again if she lives. Birds will sing no more and the laughter of little children will be gone from the land, unless I drive a stake through her heart." He shrugged. "Or cook her like a french fry. Whatever." And he lowered her another few feet.

"There's another way, Kelley," R.J. said, trying to inch closer. "The stuff you had Pauly pass me. I can put her away with that stuff."

"I don't think so," Kelley said in a reasonable tone of voice. "I think she might get a nice hefty fine out of it, which the studio would pay, and then business as usual. Not that I mean to discourage you. Follow through on it, by all means. But even if she serves time, we both know what that would be. Six months at a country club, suspended sentence. And then community service, which will mean she shows her movies at half price to inner-city school kids."

"You may be right," R.J. said. "But I can't let you do this."

"You can't stop me," Kelley said. "All I have to do is let go." And he let a few feet of rope run through his hands. "I'm sorry. You were supposed to be unconscious. That way nobody could blame you. Why don't you go lie down and pretend to wake up with everybody else."

"Sorry."

"But I have to do this," Kelley went on. "I've waited too long. I did hard time, Brooks. *Hard* time. Because she framed me for being inconvenient. And she didn't even gloat. Just tucked me away to rot and forgot about me. Do you understand? It wasn't hate that made her do it, or even distaste. It was business convenience."

"That's tough," R.J. said. "And if you'd just popped her the first time you probably would have gotten away with it. But you tagged a couple of innocent people along the way."

"They weren't innocent, Brooks, don't kid yourself. Nobody innocent works for Janine. She roots out innocence like a truffle pig and gulps it down."

"They may all have been devil worshipers, Kelley. But you shouldn't have killed them."

Kelley sighed. "I know. I really am sorry. The first one was an accident, that lawyer? I was trying to get Janine and I just missed. Bad planning. If I'd had any idea my daughter was there, I never would have—" He sighed again. "Well, there it is. I really don't have any natural talent for this. I've had to learn as I go, and that lawyer— But then it occurred to me, why not? Kill her a little at a time, like she did me. Knock off the people around her, make her squirm. Make her tremble, wondering when the ax would fall again, never knowing who would be next or if *she* would be next. Everyone around her would see that it was bad to be near her, and they'd begin to look at her for what she was—a dangerous disease." And he lowered her another few feet.

For the first time R.J. saw the glint of madness in Kelley. He had known it had to be there. Nobody knocks off a bunch of people just to worry their real target unless they're a little unhinged. But until now Kelley had hidden behind a mask of gentle good humor.

Now it was out in the open. This was a psychotic killer. He might be the world's nicest psychotic killer, and he might be harmless once Janine Wright was dead—but he might not be, too. And whatever the case, he had already killed a slew of people and he was dangerous as hell now.

"A disease," Kelley went on. "A vile, vicious psychopath who would suck your blood if only she could make it hurt a little more." He lowered the body some more.

"This won't cure it," R.J. said. "This will make her a martyr."

Kelley shook his head. "I don't think so. A martyr has to leave a legacy of some kind. And what does she leave behind? Just a bad odor—only partly from the singeing she's about to get. It won't be kind on her hair, I'm afraid."

As he spoke he dropped her almost to the lip of the volcano and sure enough, in the glow from the volcano's molten insides, R.J. could see Janine Wright's hair starting to shrivel from the heat.

"I'm sorry," Kelley was saying. "I'm not really demonic. In fact, I used to be a pretty good guy. I think that's why she was able to do this to me. But the fact is, Brooks, you really can't stop me. I know it must make you feel bad and I'm sorry, but it's true, you can't stop me. If you jump me I just drop her and it's over. If you shoot me, it's the same thing. It's as good as done. You can't stop me. I have waited for this for twenty years and now—" He shivered. The rope shook and Janine Wright slid another few inches. One side of her hair burst into flames. "You really can't stop me. Nothing can stop me."

"Daddy?"

The voice came from the darkness of the catwalk off to R.J.'s left and took him completely by surprise. It was Mary Kelley, no question about it, but—the voice was different. Softer, younger. It sounded like a little girl who woke up in the night dreaming of monsters under the bed.

"Daddy, is that you?"

R.J. and Kelley both froze at the sound. Kelley recovered first. He straightened and took a half step toward the voice. The rope in his hands came with him, tugging Janine Wright a foot or so higher, away from the volcano.

"Who is that?" he said. "Don't try anything—"

"Daddy, it's me," Mary said and stepped into the dim light from the volcano.

Kelley looked like he had been pole-axed. ". . . Mary?" he whispered. "Baby . . . ?"

She stepped a little closer and he didn't move except to sway slightly. "Daddy . . ."

He stepped toward her like he was being pulled on a string. As he moved the rope moved with him and Janine Wright's body floated slowly back up toward the catwalk.

R.J. edged forward, trying to get close enough to get a hand on the rope without any sudden movements that would alarm Kelley. But Kelley was totally focused on his daughter.

"Mary," Kelley said. "My Mary—"

R.J. was only a few feet from the rope when Kelley opened his arms to embrace his daughter. "Oh, God," he said. "My little girl." And he lunged to her with his arms wide.

And dropped the rope.

R.J. dove for it.

CHAPTER 43

The cops were milling around watching the paramedics. There really wasn't much for them to do, now that they had the killer. It was just a matter of waiting for everybody to wake up.

They had already taken Janine Wright away in an ambulance. Her hair was burned off and one side of her face was always going to be red and a little too smooth from the burns. R.J. had snagged the rope just as Janine Wright's head dipped into the cone of the volcano. She'd be all right. But she was going to look a little weird from now on, with her partly melted face.

Maybe that was justice. Kelley thought so.

They had taken William Kelley away, too. He had come quietly down from the catwalk and stood with his arm around his daughter until they cuffed him and shoved him into a car. Then she got in beside him. The cops weren't happy about that, but she just wouldn't get out. They tried to persuade her to ride in the ambulance with her mother, but she just looked at them, one hand resting on her father, and finally they gave it up and let her ride along.

And now it was just a matter of waiting for them all to wake up inside the big hangar.

As soon as the cops had let him go, R.J. had checked on Portillo and then Bertelli. Uncle Hank was lying on his face halfway across the floor toward the spot where Kelley had set up his tanks. His gun was drawn. His pulse was strong and steady. R.J. flipped him over into a more comfortable position and left him to wake up.

Angelo was slumped over beside the food table. A small plate of what looked like cannoli was beside him. R.J. checked his pulse and left him.

He went over to where Casey lay stretched out on the floor. He took off his jacket and folded it under her head. He had grabbed a bottle of sparkling water and a carton of orange juice from the food table to have ready for her when she woke up. And some aspirin, just in case she needed that.

And most of all he'd gotten himself ready, too.

Something had come together for him up there on the catwalk. Watching a family drama play out, love yanking people around in some wild directions. And as he had come back down to the floor it had occurred to him that, in a funny way, that's what this whole thing had been about. Love gone crazy.

He'd been thinking all along that he couldn't concentrate on the killer because of Casey, or on Casey because of the killer, and it hit him that maybe it was all the same problem. That maybe sometimes life set you up with a problem and you had to work it out one piece at a time before you could move on.

And maybe he was only thinking that way because he was in California. A state where the official motto, printed on the license plates, was "All Things Are One."

Sure, he might have gone mushy between the ears over the last few weeks. But he was sure about the answer he'd come up with, as sure as he'd ever been in his life.

And as he stood over Casey and watched her sleep off the

knock-out gas, watched her beautiful face that seemed so alive even when it was so still, he knew he was right. There were problems to work out, things to talk about, but that was no big deal. There were always going to be things to talk about between the two of them. That was one of the things that made it so good.

Now there was a new thing, and when she woke up they would talk about it. Because he'd thought about it and it had stuck with him, and he knew exactly what he would say to her when those beautiful blue eyes fluttered open and focused on his.

R.J. sat down to wait, running through it in his head, trying to get used to the sound of it. The words were strange, hard to say, but he would try like hell to say them:

"Will you marry me, Casey?"